Dream
NO MORE

Dream NO MORE

RISE OF A LION

BOOK I

MARRIO C. MATHEWS

ARPress
45 Dan Road Suite 36
Canton MA 02021

Hotline: 1(800) 220-7660
Fax: 1(855) 752-6001

Ordering Information:
Quantity sales. Special discounts are available on quantity purchases by corporations, associations, and others. For details, contact the publisher at the address above.

Printed in the United States of America.

ISBN-13:   Paperback   979-8-89356-086-2
           eBook   979-8-89356-087-9

Library of Congress Control Number: 2024904214

I dedicate this book to all of you, who believed in my ability to produce and prosper. To the people that constantly asked, *"You finished that book yet?"*. To my friends, who grew up writing with me. To my family, who can never be replaced. To other producers, who helped mold and shape my thoughts. Lastly to my community, the Black Descendants of American Slaves, honoring the sacred lineage and history that flow through my veins. Everlast.

CONTENTS

I used to dream of this little lion that lived on a grain of dust. The grain floated in a basin of starlight; a special place in a grand cosmos. Hosted by its parent star, the grain remained bathed in light; which bestowed an irreplaceable ingredient for life. The grain was chaperoned by three moons. The moons stationed in a harmonious triangular formation, linked by reflected light.

The grain of dust where this little lion lived was aptly named "Ni," a planet that thrived through cycles of life and death. It is here where this little lion rests amongst the chaos. And although I may know his future, it will be up to him to live, learn, survive, and prosper. It will be his life to experience—or so it would seem.

PRELUDE

(In a large home stationed in the middle of a forest, a young boy sleeps in his room as Ni's parent star rises across the horizon, bringing in the light of day. He is occasionally disturbed by the clashing of steel and thumping of running steeds echoing through the forest. Suddenly, the home and forest shake with the sound of an explosion from a distant location. The young boy sits up in his bed, hugging his legs, staring toward his window. He then hears a woman's voice outside of his room's door.)

Voice: "Lyone? You awake, Champ?"

Lyone: "Nanny Lorelei!"

(The door opens and a tall, muscular, bronze skinned woman wearing a green-and-gold tunic, with a shaved head covered with tribal markings enters.)

Lorelei: "Hey, kid. How are you feeling?"

Lyone: "What's going on outside, Nanny?"

(Lorelei notices his worried expression as the home and forest shake once again.)

Lorelei: "There's fighting going on."

Lyone: "Who's fighting?"

Lorelei: "The people that are supposed to be protecting this place. Now they're at each other's throats."

Lyone: "Where is Mom, Dad, and Auntie?"

Voice: "Lorelei! We're almost ready to move! Get Lyone ready!"

(Lyone and Lorelei turn their attention to the room entrance, hearing a woman's voice calling out to them. Then, they look at each other with a sense of urgency.)

Lorelei: "Come on, Champ. Let's get you ready to leave."

(Lyone climbs out of his bed, rubbing his eyes, looking towards his window.)

Lyone: "But, where are we gonna go?"

Lorelei: "We'll figure that out once we're safe. Now, put some clothes on. I'll help pack a bag for you."

Lyone: "Ok."

(A few minutes later, Lyone and Lorelei make their way down the stairs to the basement. Once they reach the basement, they see a person jumping into a hole in the floor.)

Lorelei: "Alright, down the hole."

(Lyone walks up to the open hatch and jumps down the hole, landing in an escape tunnel built under the home. The tunnel is lit by a bright light, shimmering from a single ember, resting on the fingertip of a dark-skinned man. He has a flowing black beard and wears a sleeveless black-and-gold tunic fit for an unarmed fighter. The man stands in the company of two women, one with a dark skin tone that matches the male among them, and another lighter shade of brown. The brown-skinned lady is fully covered by a dark-purple stealth tunic tailored for an assassin, partially concealing her face, and her long hair is braided into a rope that reaches her lower back. Standing between the other two with her back toward Lyone, the dark-skinned lady wearing a heavier, silver armor made for a knight that bears the crest of a winged lion, and a blue-hooded cape that covers her long hair. The trio discusses a plan of action in their native language as Lorelei jumps into the tunnel behind Lyone.)

Lady Assassin: <translated> "Like I said, I've scouted out both of the main camps from a distance. I spotted both Ci-Ru-Da and Ia-On in their respective camps."

Male Fighter: <translated> "Then we have to move now. This may be the only time we have to confront the two before the real fight begins."

(Lyone looks deeper into the tunnel to find a dark and damp cave entrance, illuminated by fungi emitting blue light. Suddenly, the cave shakes slightly from a faraway explosion, alarming Lyone. He runs over to the lady knight, tightly hugging her leg.)

Lyone: <translated> "Mom, what's going on?"

(The trio becomes concerned, noticing the panic on Lyone's face. The lady knight kneels to eye level with Lyone, wearing a confident smile.)

Lady Knight: <translated> "Hey, Lyone, look at me. Everything is going to be fine. Auntie Rose, your father, and I will handle this. No need to be afraid, ok? We'll protect you. Got it?"

(Lyone nods his head in agreement and gives her a hug. Lorelei takes notice to a building anger within the male fighter, causing the light from the ember at the tip of his finger to gradually intensify.)

Lorelei: "Kai, save that anger for the battlefield. No need to blood flow here."

Kai: "Don't worry. I have control."

(The ember returns to a small, manageable flame as the lady knight releases Lyone, wiping tears away from his eyes. Then, she stands firmly, turning her attention to the rest of the party.)

Lady Knight: "Rose, do you have a travel path ready?"

Rose: "Yeah, the cave up ahead is cleared, and I've already identified a vantage point over the battlefield."

Kai: "Come on Raine, let's get this over with."

Raine: "Ok."

(Raine turns toward Lyone and Lorelei with an alluring smile.)

Raine: "Lyone, listen to me carefully. Mommy, Daddy and Auntie Rose are going to put an end to this. We need you to be strong and protect Nanny Lorelei. Can you do that for me, sweetheart?"

(Lyone takes a moment to build his confidence, nodding his head once again.)

Lyone: "Ok, Mom."

Lorelei: "That's the spirit, Champ. I'm gonna need those muscles of yours!"

(Kai and Rose walk over to Lyone, kneeling to eye level, both with determination in their spirits.)

Kai: "Don't worry, son. We'll be back before you know it. Besides, I still gotta lot to teach you so you can beat your Auntie Rose."

Lyone: "You think I can?"

Rose: "From the look in your eyes, I'd say you're already there, Lyone."

(Lyone smiles, giving both Rose and Kai a hug. Suddenly, another explosion shakes the surrounding cavern.)

Lorelei: "That felt closer than the last one!"

(Kai and Rose releases Lyone from their embrace, rises to their feet, and turns to Raine. The trio reflects each other's resolve, prepared to travel through the cavern towards their objective.)

Kai: "Alright, let's go."

Rose: "Lyone, Lorelei, it's up to you two."

Lorelei and Lyone: "Right!"

(While Lyone watches them closely, the bodies of his parents and aunt becomes engulfed by resonating auras. Then, the three sprints through the cavern in an extraordinary display of speed.)

Lyone: "Holy heck, they're fast."

Lorelei: "Hey, who taught you to say that?"

Lyone: "Oops! I heard dad say it. Sorry."

(Lorelei shakes her head in disapproval as Lyone covers his mouth, laughing with embarrassment.)

Lorelei: "I should've known. Alright, Lyone, time to go. No sense in staying here to be buried in this cave!"

Lyone: "Ok!"

(Lorelei steps in front of Lyone, kneeling with her back turned toward him. Then, he climbs onto her back with his arms around her neck, holding on tightly.)

Lorelei: "Hold on tight, Champ. Here we go!"

(Lyone notices Lorelei's body, resonating with a strong aura. Suddenly, she dashes forward through the cave, disappearing in a burst of speed.

Meanwhile, Kai, Raine, and Rose stands at the top of a hill, located at the edge of a forest, observing over a large meadow plain. The party stands by, witnessing the beautiful green meadow transformed into a war-torn battlefield.)

Rose: "The two armies are engaged in the central part of the Helde Meadow. To the northwest of the Helde Meadow is the North Ryone main camp where Ci-Ru-Da awaits. To the south is the South Ryone main camp where Ia-On resides."

Raine: "Kai and I will take Ia-On. Ci-Ru-Da is all yours, Rose. It's probably best this way considering we all have a history."

Rose: "Agreed. I'll make this quick."

Kai: "The sooner, the better. Let's get going."

(Their bodies become engulfed in auras once again, taking off towards their targets; the battle between South and North Ryone rages on.

At the South Ryone camp, soldiers prepare themselves, checking equipment and practicing drills. A male knight wearing armor made of gemstones stand at a strategy table under a large open tent, positioned in front of the entrance to a closed space connected to the tent. Joined by two strategists, they discuss incoming reports from the battlefield.)

South Ryone Strategist #1: "Darn it, are you crazy? If we give up ground now, we can lose a supply line!"

South Ryone Strategist #2: "We will have a re-established supply line by the time our forces reach the appropriate retreat positions. Right now, we're moving too far into enemy territory without adequate scouting. Surely you wouldn't want our men falling into a trap without reinforcements watching their backs, right, Syian?"

(Syian sighs out of frustration, conceding to the points made by her male counterpart.)

Syian: "You're right, Kev. We don't need our countrymen dying that way."

Ruby Knight: "Then is it settled? We'll retreat to regain our second wind and scout out the way forward to avoid ambushes?"

Syian: "Yeah. Then we'll crush the lot of them once we're fully prepared."

Kev: "Commander Iekiyi, give us the order and we'll see to that it goes as planned."

Iekiyi: "Go."

Syian and Kev: "Commander!"

(Iekiyi folds his arms with his eyes closed. Both Syian and Kev bow with respect, walking away with a group of high-ranking South Ryone soldiers.)

Iekiyi: "You two do not have to sneak around. I know you're both there."

Kev: "Huh?"

(Kev and Syian turns back toward Iekiyi, wearing confused expressions, noticing Iekiyi with his arms still folded as he stands firmly in place.)

Syian: "Are you ok, Command—"

(Suddenly, Kai and Raine appears before Iekiyi, shocking Kev, Syian, and all the warriors in the area.)

Kev: "What the heck?"

Kai: "Iekiyi, stand aside."

(Kev quickly draws his weapon, a pole arm fitted with a curved blade. Syian erects horns of energy on top of her head with an electric current sparking between them. The surrounding warriors follows suit, drawing their weapons. Raine turns towards the crowd of warriors surrounding them, standing back-to-back with Kai as he continues to address Iekiyi.)

Iekiyi: "You know I can't do that, Kai."

Kai: "Worth a try. I think there's been enough bloodshed here already. Didn't want to have to contribute."

Iekiyi: "Yes, it's an unfortunate turn of events. However, it cannot be avoided. Even on such a beautiful day."

(Kai and Raine continue the standoff with Iekiyi and the rest of the South Ryone forces. The clouds above the meadow slowly move away from Ni's parent star, shining light onto Iekiyi's armor, creating a rainbow of reflecting light.)

Kai: "Iekiyi, we came here for one reason only. And considering the circumstances, we don't intend to turn back. So, either you get out of our way, or we'll make you."

(Iekiyi becomes visibly nervous as Kai balls his fist, generating an aura of pure fire element around it. Iekiyi slowly unfolds his arms, placing them to his sides, concentrating energy into the palms of his hands.)

Unknown Voice: "Stand down, Iekiyi. Even you could not stop them if you tried."

(Surprised, Iekiyi stops and looks over his shoulder at the closed part of the tent behind him. A pale-skinned woman wearing a mask which covers the right half of her face emerges from the tent, causing Iekiyi to stand aside. Kai and Raine remains standing as the surrounding South Ryonian warriors bow in respect to the half-masked woman.)

Half-Masked Woman: "No sense in getting the best fighters in the army killed here."

Raine: "Ia-On."

(Meanwhile, Rose stands alone in the North Ryone stronghold, surrounded by a force of elite warriors with their weapons drawn. A heavyset woman sits on a throne, relaxed and smiling at Rose's predicament.)

Rose: "You must have known I would be coming here, Ci-Ru-Da. But, is all of this resistance necessary?"

(Suddenly, a young lady steps before Rose, prepared to fight. She is wearing full body armor and a decorative cape, wielding a shield and short sword.)

Young Lady: "Lady Rose, you will not go any farther. As the newly elected commander of North Ryone—"

Rose: "You can't be serious, Gieya."

(Interrupted by Rose's contemptuous words, Gieya stands strong in her battle stance. Rose turns her attention back to Ci-Ru-Da with a frustrated sigh.)

Rose: "Ci-Ru-Da, call off your guard dogs so we can get this over with."

Ci-Ru-Da: "To be fair, Rose, I tried to tell them that none of them stood a chance if you or any of the others came here to confront me. But, you know, guard dogs will be guard dogs."

(Three older soldiers in the group become visibly irritated at Ci-Ru-Da's words.)

Veteran Soldier #1: "Your highness, how can you take this so lightly? It's obvious she's here to stop you!"

Veteran Soldier #2: "Agreed! She could probably kill you! How about some credit for putting our lives on the line?"

Ci-Ru-Da: "More like throwing them away."

Veteran Soldier #3: "Pal, Sarah and everyone here will do whatever it takes to see that our kingdom gets vengeance for what South Ryone did! Even if it means fighting legendary warriors like Royakose!"

(Rose becomes infuriated, hearing herself addressed by that name. An chilling sangria colored aura slowly arises around her body as a response.)

Rose: "Enough."

(Her aura fully emerges, causing the surrounding soldiers to fall to their hands and knees, weakened under a massive amount of pressure.)

Ci-Ru-Da: "Thanks for making her angry, Fredson. Good job! Negotiating with her is going to be sooo much easier now!"

Fredson: <struggling> "S-sorry, Your Highness!"

(Rose steps over her opposition, confronting Ci-Ru-Da. Unnerved by Rose's determined demeanor, Ci-Ru-Da remains seated with a smile.)

Rose: "Ci-Ru-Da, just what the heck are you and Ia-On thinking? What has happened to the North and South Ryonian Treaty? Why are there soldiers in the Meriden Forest killing each other right outside of our home?"

(Ci-Ru-Da's smile instantly shifts into a stern glare upon hearing this revelation, causing her to slowly rise from her throne and onto her feet.)

Ci-Ru-Da: "Rose, I never authorized combat in the Meriden Forest. It is a sacred place to both Ryonian Kingdoms. Those must be rogue fighters-"

Rose: "Don't lie to me! We managed to examine a few of the corpses that are now littering the forest. They're both South Ryone and North Ryone nobles fighting in there, breaking the treaties! And you mean to tell me that you know nothing of it?"

Ci-Ru-Da: "Yup, that's what I'm trying to say. During this whole mess, both Ia-On and 'mwah' sought to negotiate and, hopefully, avoid war. As you can see, that didn't turn out too well. Both kingdoms ended up kingless. And now, the rivalry and bloodlust between our kingdoms pushed us into the ole' song and dance."

(At the South Ryone camp, Raine and Kai both tightens the palms of their hands into a fist with agitation, listening to Ia-On's same explanation of events.)

Raine: "Why didn't you come to us beforehand? It's obvious that this was some sort of plan to start the warring once again! We could have helped you!"

Ia-On: "This is a matter that only concerns our kingdoms. And our kingdoms are our problem."

Kai: "That has now spilled over into your sacred lands and into our backyard! Call off this battle, Ia-On. This has gone on long enough!"

Ia-On: "If what you both say is true about the Meriden Forest, then it is quite clear that nobles are involved in breaking treaties; among other questionable acts. There will be an investigation and consequences in the near future-"

Kai: "An 'investigation' is the last thing we want to hear! Our son is in the middle of this crap! Call it off now Ia-On."

Ia-On: "Even if I wanted to, I could not. The people in both North and South Ryone has already suffered casualties. War has come, and blood will be spilled on this day. Unless you're willing to dispose of entire kingdoms, it will continue."

Kai: "Ia-On, I'm only going to say this once. You don't want to make us angrier than we already are."

(Ia-On and the other South Ryone warriors become intimidated as both Kai and Raine's auras slowly become visible, engulfing their bodies. Meanwhile, Lorelei and Lyone exits the cave, taking cover behind a nearby rock formation. Groups of North and South Ryone Noble Warriors can be heard fighting each other in the distance within the Meriden Forest.)

Lorelei: "Looks like we're going to have to go through the fighting to get to safety. Which is probably not a good idea at all. There's some serious energy being thrown around out there."

(An explosion goes off in the distance, causing Lyone to hug Lorelei in fear. Lorelei looks down at Lyone and becomes determined to find a solution.)

Lorelei: "Well, we can't fly out of here without being mistaken for an enemy. There's only one other way I can think of to solve this problem."

(Lorelei kneels to eye level with Lyone with a determined expression, accompanied by a smile.)

Lorelei: "Hey, Champ, wanna see something cool?"

(Lyone smiles back, nodding with curiosity.)

Lorelei: "Alright then, stay here."

(Lyone watches as Lorelei rises to her feet, walking further into the forest as Lyone remains in cover. Suddenly, a powerful aura engulfs Lorelei's body, and she punches her left hand into the ground. Lorelei pulls a large hammer made of stone out of the ground, emitting energy that connects to her aura.)

Lorelei: "Enough of this!"

(Lyone quickly ducks as Lorelei uses the hammer to pound the ground in front of her, breaking the hammer, sending a ground-shattering shockwave throughout the forest, whipping up dust and uprooting trees. After a few seconds, Lyone looks at the forest, noticing the silence after Lorelei's attack.)

Lyone: <translated> "That was cool as heck!"

(Lorelei looks back at Lyone after hearing him speak in his native language.)

Lorelei: "You didn't use a swear word in Huadi, did you?"

(Lyone covers his mouth with embarrassment as Lorelei shakes her head with a smile.)

Lorelei: "At any rate, that should keep those soldiers stunned and confused for a while. Let's go, Lyone!"

Lyone: "Ok!"

(Lyone runs over to Lorelei, taking her hand, keeping their heads low, proceeding through the thickness of the surrounding forest.

Meanwhile, at the South Ryone main camp, Kai and Raine grow tired of waiting for Ia-On's response. Both are engulfed in powerful auras, causing all the surrounding soldiers to fall to their knees.)

Raine: "What's it gonna be, Ia-On? Should we start with your main forces in the central Helde Meadow?"

(Ia-On becomes nervous, eagerly taking responsibility upon responding.)

Ia-On: "No. I Insist that we fight first. I am the leader, after all."

Raine: "How admirable."

(Suddenly, the blue skies above becomes darkened, shattering with crackling like thunder. An eclipsing shadow is cast upon the Helde Meadow and the Meriden Forest. Everyone turns their eyes toward the skies in confusion.)

Kai: "The heck is going on?"

(Emerging from the clouds in the shattered sky is a giant, dark orb accompanied by dark purple lightning, painting the sky with terror. In the Meriden Forest, Lorelei and Lyone watch as the mysterious object slowly descends upon the Helde Meadow.)

Lyone: "Nanny Lorelei, w-what is that?"

(Lorelei doesn't answer. She stands in awe of the sight, beginning to sweat nervously at the sudden change of events.)

Lorelei: "Why do I feel this fear? What's going on? Ni have mercy on us all."

Lyone: "Nanny Lorelei!"

(Lyone hugs Lorelei, snapping her out of her trance. Lorelei picks up Lyone and begins running away.)

Lorelei: "Whatever that thing is, Champ, we don't wanna be here to meet it!"

(At the North Ryone main camp, Rose, Ci-Ru-Da and the rest of the North Ryone warriors watch in shock as two smaller, dark-purple balls separate from the mysterious orb.)

Rose: "Ci-Ru-Da, do you have any idea what's happening?"

Ci-Ru-Da: "I'm as clueless as you are!"

(Suddenly, Rose gasps as the two smaller balls launch themselves into the North and South Ryone main camps. And, in the blink of an eye, they impact, causing two great explosions. The shockwave from the explosions blows Lorelei and Lyone away, sending Lorelei crashing through a tree and Lyone crashing onto the ground.

Minutes later at the South Ryone camp, screams from injured people can be heard throughout the camp, scorching flames smothers the impact zone. Raine lays next to Kai on the ground, slowly regaining consciousness. She pulls herself onto her feet, witnessing the sheer turmoil that has devoured the camp. After a few seconds of catching her breath, she peers toward the smoke, clouding the decorated tent. Through the smoke, Raine notices an unknown person, standing alone with their back turned.)

Raine: "Ia-On?"

(The unknown person hears Raine's cry and gazes over his shoulder, smiling devilishly. Then, he disappears before her eyes in a burst of speed, blowing away some of the surrounding smoke. Once the smoke is bended, Ia-On's headless corpse is revealed. Raine gasp as Kai begins to regain consciousness. She balls her fist in shock as the injured Iekiyi walks past them, collapsing onto his knees in shame upon witnessing Ia-On's corpse.

At the North Ryone main camp, Rose holds her head with blood covering the right side of her face. After she adjusts her sight, hearing the chaos around her, looking toward Ci-Ru-Da's throne. Then, she notices an unknown lady, repeatedly stabbing Ci-Ru-Da with a strange sword that glows around the edges of its blade. Rose quickly regains her composure and quietly charges at the unknown assailant. The assailant senses Rose's advance and disappears in a burst of speed, fleeing before Rose can strike. Rose looks down upon Ci-Ru-Da's bloody corpse as Gieya and Fredson rushes over, gasping in terror at the scene.)

Fredson: "Y-Your majesty?"

(Gieya becomes enraged, drawing her sword and turning it against Rose once more.)

Gieya: "You! This is your fault!"

Rose: "Don't be foolish."

(Gieya glares at Rose with intense conviction. Yet, Rose turns, fixing her sight on the dark orb as it begins to move closer toward the ground at the Helde Meadow.)

Rose: "This is obviously THAT thing's fault. And, if I didn't know any better, I'd wager that this was a planned assassination."

(Rose looks at one of the medics running around the camp helping the wounded.)

Rose: "You! Medic!"

(The medic stops, becoming overtaken by fear, panting upon the sight of Ci-Ru-Da's corpse.)

Rose: "Get over here and boost my Energy Stream."

(The medic is unresponsive, horrified at the corpse of his now-deceased ruler. Rose suddenly appears in front of the medic, startling him as she glares with an angry expression.)

Rose: "Listen, whoever did this came from whatever the heck that is in the sky. The longer you wait to help me, the higher your chances of ending up like Ci-Ru-Da. So, snap out of it, fool!"

(The medic becomes highly intimidated by Rose. Gieya walks up to the two and smiles softly at the medic.)

Gieya: "It's ok. Boost her Energy Stream. She is our ally now, and we need her help."

(Upon hearing Gieya's order, the medic snaps out of his debilitating fear. He stands before Rose and holds both hands out toward her. A blue aura engulfs his body, as he begins to transfer energy to her.)

Rose: "Darn, one isn't going to be enough. Gieya, get me at least two more medics."

Gieya: "Two more? Do you not see the chaos surrounding us, Rose? We can't afford to—"

Rose: "Do you want to die today?"

(Gieya pauses, tightening her teeth with frustration. Rose glares towards her, waiting for a decision.)

Rose: "Then get me two more."

(Gieya calms herself, conceding to Rose's demands.)

Gieya: "Ok."

(Minutes later at the South Ryone main camp, Kai and Raine both stare at the giant dark orb, sitting on the battlefield at central Helde Meadow. They close their eyes, focusing their minds as Iekiyi, Syian and Kev directs people to safety. The two begin to communicate with Rose telepathically in their native language.)

Kai: <in Huadi> *"Rose, can you hear us?"*

(Rose stands alone, staring at the dark ball with her arms folded, unfazed by her bloodied face.)

Rose: <in Huadi> *"Yes, I can hear your thoughts."*

Raine: <in Huadi> *"What is the status of the North Ryone main camp?"*

Rose: <in Huadi> *"It's destroyed. Whatever that thing is, it's responsible."*

Kai: <in Huadi> *"What about you? Are you ok?"*

Rose: <in Huadi> *"I was hit pretty hard. A group of Huma medics here at the camp managed to help with my Energy Stream, but my body is still not at a hundred percent."*

(Rose looks over her shoulder, glaring at the fatigue-stricken North Ryone medics. While, Fredson and Gieya assist them, Rose shakes her head with pity, refocusing unto the giant dark orb.)

Rose: <in Huadi> *"Weaklings."*

Kai: <in Huadi> *"Ok. We need a plan of action, especially considering all three of us are in the same boat. None of us are at full strength."*

(Suddenly, the ground begins to tremble, and the sky above cracks. Dark-purple lightning randomly strikes the ground below, invoking a perilous environment. The giant dark ball begins to shrink, burrowing into the ground, creating a crater in the central plains of the Helde Meadow.)

Rose: <in Huadi> *"Everything is falling apart around us!"*

Raine: <in Huadi> *"This is only going to get worse! We need to confront the enemy and provide cover for people to retreat!"*

Kai: <in Huadi> *"Darn it, this is pretty bad circumstances. But, not much of a choice at this point. Let's do this."*

(Rose turns her attention to Gieya, arguing with Sarah and Pal about their swift retreat.)

Sarah: "We can't just leave the rest of our men out there in the central plain! We have to . . ."

(Sarah grunts in pain, holding her ribs. Pal places his hands onto her shoulders, helping her stand.)

Gieya: "We have no choice, Sarah. We've sustained so much damage that we couldn't go save them even if we wanted to. We have to retreat and regroup."

(As Sarah hangs her head in shame, Rose walks up to Gieya, determinedly posturing herself.)

Gieya: "We're retreating as we speak. What's your plan?"

Rose: "Whatever the heck that orb is, Kai, Raine, and I plan to challenge it. That should provide cover for your people to retreat safely."

Sarah: "Please take me with you!"

(Rose looks at Sarah out of the corner of her eyes with a piercing glare, heavily intimidating her. Afterward, Rose turns toward her objective as Gieya moves to Sarah's side to comfort her.)

Gieya: "Rose?"

Rose: "What?"

Gieya: "Good luck."

Rose: "Sure."

(Rose summons her aura, disappearing in a burst of speed, heading toward the Helde Meadow's central plain. At the South Ryone main camp, Kai and Raine takes off towards the central plain as well. Iekiyi watches them, retreating with the last of his men. At the Helde Meadow's central plain, the battleground is covered in death, littered with the corpses of dead soldiers from both factions. Two mysterious people stand in front of a giant crater, created by the shrinking dark ball.

It finally reaches full compression, morphing into the shape of a person made of pure energy. Slowly floating to the top of the crater, the body of the mysterious entity frequently discharges a strange flux of energy, striking randomly into its environment. It reaches the top of the crater where the other two unknown assailants await.

Suddenly, Kai, Raine, and Rose appear before their three mysterious opponents. Kai's fist becomes engulfed with pure flames, Rose summons a short sword with an ebony blade, and Raine materializes a long sword and a shield brimming with an ethereal shine. The two teams of three stand before each other in their fighting stances, anticipating a great battle.

In the Meriden Forest, after some time passes, Lorelei regains consciousness, slowly lifting herself onto her hands and knees. She notices Lyone, standing alone with his back turned toward her. As he stands motionless, looking toward the Helde Meadow, a bright light engulfs everything in front of him. Lorelei adjusts her eyes, noticing the nature of the light; an enormous explosion of unknown energy, traveling fast in their direction. She reaches out to Lyone, desperately calling his name.)

Lorelei: "LYONE!"

(Lyone looks back at her, confused and scared. Lorelei tries to speak. But, the sound of the explosion overwhelms her voice. And, in an instant, the light engulfs them.)

Narrator: "Beginnings are always the hardest. At the time, I didn't remember much of that day. It all just . . . happened so fast. To be honest, I can barely recall how I survived."

(Lyone opens his eyes slightly in a daze, unresponsive. He notices himself, floating through the air. Unable to move a muscle.)

Narrator: "I remembered someone or something carrying me through the wind. I felt cold and weightless. I was hurt so badly. I frequently passed out between my glimpses of consciousness."

(Lyone glances at a giant winged monster, covered in scales, carrying him. The next moment, he blackout once again.)

Narrator: "And, once I woke up, I found myself in a very weird situation."

THE STRENGTH TO OVERCOME

(Lyone slowly opens his eyes, awaking to the sounds of singing birds. Regaining consciousness, his eyes captures glimpses of light, entering the room through holes in the surrounding walls. He sits upward, laying on a bed made of leaves inside a hollowed tree. Then, he climbs onto his feet, noticing his body, woundless.

Noticing he is alone, Lyone decides to walk outside. He finds himself in a vast jungle, reaching far past the horizon, surrounded by a great mountain range. He glances toward the sky, shielding his eyes from an ethereal light of an unknown source. Squinting through the shining light, he witnesses a menacing black vortex, looming above the land.)

Lyone: <in Huadi> "Where am I?"

(Lyone walks around the hollowed tree, attempting to strategize.)

Lyone: <in Huadi> "Ok, think, think, think. Ok, so, Dad and Auntie Rose took me camping a lot. I should just treat this like training camp! Yeah, then maybe I can find Nanny Lorelei. She has to be around here somewhere . . ."

(Lyone stops, taking another look around the jungle, intimidated at the thought of being alone.)

Lyone: <in Huadi> ". . . I hope."

(As he explores the area, the sudden sound of rustling bushes command his attention. The sound becomes louder, drawing closer by the moment. Deciding quickly, Lyone runs into the hollowed tree, peeking through one of the holes. A rabbit-like monster with three ears and white fur runs out of the bushes, chased by a bigger, vicious, foxlike predator. The two races around the hollowed tree and a sudden arrow flies from the top of a surrounding tree. The arrow pierces the skull of the fox monster, killing it instantly, allowing the rabbit-like monster to escape.

Lyone continues to watch as a little girl jumps from the treetops. She wears purple hair, strange purple scale armor infused into her skin, brandishing rows of sharp teeth as she smiles. The wild girl walks over to the downed fox monster with a nocked arrow. Then, she playfully pokes her game with her foot.)

Wild Girl: "Dead enough? Alright! Dinner!"

(While Lyone watches in confusion, the wild girl celebrates, freely dancing. Afterwards, she stops, turning her attention in his direction. He nervously ducks away from the hole and the wild girl gleefully smiles. She grabs the big fox's tail, dragging it toward the hollowed tree, walking through the entrance, finding Lyone hidden behind his guard. A sudden thunderstorm can be heard in the skies above as Lyone stands ready to defend himself. The wild girl continues to smile, hauling the big fox farther into the hollowed tree, eventually tossing it onto a makeshift table made of stone.)

Wild Girl: "Dinner!"

(The wild girl erupts into dance once again. Lyone stands about with growing perplexity.)

Lyone: "Um . . ."

Wild Girl: "You not hungry?"

Lyone: "Umm, who are you? Where am I?"

(Lyone stomach growls and the weather changes to a scorching sunshine. The wild girl gives Lyone a big grin and he stands about with an embarrassed smile. Then, he turns his attention over to the big foxlike monster.)

Lyone: "So, you have a Friorion there, huh? My dad and auntie taught me how to prepare those. Do you mind ha ha?"

(A few hours later at nightfall outside of the hollowed tree, Lyone and the wild girl sit near a campfire, finishing their dinner. Lyone stares at the wild girl puzzled as she throws discarded bones over her shoulder, devouring her last bite of meat, smiling with satisfaction.)

Lyone: "Did you really eat that raw meat from the Friorion? I cooked enough for the both of us you know! You can die from uncooked food!"

(The wild girl turns to Lyone with a curious expression amidst his concerns.)

Wild Girl: "Huh? What is this? Cook?"

Lyone: "You don't know what cooking is? How do you drink groundwater? Do you even filter and boil it to kill germs?"

(The wild girl burps and smiles at Lyone, chanting in celebration.)

Wild Girl: "Full! Full! Full! Full! Full!"

(Lyone sighs, controlling his frustration, watching the wild girl continues her chant.)

Lyone: *"Guest I can't complain too much. I'm full myself."*

Wild Girl: "You're full! You're full! You're full!"

Lyone: "Huh? Wait a minute, how did you know that?"

Wild Girl: "Huh? Know what?"

(After a brief silence, Lyone shakes his head with disregard.)

Lyone: "Forget it."

(He places his back to the ground, trying his best to relax, noticing the dark vortex in the sky among the stars.)

Lyone: "Hey, I never got your name."

Wild Girl: "Name? Hmm."

Lyone: "You do have a name, right? I'm Lyone. Whats your name?"

Wild Girl: "Tuki."

Lyone: "Tuki? You just made that up, didn't you?"

(Tuki gives Lyone a big grin, repeatedly chanting her name.)

Tuki: "Tuki! Tuki! Tuki! Tuki!"

Lyone: "Ok, ok! I got it. Tuki! Great name."

(Lyone turns his attention back to the skies, becoming increasingly concerned.)

Lyone: "So, Tuki, where are we anyway? I've been having weird feelings about this place ever since I woke up. Even the stars seem a bit. . . weird. And that giant hole in the sky. None of this seems strange to you?"

(Lyone looks over to Tuki; she carelessly stretches and yawns.)

Lyone: "Did you hear me, Tuki?"

Tuki: "Dreams are real! Dreams are real! Dreams are really, really real!"

(Annoyed by her chanting, Lyone turns his attention back to the sky.

The next morning, Tuki sleeps on the floor of the hollowed tree, snoring with saliva sliding out of her mouth. Lyone stands at the entrance with his arms folded, watching the rainfall from a cloudless sky, pondering the whereabouts of his parents.)

Lyone: <In Huadi> *"I hope they're all safe. I have to find them, but I don't even know where I am."*

(Lyone looks over his shoulder at Tuki, bothered at her slumber mumbling. Then, he turns back to the doorway, sighing in frustration.)

Lyone: <In Huadi> *"I really wish Tuki was more help. What a waste of time."*

(He stares up at the sky, noting the vortex has shrunken. Suddenly, Tuki yawns loudly, gaining Lyone's attention. She abruptly lifts her legs into the air, hopping onto her feet with a big grin.)

Tuki: "Parents!"

Lyone: "Huh?"

Tuki: "Mommies, Daddies, Aunties, Nannies!"

(Lyone grows anxious, listening to Tuki's chanting.)

Lyone: "Tuki, you know where my parents are?"

(Tuki pauses, carefully thinking, increasing Lyone's restlessness.)

Tuki: "Hmm."

Lyone: "Tuki?"

Tuki: "Hee hee! I know!"

Lyone: "You know where they are?"

Tuki: "Follow! Follow! Follow!"

(Lyone's face brightens with happiness as Tuki runs out of the hollowed tree and into the surrounding wilderness. With clear skies and light shining from above, he runs behind her. They travel through the jungle, surrounded by tall, intimidating trees and thick vegetation. Then, Lyone loses track of Tuki, looking around with uncertainty.)

Lyone: "*Where'd she go?*"

Tuki: "Parents! Parents! Parents!"

Lyone: "What the . . .? Hey, wait up, Tuki!"

(Lyone runs through the wilderness, searching for Tuki, trailing the sound of her voice. Suddenly, he stops, hearing the mysterious sound of a heavier voice, breathing slowly, echoing from his right.)

Lyone: "What is that?"

(Curious, he walks toward the heavy breathing; it grows louder with each step.)

Lyone: "Something breathing?"

Tuki: "Parents! Parents! Parents!"

(Lyone pauses, listening to Tuki's chants in the distance. Yet, he decides to continue toward the heavier breathing. A blanket of fog settles across the area as Lyone nervously travels onward. Then, he steps out of the jungle into a grassy field, discovering a giant cave covered with moss and vines.

Lyone stands silent, listening to the heavy breaths emerge from the cave. He starts to back away into the jungle and a sudden roar erupts from the cave; along with a menacing red aura. Lyone instantly stops, standing still, gazing at the cave entrance; the pupils of his eyes glows red. The skies above converts into pitch-black, unpredictably expelling red bolts of lightning.

Tuki heeds the destructive weather, wearing an expression of bewilderment. Then, her uncertainty transforms into resolve, taking off in a burst of speed toward the cave's red aura. Lyone begins to slowly walk toward the cave entrance, hypnotized by the red aura. Suddenly, Tuki appears, noticing Lyone's lack of self-control. Quickly acting, she punches onto the ground, fracturing it into parts. Then, she lifts a giant slab of rock out of the ground, infusing the boulder with energy. Finally, she tosses the boulder into the cave entrance, completely blocking it.

As the menacing red glow from the cave subsides, Lyone stands in place with his eyes still glowing. Tuki runs up to him, noticing his hypnosis. Then, she slaps him on the neck, making him flinch. Lyone grabs his neck in pain, intensely scowling at her.)

Lyone: <in Huadi> "Hey, what the heck?"

(Lyone rubs his neck, feeling confused and drained. The weather changes from a pitch-black sky to a harsh shine, accompanied by a humid mist.)

Lyone: "Tuki? What did you hit me for?"

(After examining Lyone, Tuki gives off a big grin and runs back into the jungle, chanting.)

Tuki: "Parents! Parents! Parents!"

(Lyone watches Tuki skip back into the jungle, briefly turning his attention to the cave entrance; now blocked by a giant boulder.)

Lyone: *"When did that happen?"*

(Lyone regains his composure, walking toward the jungle, watching the cave over his shoulder, running away. He follows behind Tuki, breathing heavily and feeling weak. After some distance, he stops next to a tree, catching his breath. Closing his eyes for a few seconds, he opens them to find Tuki, playfully grinning.)

Lyone: "Give me a minute, Tuki."

Tuki: "Parents near!"

(Lyone gains a hopeful second wind, receiving her words with a smile. As the day converts into clear skies and a soft breeze, Tuki extends her hand toward Lyone, helping him onto his feet. The two presses forward through the jungle together. In a short amount of time, they walk out of the jungle and into an open, grassy field. The prairie is home to three large pillars of stone. Lyone examines the area as Tuki playfully runs through the prairie.)

Lyone: "Tuki?"

(Tuki stops, turning towards Lyone, noticing his face riddled with disappointment. The cloudless sky alters into a somber grey color, as Lyone finds no one around.)

Tuki: "Huh?"

Lyone: "My parents. I thought we could find them here."

(Tuki grins, carelessly running through the field. Then, she reaches the three pillars, chanting and dancing.)

Tuki: "Parents! Parents! Parents!"

(Lyone walks in front of the pillars of stone, curiously resting his hand onto one of them. After a few seconds of standing silently, he sits onto the grass at his feet, fatigued and depressed.)

Lyone: *"This is so stupid. I don't know where I am, how I got here, and I don't know where my family is."*

(Lyone watches Tuki aimlessly play around the prairie, annoyed by her carelessness. As Tuki continues to play, the weather changes once again with shaking grounds and harshly blowing winds.)

Lyone: *"And she is no help. Urgh."*

(Lyone stomach growls, catching Tuki's attention as the weather calms.)

Tuki: "Hungry! Hungry! Hungry!"

Lyone: "Uh, did we have more food back at that big tree?"

Tuki: "Nope!"

Lyone: "Great."

(Lyone rubs his stomach, hungrily looking back toward the jungle. Then, he spots three rabbit-like monsters, obliviously roaming the prairie.)

Lyone: "Hey, Tuki! Want some target practice?"

(Later that night, Lyone and Tuki sit outside of the hollowed tree in front of a campfire, eating the last bits of their meal. Lyone takes notices to the food, keenly observing the meat.)

Lyone: "You know what's weird, Tuki?"

(Promptly turning toward Lyone, Tuki listens with a mouth full of meat and bones.)

Lyone: "Friorions and Gums are two of my favorite monsters to eat when I'm camping with my family. They taught me all about survival, and good sources of food like these monsters. But I noticed that these tastes different than normal. Both were pretty bland. Did you notice that?"

(After explaining his observation, he turns to Tuki and she continues to chew with her mouth full.)

Lyone: *"Should've seen that one coming. Well, at least I'm not hungry anymore."*

(Lyone rises to his feet, soothingly stretches, and walks over to a nearby tree. Assuming a novice fighting stance, he punches the tree as hard as he can, slightly shifting its position. Tuki gawks at Lyone with her signature grin, standing to her feet, applauding.)

Tuki: "Yeahhh!"

Lyone: "Um, ok."

Tuki: "Who taught you?"

Lyone: "What? How to fight? My parents. Well, at least, they started to teach me . . . before I lost them."

(Lyone folds his arms, staring towards the ground, adrift.)

Lyone: "You know, once my Nanny Lorelei told me that my parents are the strongest fighters on the planet."

(Tuki watches as Lyone slowly walks over to the campfire; the night stars becomes dim. Lyone takes a seat, silently contemplating his dilemma.)

Lyone: "Tuki, I'm leaving this place tomorrow. I have to find my family. I know they're out there somewhere waiting for me."

(Lyone folds his legs as Tuki's eyes roams around aimlessly.)

Lyone: "You can come with me if you like."

Tuki: "Huh?"

Lyone: "Well, you don't seem to have parents or anything. Sticking together is better than being alone in the middle of nowhere, right?"

(Lyone looks at Tuki, noticing her laying on the ground near the campfire in a fetal position. She is already asleep, loudly snoring. Lyone smiles, charily shaking his head, deciding to make his way toward the hollowed tree.

Late in the night as Lyone sleeps, Tuki floats high in the sky with wings sprouted from her back. She floats in front of the vortex, and black electricity shoots from her fingers to the edges of the abyss. After a few seconds, she manages to close it completely, floating about with a victorious grin. The next day, Lyone awakens inside the hollowed tree, instantly detecting his body in a debilitated state.)

Lyone: *"Urgh, what's going on? I-I can't talk."*

(Trying to move out of his bed, he falls to the floor, sweating with a short of breath. His vision loses focus. His environment scatters in a mix of colors. He falls within a blinding void of light.)

Lyone: *"What's going on? Am I seeing things? Am I dreaming? Am I going to die? Mom. Dad. Aunt Rose. Nanny Lorelei. I'm sorry. I couldn't find any of you. Forgive me."*

Voice: "Don't worry!"

Lyone: *"Huh?"*

(Suddenly, Tuki floats through the void, catching Lyone in her arms, wearing her signature grin.)

Lyone: *"Tuki?"*

Tuki: "The hard part's over, Lyone."

(Lyone observes Tuki's face, watching her mature in age before his eyes. Her purple hair and scale armor darken to black, gorgeously contracting her light brown skin. Then, he slowly closes his eyes, becoming engulfed by the light of the void.

After an unspecified amount of time passes, Lyone gradually awakens, laying in bed within a comfortable home. Various parts of his body is wrapped in bandages and attached to machines through IVs.)

Lyone: <in Huadi> "*W-what? What's happening?*"

(He shifts his head to observe the room, noticing a photo of a family of four, elegantly sitting near a window filled with the light of day. Then, he turns to the door of the room, detecting someone slowly walking in. A young dark-skinned girl in her early teens steps into the room, carefully juggling a bowl of soup on a food tray. She walks to the desk at Lyone's bedside, placing the tray on it. Afterwards, she turns around towards Lyone, gasping at the sight of his renewed consciousness.)

Young Girl: "Oh! You're not a vegetable anymore!"

Lyone: "Who are you? Where am I?"

Young Girl: "Hold on one sec. I'll get my mom to help!"

(Lyone watches as the young girl leaves the room, quickly moving, calling out to her parents.)

Young Girl: "Mom! Dad! He's awake! I'm not making it up this time! I swear!"

(Minutes later, Lyone notices as an older, bronze-skinned man with a short, grayed beard and a fit physique walks into his bedroom with the young girl from before. The elderly man momentarily weighs Lyone's disorientation, silently standing at his bedside.)

Elderly Man: "Lisa, go and tell your mother to make sure to bring her medical equipment."

Lisa: "You think she'd forget, Dad?"

Elderly Man: "Hey, I didn't say that. More like she might need some help carrying things."

Lisa: "Ha ha! Sure, Dad. Alright then, I'll go help her."

(Lisa leaves the room as the elderly man grabs a chair, taking a seat, gaining Lyone's full attention.)

Elderly Man: "You certainly took quite the beating for a child out in the middle of nowhere."

Lyone: "W-What?"

Elderly Man: "My name is Dior Kendric. You are at a home located south of the Federal Union. My daughter and I found you badly injured at the foot of Mount Hoviros, located further south from here. If we hadn't shown up when we did, you would have been dinner for the native monsters."

(Dior inspects Lyone, watching him stares at the ceiling of the room. Lyone lingers in his confusion, warily responding.)

Dior: "Do you remember why you were out there?"

Lyone: "I-I don't know."

Dior: "How about who you were with?"

Lyone: "I-I said I don't know."

Dior: "Tell me, do you remember anything prior to being injured and lost?"

Lyone: "I don't remember!"

(Dior is silenced by Lyone's sudden outburst, patiently withdrawing his interrogation. Lyone places his hand on his forehead, struggling with the circumstances.

As silence fills the room, the door opens. Lisa walks into the room, pulling a cart of supplies and machines. With her, an elderly lady of a dark complexion, wearing glasses and a lab coat with a fluffy afro. She walks into the room, brightly wearing a soft smile.)

Elderly Lady: "Ok, ok, I get it! I'm getting old. But must you remind me, dear?"

Dior: "Ha ha, what's age gotta do with it? You've always been forgetful, honey."

(The elderly lady observes both Dior and Lyone, intuitively noticing his confusion and distress.)

Elderly Lady: "Hm, dear, what did you do?"

Dior: "I just asked him a few questions is all."

(She sighs with irritation, removing both Dior and Lisa out of the room.)

Elderly Lady: "Alright, thanks for the help you two. Now, out."

Lisa: "Um, you sure Mom?"

Dior: "We could still help if you need us."

Elderly Lady: "I believe you've helped enough, Dior. Now, out of here. I'll talk to you two afterwards."

Dior: "Alright then. See what you did, Lisa? Come on, let's go."

Lisa: "Wait, what? You were the one that did whatever it was!"

Dior: "Now, now, Lisa. You can apologize later. Ha ha!"

(The elderly lady wears a weary smile as Dior guides Lisa out of the room by the shoulders; despite Lisa's continued objection to his deflection.)

Elderly Lady: "What am I gonna do with those two?"

(After they leave the room, she gives her undivided attention to Lyone. He remains silent, unhappily staring at his bed sheets.)

Elderly Lady: "Did you have lunch yet, young man?"

(Lyone turns away from the elderly lady, attempting to ignore her. But, his stomach growls, frailly causing his face to drop.)

Elderly Lady: "You're gonna ignore your stomach like you're ignoring me, huh?"

(She kindly guides his eyes to the bowl of soup. He is slightly hesitant, eventually deciding to take the food. Minutes later, Lyone sits in his bed holding an empty bowl with the elderly lady sitting at his bedside.)

Elderly Lady: "Feeling better?"

(Lyone sits quietly with his head down towards the bedsheets, visibly disheartened.)

Elderly Lady: "My name is Jel Kendric. Mind telling me your name, sweetheart?"

Lyone: "It's Lyone."

Jel: "Lyone? That's a very strong name filled with pride and majesty. You wanna know a secret about that name?"

Lyone: "A secret?"

Jel: "Yup. You see, the origin of your name, is from a species of monsters called 'Lyon.' They are amongst the strongest monsters in the world; due to their latent abilities. You know what that means?"

(Jel wears her inviting smile, bringing comfort to Lyone's genuine curiosity.)

Lyone: "No. What's it mean?"

Jel: "It means as they grow up, they can easily surpass most other monsters in strength and dominance because their hidden power matures over time."

Lyone: "Hey, my parents told me the same thing once."

Jel: "Oh really? Well, I think they chose a very good name for you, Lyone. You'll grow to be a strong man."

Lyone: "Thank you."

Jel: "No problem, sweetheart."

Lyone: "Um, Mrs. Kendric, have you seen my parents and my nanny?"

Jel: *"So, he doesn't know where they are."*

(Jel becomes attentive, grabbing a clipboard and pen, analyzing the situation.)

Jel: "Oh, I haven't seen them. But I can help you find them. Would you like that?"

Lyone: "Yes, please!"

Jel: "Ok, then. But I need your help as well."

Lyone: "My help? With what?"

Jel: "Well, sweetheart, when my husband and my daughter found you, you were badly hurt. I need you to help me check your condition. And I promise I'll help you find your parents. Ok?"

Lyone: "Ok."

(An hour later, Jel walks into the kitchen, dishearteningly sighing, as Dior and Lisa eat together.)

Lisa: "Everything ok, Mom?"

Jel: "Honestly that depends, sweetheart."

Dior: "Go ahead, dear. We're all ears."

Jel: "Ok then. So, his name is Lyone Kindle. The last thing he remembers is a bright light following a large explosion of some sort and being carried through the air. He lost contact with his mother, father, aunt, and nanny. And, worst of all, he is paralyzed from the waist down."

(Dior and Lisa digest the news, discouragingly matching Jel's concern.)

Lisa: "That's horrible! Can we do anything to help?"

(Dior slowly walks around the kitchen, thinking back to where they found Lyone.)

Dior: "Hmm, an explosion, you say? There was a hole in the ground where we found him, but there was no explosion in the area before we arrived. It's more likely that he landed there, rather than an explosion around him. Though I could be wrong."

Jel: "Considering his accent, he definitely didn't grow up in the Federal Union."

Dior: "Being carried in the air . . . If I didn't know better, I'd say it sounds like he flew here from somewhere. We should talk to him and see if we can gather more information."

Jel: "Honey, remember the first time you tried to 'gather information'? You confused and frightened him."

(Dior becomes silent, sipping his tea as Lisa sassily smiles at him.)

Dior: "You're right. My apologies."

Jel: "Good. For the time being, he is my patient. I believe he has a chance to regain his motor skills. However, too much stress can be detrimental."

(Dior considers the situation, firmly turning his attention to Lisa.)

Dior: "Lisa, go ahead and practice your math in the classroom."

Lisa: "What? Really, Dad? Do I have to though?"

(Dior responds to her objection with a stern stare, and Lisa hangs her head with a sad face.)

Lisa: "Can I at least practice my stances instead?"

Dior: "Math."

Lisa: "Ok."

(After a sad whimper, she leaves the kitchen, reluctantly heading towards the classroom in the back of the house. Once Lisa leaves, Dior and Jel continues their conversation.)

Dior: "Now, about your colleagues. We've been lucky these past few days. But, if someone finds out we're harboring an undocumented person, we'll have Arbitrators on us in no time."

Jel: "Don't worry, I'm already on it. I've sent out a settlement-wide notice about information gathering at experimental unit GH-10. Appointments and meetings at this location are off limits for all personnel below administration ranks unless ordered and/or approved."

Dior: "That should give us a paper trail and a fair warning. Always thinking ahead, dear."

Jel: "You know it."

Dior: "In the meantime, I'll retrace our steps and try to piece together this puzzle."

(Jel smiles, walking closer to Dior, affectionately wrapping her arms around his neck.)

Jel: "Sounds like we have a plan, dear."

Dior: "That we do."

(After the couple share a kiss, Dior touches her face with his hand, lovingly preserving eye contact.)

Dior: "You really think he'll be able to walk again?

Jel: "With our help, his chances are the best."

Dior: "Getting a 'yes' from a doctor is the hardest thing ever."

Jel: "Hey, you're one to talk, mister explorer, historian, all around know-it-all. I'll never forget anything with you around."

(Jel playfully pushes Dior away, walking out of the kitchen.)

Jel: "I'll help Lisa with math."

(Dior smiles, confidently turning toward the kitchen, collecting dishes. Meanwhile, Lyone remains in bed, drearily staring out the window of his room. For the next few days, he lingers in his depression, attempting to focus his mind on his legs, desperately trying to move his muscles. At night, he hums a song to himself in Huadi, falling asleep shortly afterwards.

One day, Lisa quietly walks into his room with a tray of food. She notices Lyone, watching the daylight beam through the window, inattentive to her presence. Lisa places the tray of food on the desk at his bedside, silently proceeding toward the door.)

Lyone: "Hey."

Lisa: "Huh?"

(Lisa turns toward Lyone, noticing him seated upwards. He curiously stares at her, shyly craving to ask a question.)

Lisa: "Oh, hey! Everything's all good?"

Lyone: "You mind if I could get another cookie?"

(Lisa peers over to the cookie on Lyone's tray of food, playfully turning her attention back to him.)

Lisa: "I can get you another one. But I'll have to sneak past Mom and Dad to do it. That's pretty dangerous. I think I'm gonna need something from you in return for this job."

Lyone: "You can't just ask them to get me a cookie?"

Lisa: "Um, no. Cookies are limited supplies. We have to ration them you know."

Lyone: "Oh, ok then. So, what do you want from me?"

Lisa: "Your name is Lyone, right?"

Lyone: "Yeah."

Lisa: "I'm Lisa. Nice to meet you."

Lyone: "Nice to meet you."

Lisa: "You know, I was with Dad when we found you at the foot of that mountain."

Lyone: "Really? Did you see my parents there?"

Lisa: "Nope. It was only you. You were inside of this huge hole. Dad thinks it may have something to do with that explosion you were talking about."

Lyone: "No. That wasn't created by the explosion. My nanny was with me and we saw the explosion. Everything was lit up."

Lisa: "Oh. I see."

(After a brief silence, Lisa decides to leave in support.)

Lisa: "I'll go get a cookie for you."

Lyone: "Thanks."

(Later in the day, Lyone stares at a family picture held within a decorative frame: A family of four standing together, joyfully smiling. He recognizes Jel, Dior, and Lisa in the photo. However, the fourth man with a bald head, tall, and muscular remains a mystery. Afterwards, Jel walks into the room, happily pushing a wheelchair.)

Jel: "Hey, sweetheart. Hope your day is going well."

Lyone: "It is. Thanks for the food, Mrs. Kendric."

Jel: "Please, call me Jel, dear. Now, after your physical today, how about we take a stroll outside for a bit?"

Lyone: "Sounds good."

(Jel lifts the bedsheets, exposing Lyone's feet. She takes a pen out of her lab coat pocket, slightly moving the tip of the pen along Lyone's feet until a toe twitches on each foot. Lyone notices the smile on her face, delightfully placing her pen back into the pocket of her coat.)

Jel: "Great news, sweetheart! The nerves in your feet are recovering very quickly. You'll be up and about in no time."

Lyone: "Really? Yes!"

(Brimming with confidence, Lyone pumps his fist. Jel continues with his physical, moving his legs and bending his knees.)

Jel: "I gotta admit, this is very quick progress."

Lyone: "Well, I've been trying to focus my mind on moving my feet. Looks like it's paying off."

Jel: "That's a lot of willpower you have there, young man. Lyone was the right name for you after all!"

(After a few minutes, Jel finishes Lyone's physical, preparing his wheelchair.)

Jel: "Alright, Lyone, everything is healing well. Let's go on that stroll, get you familiar with the surroundings, and talk more about your parents. Sounds good?"

(Lyone nods his head, cheerfully smiling as Jel helps him out of bed. The two take an elevator from the second floor to the first floor, making their way to the front porch. Lyone takes a deep breath of fresh air, being wheeled by Jel down a ramp connected to the porch. As Jel pushes his wheelchair, he tunes his ears, listening to the sounds of massive construction cranes and machines, echoing from the north.)

Lyone: "What is that?"

Jel: "Construction is taking place for the new town of Wisden. It's a new settlement of the Federal Union, and the people there wish it to be the next big city. They work very hard all the time. A little too hard, really. Considering how often I see the paperwork of patients from there Ha ha!"

(Lyone turns his attention to the forest behind the home, curiously observing the green-and-yellow leaves of the trees. Then, he grows concerned, gazing upon the abnormally darkened trail that leads deeper into the forest.)

Lyone: "What's the name of this forest?"

Jel: "Oh, well, it doesn't really have a name yet. You see, this entire area, including Wisden, was a uninhabitable zone up until about a year ago. Before the Federal Union settlement was established a lot of powerful native monsters had control of this area, along with the different beast species that used to live with them. So, since this is all fairly new, a name for the forest hasn't been selected yet."

Lisa: "I call it Yellow Shadow Forest!"

(Jel and Lyone look toward the home, watching Lisa jump off the front porch. Lisa walks up to them, cheerfully grinning.)

Lyone: "Yellow Shadow Forest? Why that name?"

Lisa: "See the yellow parts of the leaves? They absorb so much of the light from Yunyi that almost none of it reaches the forest floor. That's why it's so dark in there, even in the daytime. At least that's what Dad told me!"

(Confused by Lisa's explanation, Lyone stares at her, eagerly searching for clarity.)

Lyone: "Yunyi?"

Lisa: "Yeah. Yunyi. You know, the parent star to our solar system."

(As Lyone remains confused, Jel takes notice of his lack of knowledge, becoming intrigued.)

Jel: "Oh my, you don't know what these things are? Or is it that your injuries caused you to forget?"

Lyone: "Um, I'm not sure. I don't think I've heard those things before."

(Lyone lowers his head with roaming eyes, juggling with memories of his family, recalling a moment shared with Rose and Kai. The three speak to each other in Huadi during a camping session at night.)

Kai: <in Huadi> "You see those three glowing circles in the sky, Lyone?"

Lyone: <in Huadi> "You mean the three that makes a triangle, Dad?"

Kai: <in Huadi> "Yup, those are the ones I'm talking about. There is an old Renzido legend that tells you about 'em. Wanna hear it?"

Lyone: <in Huadi> "Yeah! Please tell me!"

(Lyone grabs a piece of roasted meat from the large plate of food next to the campfire, attentively crossing his legs, listening to Kai's story.)

Kai: <in Huadi> "Alright then. Long ago the creator of this world had four children. The creator wanted to raise the children to be free. So, it let them grow on their own with no rules or limits. All four children grew up with amazing powers and potential. But, they also grew up hating each other."

(Lyone interjects, chewing with a mouth full of food.)

Lyone: <in Huadi> "Huh? Really? But why?"

Kai: <in Huadi> "Well, although they grew up free, they were always in competition with each other for survival. They never learned how to work together, so they hated each other. The creator saw this and became ashamed of itself for allowing its creations to be corrupted by hate. And so, the creator made one more child . . . and Ni was born."

Lyone: <in Huadi> "Hey, isn't that the name of our planet?"

Rose: <in Huadi> "Lyone, show some respect and swallow your food before talking!"

(Lyone urgently turns his attention to Rose, instantly noticing her scolding leer. As she leans on a tree with her arms folded, he swallows his food, remorsefully turning his body towards her, respectfully bowing.)

Lyone: <in Huadi> "Sorry, Auntie Rose! So, so sorry!"

(Rose lowers her head, cloaking a smile at Lyone's adorability.)

Rose: <in Huadi> "Apology accepted."

(Lyone briefly maintains his bowing position, slowly raising his head to the sight of Rose's smile. Feeling better, Lyone turns back towards Kai, respectfully bowing as well.)

Kai: <in Huadi> "Ha ha, it's all good, Lyone. You are excused."

(Satisfied with their approval, Lyone raises his head, continuing his dinner with a smile of his own.)

Kai: <in Huadi> "So, the creator made Ni, the very same Ni that has given us all life. And this time, the creator decided to not only impose order upon Ni's life, but also to nurture Ni with a plan for success. And when Ni grew up, she became the planet that we all have come to know. But the other children of the creator became jealous of Ni and her amazing power. Although the four hated each other, their hatred for Ni trumped all else. They vowed to destroy Ni. Once the creator learned of the vows its children had taken to destroy Ni, it went to three of the strongest citizens and made them the champions of Ni. Their new powers were so strong, they turned the champions into the three moons we have now. The first champion, Eargorh, protects Ni's lands. The second champion, Vehathe, protects Ni's seas. And the third champion, Rehtoris, protects Ni's skies. And that's the old Renzido legend of Ni and her three protectors. At least the beginning of it, anyway."

(As Lyone finishes the last bite of his meal, he looks to Kai, pondering with questions.)

Lyone: <in Huadi> "Wow, so did all of that actually happen?"

Kai: <in Huadi> "Well, I'm willing to bet it didn't happen exactly that way. But, in most Renzido cultures, those are the names of the three moons."

Lyone: <in Huadi> "And what about the other ball in the sky? The one that's always dark with that weird golden glow around it?"

Kai: <in Huadi> "Ahh, that one is the creator's home: Jiloron. It's the source of all life as we know it."

(Kai abruptly pauses, discerning Lyone's previous statement and becomes puzzled.)

Kai: <in Huadi> "Wait, 'dark ball with a golden aura'? You're talking about the one at daytime, right?"

Lyone: <in Huadi> "Yes. So, it's Jiloron, right?"

(Rose and Kai glances over at each other with suspicion.)

Kai <in Huadi> "Y-Yeah, son."

Rose: <in Huadi> "Kai, that's enough for now."

(Rose stands onto her feet, walking to the rest of the party, capturing their attention.)

Rose: <in Huadi> "Training continues at dawn. It's best that we all get some sleep."

Kai: <in Huadi> "Oh crap, I forgot all about that."

Lyone: <in Huadi> "Um, bad word, Dad."

Kai: <in Huadi> "Oh cra—, err, I mean, shoot! Sorry! Ha ha! A-Anyway, let's clean up and call it a night, eh?"

(At the dawn of the next day, Kai and Rose instruct Lyone, preparing equipment and supplies for an early morning hike. During his task, he briefly stands, silently staring at the parent star of the planet.)

Rose: <in Huadi> "Lyone, we're ready."

Lyone: <in Huadi> "Huh? Ok!"

(Hearing Rose's voice, he turns away, following them along the trail. As Lyone's memory comes to an end, he glances towards the sky, blissfully staring at the planet's parent star. Suddenly, Jel covers his eyes, looking toward Lyone with confusion.)

Jel: "Hey! Don't stare directly at Yunyi! You'll burn out the retina of your eyes!"

Lyone: "Huh? 'Ret-na?' What's that?"

Jel: "Well, I can teach you about that. But don't stare at Yunyi, dear. Its rays can damage your eyes if you focus them directly at it."

Lyone: "Really? I've done it before. When will that happen to me?"

Jel: "Wait, you've done it before?"

Lyone: "Yeah. I've stared at Jiloron a lot. It looks pretty cool."

(Perplexed by Lyone's words, Jel becomes surprised at his candor.)

Jel: *"He didn't have any vision problems in the physical. Weird."*

Lyone: "Now that I think about it, why do you guys call it Yunyi? Isn't the name of the creator's home Jiloron?"

(The perplexity spreads as both Lisa and Jel look toward each other.)

Lisa: "'Jiloron?' I've never heard of that name before. Did you just make that up?"

Lyone: "My dad told me it's called 'Jiloron.'"

(Lisa teases Lyone, jokingly mocking his knowledge with a smirk.)

Lisa: "Come on Lyone, why would anyone teach you such a silly name for Yunyi? Just admit you made it up."

(Lyone becomes irritated, turning away from Lisa, attempting to ignore her.)

Lyone: "I didn't make it up."

Lisa: "Ha! My dad says liars soar higher but always crash in a pillar of fire."

(Lyone slams his fist onto the arm of his wheelchair, causing both Jel and Lisa to step back at his sudden outburst.)

Lyone: "I'm not lying, so shut up!"

(Lyone folds his arms, angrily turning away from Lisa once again.)

Jel: "Alright, that's enough, you two. Lisa, go help your father with dinner plans."

Lisa: "B-But what did I—"

Jel: "Lisa, go ahead and do what you're told. I will talk to you about this later."

(Lisa sighs, begrudgingly walking back to the family home.)

Jel: "Lyone, I apologize for letting that happen. The last thing we need to do is to burden you with unnecessary stress."

(As Jel pushes him back to the house, Lyone unfolds his arms, unhappily hanging his head.)

Jel: "So, your father taught you the name of our parent star?"

Lyone: "Yeah."

Jel: "I see."

(The two remain awkwardly silent, making their way up the ramp and onto the front porch.)

Jel: "You must excuse me, Lyone. I didn't intend to talk about your parents in such an—awkward manner."

(Lyone's head remains hung, unresponsive to Jel's apology.)

Jel: "We'll pick up this topic at a later time. Dinner should be soon. Are you hungry?"

Lyone: "Maybe."

Jel: "Maybe? You sure it's just maybe?"

(Lyone's stomach growls, causing him to laugh nervously. Reassured at Lyone's renewed sense of humor, Jel also smiles .

Later that night, Jel, Dior, Lisa, and Lyone sit at the dinner table, joyfully sniffing the aroma of meat cooked with herbs and spices. Lyone salivates, gawking at the dinner table covered in different plates of food.)

Dior: "It's been some time since you came to our home, Lyone, and we haven't had a formal dinner with you yet. So, I made this feast as a 'welcome to our home' gesture."

Lyone: <in Huadi> "Wow! This is amazing."

Dior: "Hmm?"

(Everyone watches as Lyone stares at the dinner table, licking his lips with anticipation.)

Lisa: "Ha ha, maybe Lyone wants to say prayers before we eat?"

(Lyone turns his attention to everyone, wondering the meaning of Lisa's suggestion.)

Lyone: "Huh? Prayers?"

Dior: "Yes, go ahead, Lyone. We'll wait for you."

(He hangs his head, timidly responding to Dior.)

Lyone: "Um, I've never done that before."

(Noticing Lyone's shyness, Jel gently places her hand on the table in front of him, gaining his attention.)

Jel: "It's ok, Lyone. I can do it this time. Don't worry."

Lyone: "O-ok."

(Jel leads the prayer, bowing her head and closing her eyes. Lyone watches Dior and Lisa, following Jel's example. He slightly bows his own head, cautiously keeping his eyes on them.)

Jel: "By the grace of Ni, we thank our mother for the vigor, valor, and wisdom given to us to assemble this feast. We also thank our mother for Lyone's company, and may his recovery be swift. Ni'Ador."

Lisa and Dior: "Ni'Ador."

(After the prayer, Lyone follows the others, peacefully raising their heads with smiles.)

Jel: "Please, allow me, Lyone."

(Jel and Dior receives Lyone and Lisa's plates respectively, happily serving them food. Thirty minutes later, everyone at the table stares at Lyone, amazed at the amount of food he has eaten. Lyone finishes another plate, cheerfully looking about the table once more.)

Lyone: "May I have some more, please?"

Dior: "Oh! O-of course!"

(Jel and Lisa watches Lyone in amazement as Dior prepares another plate for him.)

Lisa: "Geez, Lyone! You eat faster than my big brother!"

Jel: "Chris would be impressed. That's for sure."

Lyone: "Ha! If you think I can eat, you should see my dad and my aunt!"

(Lyone receives his plate from Dior, cheerfully continuing his dinner. While Lyone eats, Jel looks over to Dior, signaling him with a nod.)

Dior: "So, Lyone, about your parents. Have you managed to remember where they are?"

(Silence takes over the dinner table as Lyone swallows his food, growing worried, remembering memories about his family once more.)

Lyone: "No. But I have to find them."

Jel: "Do you remember the last place you saw them?"

(Lyone closes his eyes, carefully recalling the chain of events in the last moments he shared with his family.)

Lyone: "It was at our home. My nanny and I were trying to make it out of the Meriden Forest, while my parents were on some kinda mission."

(Jel and Dior becomes instantly troubled as Lisa curiously listens to the conversation.)

Lisa: "Meriden Forest? I heard that before somewhere."

Jel: "Maybe from radio and T.V broadcasting, considering that's all there was to talk about a few weeks ago."

Dior: "Lyone, you sure that's the forest your family lives in?"

(Lyone stares at Dior, nodding his head, unwavering in his certainty.)

Jel: "Lyone, go ahead and tell us what you remember. Hopefully, we can provide you with clarity."

(Lyone sit back in his chair, collectedly sighing before continuing.)

Lyone: "Ok."

(Ten minutes later, everyone sits silently, absorbing the details of Lyone's story. Dior sits with his eyes closed and arms folded. Jel leans forward with her elbows on the dinner table, mouth hidden within her hands. Lisa slowly sips the last of her drink, trying to understand Lyone's dilemma.)

Lyone: "That's all I remember."

Jel: "Lyone, there is a lot that happened that day besides what you've experienced."

Lyone: "You know what happened to my family?"

(Lyone awaits an answer from Jel, ineptly holding his growing concern.)

Dior: "Lyone, you must know that the events that occurred that day on the Helde Meadow were news around the world. That battlefield was decimated by some unknown explosive power. Nearly every single soldier that didn't evacuate in time died. And it's been reported that those who survived that explosion have all been experiencing some sort of unknown psychosis that drives them to madness."

Lyone: "W-what? Are you saying they are . . .?"

(Lyone balls his fists tightly, tensely thinking about his family vanishing on the Helde Meadow battlefield.)

Dior: "No."

(Lyone turns his attention back to Dior, noticing his confident demeanor.)

Dior: "Due to the fact that you're here and you don't have any of the illnesses attributed to the aftermath of that battle, there is a chance that more people are in a position such as yourself."

Lyone: "You mean, unable to walk?"

Jel: "Yes, it is a serious situation you're in. But, as a doctor, I believe it's safe to say that having paralysis is better than death or being driven mad to the point where you kill yourself."

(Lyone hears their rationalizations, worriedly falling into the depths of his mind.)

Lyone: "*Can they really be gone?*"

(Lyone steels himself, calming his breathing, strengthening his resolve.)

Lyone: "If I can get back on my feet again . . ."

(He lifts his head, burning with passion and determination, drawing the attention of the family.)

Lyone: "If I made it out alive, then I'm sure my family is alive as well. I'll just have to find them, no matter what."

(Dior, Lisa, and Jel watches in awe as Lyone smiles with confidence, taking another bite of his dinner.)

Jel: "If we plan to get you on your feet, then we better get you on a good sleeping pattern. I'll go ahead and get a bath ready for you, and then your bed."

Dior: "I'll clean the kitchen. Lisa, could you give me a hand please?"

Lisa: "Yeah, of course, Dad."

(Later that night, Lyone sits upright in his bed, quietly humming a song. Lisa carefully steps up to the door of Lyone's room, listening to the humming. After a few seconds, she decides to gently knock on the door, interrupting Lyone's song.)

Lyone: "Umm, yes?"

Lisa: "Hey Lyone, it's Lisa. Is it ok if I come in?"

Lyone: "Yeah, sure."

(Lisa quietly walks into Lyone's room, noticing his loneliness.)

Lisa: "Hey, that was a nice song you were singing."

Lyone: "Thanks."

Lisa: "Who taught you that song?"

Lyone: "My mom."

Lisa: "Ha ha, my mom teaches me everything but singing. Although I've been told I have a pretty good singing voice by some people in Wisden."

(Lyone doesn't respond to Lisa, refusing to look at her. She becomes remorseful, nervously rubbing her arm.)

Lisa: "Hey, so I just wanted to say I'm sorry for earlier. I didn't mean to stress you out or anything. I was just trying to get you to lighten up. But I know that was the wrong way to go about that. Can you forgive me?"

(After listening to her apology, Lyone sighs, giving his attention to Lisa.)

Lyone: "That depends. Did you do this because you wanted to? Or because Mrs. Kendric told you to do it?"

(Lisa nervously laughs at Lyone's question.)

Lisa: "Would it be ok of I said both?"

Lyone: "Alright then, I believe you. Apology accepted."

Lisa: "Thanks, Lyone."

(Lisa takes a moment to bow, showing Lyone a sign of respect.)

Lisa: "Cool, I better get going to bed myself. We have a big day tomorrow."

Lyone: "Huh? We do?"

Lisa: "Yup. Tomorrow we start your rehabilitation. And I'm going to do whatever I can to help you get back on your feet."

(Lyone watches as Lisa lifts her fist, giving him a confident smile. Lyone answers with a smile of his own, agreeably nodding.)

Lisa: "Alright then, good night, Lyone. See you in the morning."

(As Lisa turns towards the door, Lyone feels a sudden desire to ask a question.)

Lyone: "H-Hey, wait. Lisa, can I ask you a question?"

Lisa: "Oh? Yeah, sure. What is it?"

Lyone: "At the dinner table. That 'prayer.' What was that all about?"

Lisa: "You've never prayed to Ni before? Ni is our world! Our planet! Our source of life! Where have you been living since forever? In a den of monsters? Ha ha!"

(Lyone considers Lisa's answer, hanging his head in shame.)

Lyone: "Fine, forget I asked."

Lisa: "Hey I wasn't trying to make you feel bad! I was just . . . I mean . . . I'm sorry. Darn it."

(Lisa hears a chuckle, turning to Lyone, noticing a mischievous grin on his face. She's instantly taken aback by Lyone's antics.)

Lisa: "Y-You're not sad! You tricked me!"

Lyone: "Ha ha, that's what you get, smart butt!"

(He laughs at Lisa's gullibility as she is overtaken by laughter herself.)

Lisa: "Alright, alright. You got me. You realize that this means war though, right?"

Lyone: "Ha ha, bring it!"

Lisa: "Well, you asked for it!"

(To Lyone's surprise, Lisa waves goodnight, opening his room door.)

Lyone: "Hey, where are you going?"

Lisa: "I'm going to bed."

Lyone: "I thought you were going to get me back?"

(Lisa looks at Lyone over her shoulder, playfully glaring with a spiteful smirk.)

Lisa: "Oh, I am. Just when you least expect it!"

(Lyone laughs, nervously realizing Lisa's seriousness as she leaves the room quietly.)

Lyone: "Hey, not in my sleep though, alright?"

Narrator: "I woke up with a fake spider on my face that morning. It scared the crap out of me. Actually, no. It wasn't the spider that woke me, it was pee. I sorta, kinda, wet myself. Ha ha."

(Lyone takes a final look at his legs, wearing a confident smile, laying down and going to sleep for the night.)

CHAPTER

FAMILY BONDS

Narrator: "It only took me about a month to get back on my feet with full functionality. It surprised everyone; especially Jel. During that time, they learned a lot about me and my family. But I also learned a lot about them and their culture. Soon enough, they would start to place the pieces about me together and realize that I'm not what they perceived. I'm not a Huma."

(A month after Lyone's rehabilitation, Dior instructs Lisa on combat training routines in front of their home at dawn. She can hear the singing of birds over her own grunts after every push up. Dior stands at her left, watching the sky turns crimson with Yunyi rising across the horizon.)

Lisa: "Urgh, was one hundred pushups really necessary though?"

Dior: "You knew what the deal was before you lost, Lisa. This old man takes no prisoners."

Lisa: "Seriously though, Dad, how are you so fast?"

Dior: "It's called 'staying in shape,' Lisa. Well, that and knowing your Energy Stream. Remember: Knowledge is—"

Lisa: "Knowledge is power. Got it!"

(Inside of the home, footsteps can be heard traveling down a set of stairs, heading toward the front door as Lisa and Dior continue their conversation.)

Dior: "You know, when I was your age Lisa, I could utilize my Energy Stream and move five times faster than you."

Lisa: "Stop lying, Dad! At the speed you move, you probably moved twice as slow as me, at best!"

(Dior smiles at Lisa's sassiness. She climbs to her feet, readying for more training.)

Lisa: "Alright then, how about we focus on Energy Stream training this time since I'm 'too slow'?"

Dior: "Ha ha! Sounds fine to me."

(Stepping out of the home, Lyone emerges onto the porch with a smile, appearing happy, healthy, and confident.)

Lisa: "Hey! Li'l L!"

(With joy at the sight of Lyone, Lisa greets him with a wave. He waves back in return, walking off the front porch.)

Narrator: "Lisa really got the hang of treating me like a younger brother. She even took it upon herself to help me figure out the answers to any questions I had. And, as much as I hated it at first, she even started calling me Li'l L as a nickname. It grew on me over time."

Lyone: "Still calling me 'Li'l L', huh?"

Lisa: "Ha ha, why not? You haven't grown an inch since we met you!"

Lyone: "Can we stop mentioning my height already?"

Dior: "Careful, Lisa. It's not uncommon for women to grow up short."

Lisa: "Why do you have to jinx my chances, Dad?"

(Lyone and Dior laugh as Lisa folds her arms, pouting at them.)

Narrator: "Dior was a great help in my recovery. Our meditation sessions gave me a much-needed sense of control and focus. I even managed to visualize my subconsciousness; 'The Inner World' as it's called. Dior once told me that the inner world is a collective representation of experiences, emotions, and history of your lineage; all the things that makes you 'you.' But, this is also where I met Tuki. Strangely enough, I wasn't able to find her there."

Voice: "Hey!"

(Everyone looks towards the front door, noticing a puzzled Jel searching for something.)

Dior: "Oh, you're awake, dear?"

Lyone: "Did you misplace something, Mrs. Kendric?"

Jel: "Yes, it was a schedule with my list of clients. I remember having it here on the bench."

(Lisa leans over to Lyone and Dior, covering her mouth with her hand, speaking silently.)

Lisa: "At this rate, we're gonna have to record everything mom does."

Narrator: "As forgetful as Jel was, getting to know more about her and her profession was pretty insightful. She was one of the top surgeon generals of the Federal Union. In short, if there was any place to be injured, in her presence was the best place. I didn't realize how lucky I was at the time."

Dior: "Lyone, why don't you continue this meditation session on your own while Lisa and I help Jel?"

Lyone: "Oh sure, no problem."

Dior: "Alright then. Lisa let's go."

(Lisa places her hands on her hips, rolling her eyes with a grin, watching Jel fumble around the front porch.)

Lisa: "Figures."

(Watching with a smile of his own, Lyone stands back as Lisa and Dior walk over to Jel, lending her their aid.)

Narrator: "Days like those were fleeting. At least for me."

(Minutes later, Lyone sits in front of the Kendric family home with his eyes closed and legs folded, calmly controlling his breathing. While meditating, he plunges into his subconsciousness, summoning his inner world. He opens his eyes to find himself standing in a familiar place: a large hollowed tree surrounded by a beautifully, untamed jungle and rugged mountains. The blue skies are calm and filled with the singing of birds that has no presence, and a bright shimmer of light from an unknown source, serenely causing Lyone to look up and smile. He turns his attention toward the jungle, walking through, carefully surveying the environment with his senses.

As Lyone travels and searches through a seemingly endless forest, he comes to a sudden stop, discovering an odd boulder with a smooth surface. Lyone examines the large rock, observing the strange crimson color and the fractures in the exterior.)

Lyone: "*What the . . .? Such a weird boulder. Was this here before?*"

(He curiously places his hand on the object, noticing a pulse that matches his own heartbeat.)

Lyone: "*Since when did boulders have a—*"

(Suddenly, Lyone falls to his knees, holding his heart as cracks in the object erupt across its exterior. As pieces of the object falls off, Lyone's heart races, forcing him to dedicate his mind to maintain his meditation. Then, the mysterious boulder shatters, unleashing a massive crimson inferno, setting ablaze the surrounding jungle of Lyone's inner world.

Meanwhile, Lisa, Dior, and Jel continue their search for Jel's missing records in their home.)

Dior: "Hey, honey! I'm gonna check in the kitchen!"

Jel: "Ok, I'm checking in the basement!"

Dior: "Why would it be in the basement, honey?"

Jel: "I don't know. Could be there though! Haven't checked there yet!"

Lisa: *"Geez mom, could you be more clueless?"*

(Teasingly shaking her head, Lisa walks back toward the front of the house.)

Lisa: "I'm gonna check on the front porch one more time!"

(As Lisa walks out of the home to the front porch, a powerful crimson red aura surges around Lyone's body, immediately forcing Lisa to fall onto her hands and knees in pain.)

Lisa: "W-What the heck?"

(At the same time, both Jel and Dior feel a sudden eruption of pressure upon them, shooting a menacing jolt to their spines.)

Dior: "Is that Lyone?"

Jel: "What is this, imperial force?"

(Jel falls to her knees, visibly weakened under the magnitude of pressure. Dior moves swift, taking off in a burst of speed, appearing at Jel's side in the basement, embracing her. With Jel in his arms, he moves swiftly once again, appearing next to a heavily burdened Lisa on the front porch. Next, he creates a barrier around them using energy, shielding them from adverse effects. Dior maintains the protective barrier, urgently turning his attention to Lyone, noticing a wildly resonating crimson red aura around his body.)

Dior: *"What in Ni's name is going on?"*

(Dior watches as Lyone's body begin to change, developing in height and weight, instantly transitioning to an adolescent male from a young boy.)

Dior: *"What's happening?"*

(Within Lyone's inner world, he remains on his knees in pain as the crimson inferno subsides. The jungle returns from ashes to a more luscious scene, with brightly-colored flowers and mature trees bearing fruit. After climbing to his feet, Lyone shakes his head, ridding himself of the lingering fatigue.)

Lyone: <in Huadi> "Urgh, what the heck was that all about?"

(Lyone hears a sudden growl at his feet, demanding his attention. Looking down, he notices a small, cat-like creature with crimson red fur, a small black mane, little wings, and two tails with afro puff hair at the tips.)

Lyone: "Where did you come from?"

(He looks at the remains of the large object, observing the pieces of shattered egg shells on the ground.)

Lyone: "You came from that?"

(Minutes later, Lyone arrives back at the hollowed tree, detecting the colorful leaves and fruit now hanging from the hollowed tree's branches.)

Lyone: "Hmmm, am I missing something? Did this place just change all of a sudden?"

(The puffy-tailed creature yawns, capturing Lyone's attention once again.)

Lyone: "And you. Hmmm, you know, you're the first living thing I've seen here since my time with Tuki. Can you speak?"

(The puffy-tailed creature stares back at Lyone, adorably grooming itself without responding.)

Lyone: "Well, if this is my inner world, then you must be a part of me somehow."

(Lyone kneels next to the creature with joy, attempting to pet it. But, he suddenly stops inches away from its fur, noticing a startling increase in his blood pressure and body temperature. Taking a step back, he rubs his head from the sudden rush of dizziness as the puffy-tailed creature wanders around aimlessly.)

Lyone: *"Whoa! The heck was that? Did that thing just do that to me?"*

(He watches the puffy-tailed creature cautiously, following with his eyes as it wonders back into the jungle.)

Lyone: "So weird."

(Lyone's stomach starts to growl, rubbing it with a famished smile.)

Lyone: "Wonder if it's breakfast time."

(Lyone breaks his meditation, surfacing back to reality, opening his eyes with renewed awareness. Afterwards, he walks towards the Kendric house with concern, noticing Dior helping Lisa and Jel into seats. Walking onto the porch, he becomes worried, realizing Lisa and Jel's weakened state.)

Lyone: "H-Hey, what happened to Lisa and Mrs. Kendric?"

(Dior holds his hands in front of Lisa and Jel, transfusing energy to them both at once.)

Dior: *"He doesn't know his role in any of this?"*

Lyone: "What's going on, Mr. Kendric? Are they ok?"

Lisa: "Urgh, you did this to us, you idiot!"

Lyone: "Huh? Me? But how?"

(Dior turns his attention onto Lyone, instantly becoming shocked. Taking notice at Dior's awareness to his face, he becomes nervous.)

Lyone: "What's wrong? Is there something on my face?"

(Lyone wipes himself off, drawing Lisa and Jel's attention, shocking them as well.)

Lisa: "Lyone, what happened to you?"

Dior: "You don't notice anything different about yourself, Lyone?"

Lyone: "Well, these clothes are a bit tighter than usual, I guess."

(Minutes later, Dior finishes tending to Lisa and Jel. Then, the family turns their full attention to Lyone, gawking at his sudden change in appearance.)

Lisa: "Hold on! I'll go get the mirror!"

Jel: "Lyone, you really didn't notice a change in your height? Weight?"

(Lyone looks at his body, spotting the oddly subtle differences.)

Lyone: "No, not at first. But, I'm starting to see it. Weird."

(Lisa runs back onto the porch, holding a small mirror.)

Lisa: "Look!"

(Lyone takes the mirror, looking at his reflection, investigating the differences in his face and large afro.)

Dior: "Hmm."

Lisa: "Something wrong, Dad?"

Dior: "Well, besides the burst of imperial force that nearly killed you and your mother, I suppose not."

Jel: "Just what was that, anyway?"

Dior: "Hmm."

(Dior briefly eyeballs Lyone, concealing his initial answer to the situation.)

Dior: *"I shouldn't say anything. Not until I'm sure what's going on."*

Lisa: "I thought I saw Lyone's Energy Stream going crazy! Maybe that was the source of the imperial force."

(Captivated by his reflection in the mirror, Lyone ignores the conversation, affectionately responding with a smile.)

Jel: "Are you sure, Lisa?"

Lisa: "Yeah, I thought so, at least."

Dior: "No."

Lisa: "Huh?"

Dior: "Your Energy Stream and body were under a great amount of strain. It's safe to say that your mind was also affected. You were probably hallucinating."

Lisa: "Oh, then what was that?"

(A cell phone rings inside the house catching their attention.)

Jel: "It's my work phone."

(Jel quickly walks into the home to answer the phone. Once Jel reaches the stairs heading to the upper floor, Dior suddenly grabs her arm, assertively gaining her attention.)

Dior: "Jel, tell them the problem was handled by me. Ok?"

(She stares at Dior, discerning his seriousness. Then, she nods her head, agreeing and proceeds up the stairs.)

Dior: *"I need time to figure out what's going on with Lyone."*

(Dior walks towards the kitchen with his arms folded, thoroughly assessing the situation. On the front porch, Lyone continues to look at himself in the mirror.)

Lisa: "So weird. Just a while ago, your hair wasn't that long. And your skin got a bit darker, almost like mine. Ha ha, you're still shorter than me, though!"

Narrator: "When I saw myself as an adolescent for the first time, I couldn't help but think of my dad. I could even see my mom in my own eyes. It felt as if they never left me. They were a part of me. And then, I heard a voice."

Faint Voice: <in Huadi> *"It's——birthday."*

Lyone: "Birthday?"

Lisa: "Huh? Birthday? Whose birthday? Your birthday?"

Lyone: "Wait, did you hear a voice just now?"

Lisa: "No."

(Lyone scratches his head, guardedly looking around.)

Lyone: "Urgh, I-I'll be right back, Lisa."

Lisa: "Is something wrong?"

Lyone: "Yeah, I think so."

(Lyone gives the mirror back to Lisa, walking into the home. He walks up the stairs, hearing Jel's voice as she talks on her phone. He makes his way to the upper-floor bathroom, parking himself in front of the sink and mirror. After splashing water in his face, he stares at his reflection once more, anxious.)

Jel: "You ok?"

(He looks toward the doorway, noticing Jel with her smile. She leans on the door frame with her hands in her lab coat pockets, staring at him with wonder.)

Lyone: "Yeah. It's just that I changed out of nowhere, you know?"

Jel: "Indeed. Such a sudden metamorphosis can mean that you're not what we all thought you were."

Lyone: "Me-tha-morp-assist? Wait, what?"

Jel: "'Metamorphosis,' Lyone. It means change in shape and size. A physical change. Looks like I'm going to have to start homeschooling you like Lisa, ha ha."

Lyone: "I see. I think I get it. But you just said I'm not what you thought I was. What did you mean by that?"

Jel: "Oh? I meant you're not a Huma like we are. That much is obvious. But I don't recall Parations, or Signas, or any other member of the Humanoid Species having growth periods like you."

(As Jel continues to openly ponder about Lyone's species and race, Lyone grows cautious by the moment.)

Jel: "Maybe you're Humanus? I suppose I can research it."

Lyone: "Don't!"

(Startled by his sudden outburst, Jel stands about as Lyone sighs, calming himself.)

Lyone: "I-I'm sorry. I just . . . too many big words."

Jel: "Oh. Ok, then. It's ok, Lyone."

(The smell of breakfast floats up the stairs, delightfully reminding them both of their hunger.)

Lyone: "That smell . . ."

Jel: ". . . is amazing! Ha ha. Let's go get some food, Lyone."

Lyone: "Yeah."

(Once Jel moves aside, Lyone heads out of the bathroom, walking downstairs to the kitchen. She follows closely behind him, skeptically pondering her interaction with Lyone.

Minutes later, everyone sits at the kitchen table, eating breakfast and joking with one another.)

Lyone: "This is great food, Mr. Kendric!"

Dior: "Thank you, Lyone. I actually used some of the fresh mushrooms Lisa managed to find on our last hike."

Lisa: "I kinda found those by luck!"

Dior: "Don't be so modest, Lisa. You've improved a lot compared to when you first started hiking."

Lisa: "But Dad, I almost fell on my face before I found those!"

Dior: "Oh yeah, you did. That's right."

(With a warm smile, Jel watches as Dior and Lisa chuckles together and Lyone stuffs his face with food.)

Jel: "Well, I'd better get going. I've got a long day ahead of me at work."

Dior: "I made lunch for you, dear. It's in the refrigerator."

Jel: "Thank you, dear. Any plans for today?"

Dior: "I've already filed the paperwork at the Federal Union Adventurer's Guild for a second expedition to the South. I'll have to check camping supplies, restock, and figure out the safest travel route."

Lisa: "We're going camping again? Yes!"

Dior: "I'm still figuring things out. But I plan to take Lyone back to where we found him. Hopefully, we can find some clues about his parents and nanny, or at least jog his memory."

Lyone: "That sounds like a good plan."

Dior: "In theory, yes. But I'm planning to make this trip more than that. If my intuition is correct, you're gonna need all the help you can get, Lyone."

Lyone: "In-tu-e-tion?"

Lisa: "It means perceptive thought, Li'l L. Proactive awareness! You know, the thing you don't have when you wake up with bugs on your face ha ha!"

(Lyone becomes annoyed at Lisa's playful cheekiness.)

Lyone: "Yeah, yeah, ok."

Jel: "Ha ha, I'll see you three later. Call me on my smartphone if you need anything."

Dior: "Ok dear. Have a great day! Love you!"

Lisa: "Love ya' mom!"

Jel: "Always?"

Dior and Lisa: "Always!"

(Jel stands from her chair, happily walking from the kitchen table. After collecting her lunch, she leaves the kitchen as Dior teases Lisa, making Lyone laugh. Later in the day, Dior stands in the garage of their home, tallying their current camping equipment. He glances over at the large highly advanced supercomputer terminal in the corner of the garage with curiosity.)

Dior: "This technological boon in the Federal Union is starting to gain a lot of attention worldwide."

(Peering over his shoulder, he finds a mysterious elderly woman, stepping up to him. She stands firmly, with her light-pink skin and short brown hair covered by a hood, connected to her loose-fitting clothing.)

Mysterious Woman: "I'm aware. Even my clan members in the Second Division is taking notice to the sudden changes. The Federal Union is a military nation-state quickly on the rise. If you're looking to know the full extent of their technological advancements, why not join their military? Everyone knows you'd be given one of the highest of honors, allowing you easy access. But you know this already, don't you?"

Dior: "Yes, I do. And it's not necessary to fulfill my priorities, Bhaja."

Bhaja: "Then how about we diverge into my priorities? Follow me."

Dior: "Where to?"

Bhaja: "The shaded forest near here is good enough."

Dior: "Hmm."

Bhaja: "Problem?"

Dior: "I'm watching over the kids."

(After a deadpan glare from her daunting light grey eyes, Dior sighs, directing her with a hand gesture.)

Dior: "After you."

(Bhaja walks toward the Yellow Shadow Forest as Dior follows closely behind.

Meanwhile, Lyone walks into his room, tiredly yawning, stopping in front of his room's window. He examines the family photo; specifically, the fourth person, who remains missing from the household. Then, he turns his attention outside the window, watching Lisa sneaking about. She suspiciously runs off into the nearby forest, heading north toward Wisden.)

Lyone: "Huh? Where is she going?"

(As Dior and Bhaja stop in a random spot under a nightshade within the Yellow Shadow Forest, Dior turns back with a sudden sense of urgency.)

Dior: "Really Lisa?"

Bhaja: "Let her go."

Dior: "She's my main priority."

Bhaja: "We both have clan members within the area do we not? The record keeper won't be harmed."

(Dior calms himself, turning his attention back toward Bhaja.)

Dior: "Alright then, let's get this over with."

Bhaja: "Indeed. Before I continue, I'd like to thank you for your part in this situation. Considering that I am out of my jurisdiction."

Dior: "It's fine. None of us knew that this would happen."

Bhaja: "Agreed. Now, the Cradle's progress: I see that he is walking now."

Dior: "Yes. His condition improved very quickly."

Bhaja: "Would you say he is fit for training?"

Dior: "Yes. Since we can't keep him in Federal Union territory without complication. I plan to take him back to where they crashed landed in order to have a place where I can train him uninterrupted."

Bhaja: "Way ahead of us, I see. Nice to know that hasn't changed. Now, do any of the people in your household remember anything from the past two months?"

Dior: "I can confirm that they only remember what they were allowed to."

Bhaja: "Good. Lastly, is everything under control?"

Dior: "I'll be able to manage the situation with ease."

Bhaja: "To be more specific, I meant with yourself."

(Dior pauses, detecting Bhaja's sharp eyes of judgement.)

Dior: "I'll manage."

Bhaja: "Very well, we'll be in touch if we have any updates of our own."

(Bhaja walks away, fading into the shadows of the forest, leaving Dior to linger about alone. Then, he hears her voice, echoing through the forest.)

Bhaja: "Better go find your daughter."

(Dior turns, walking in the opposite direction, thinking about the situation.

Fifteen minutes later, Lisa walks through Wisden. Homes and utilities are being built by robotic workers supervised by Federal Union soldiers, scientists, and engineers. Feeling out of place, she acts normal, making her way to a large marketplace filled with tents. She shuffles through the large crowd of military officials, observing them socialize and buy various items from merchants. Men and women soldiers watch her with suspicion as Lisa follows the signs to her destination.)

Lisa: *"Ahh, there it is."*

(She walks into one of the tents, greeted by the smell of fresh bread being delivered to and from their destinations. Once within, she notices a lady store owner directing haulers to properly store her goods.)

Lisa: "Um, excuse me."

Owner: "Huh? Hey, it's Lisa! How are you?"

Lisa: "I'm fine. Thank you."

Owner: "Here to buy more pastries?"

Lisa: "Actually, I wanted to get a birthday cake."

Owner: "Oh! Is it your birthday today? I bet Jel and Dior are so excited!"

(Lisa stares at the shop owner with skepticism, noticing her fake facade of happiness.)

Lisa: "It's not my birthday."

Owner: "Oh? Then for Dior or Jel?"

Lisa: "It's for my friend Lyone, and I need a customized cake with his name on it."

(The store owner becomes suspicious, hiding her intention as she continues aiding Lisa with a smile.)

Owner: "Ok then, I can do that. I'll need a few more details."

Lisa: "Fine. Whatever. And can you charge it to my family prestige please? Thanks."

(Fifteen minutes later, Lisa steps out of the bakery tent, carrying a box in her arms. Not paying attention, she bumps into someone, managing to keep both her balance and her gift safe.)

Lisa: "Hey, I'm walking here!"

(Lisa looks up to find a towering, elderly male soldier wearing a black uniform decorated with medals on the front. Lisa nervously swallows as the soldier turns toward her, revealing his big bushy eyebrows, and shiny bald head. Four other soldiers wearing blue uniforms turn their attention to Lisa.)

Towering Man: "Lisa Kendric? Where are your parents?"

Lisa: "Umm . . ."

Voice: "Really, Lisa? What's gotten into you?"

(A jolt of fear shoots up Lisa's spine upon hearing a familiar voice. She turns to her right, nervously smiling as Dior sternly walks toward her. He stops beside her, quickly taking notice to the towering soldier and his guardsmen.)

Dior: "General Idol, sir. It's been a long time."

Idol: "Dior! It has been a long time! How are you?"

(While Lisa observes, Dior and Idol offers each other salutes, politely easing their stances after a couple of seconds.)

Dior: "Living the glory years, sir."

Idol: "That makes two of us. 'Old age brings profound wisdom and strength through the blessings of Ni,' says my church pastor. Ha ha!"

(Idol looks down at Lisa, noticing the shy tension about her.)

Idol: "Lisa, you're getting bigger by the day. Try not the bump into people, eh?"

Lisa: "Sorry, sir."

Idol: "Hmm, is that a birthday cake? Looks good."

Lisa: "Y-Yeah, it is."

Dior: "Lisa, did you use the family prestige to buy sweets again?"

Lisa: "I-It's not for me! It's for Lyone."

(Upon Lisa speaking Lyone's name, Dior becomes tense, quickly composing himself, intuitively forming an alibi.)

Idol: "Lyone? You guys keeping overpowered pets now? Ha ha!"

Dior: "Actually, Lyone is a visitor from a friendly Paration family that helped with information regarding uninhabitable zones south of here. In exchange, we took him in for quick medical treatment. Temporarily, of course."

Idol: "I see you're as resourceful as ever, Dior. Although we didn't receive a report regarding this situation."

Dior: "You're right. Jel restricted visitation to the property to give the patient privacy and to maintain a controlled environment for data collection."

Idol: "Hmm, definitely makes sense."

Dior: "Well then, we'll be off, general. Hope to see you around so we can catch up."

Idol: "Sounds like a plan, Dior. That may happen sooner rather than later! Ha ha!"

Dior: "Alright then, sir. We hope to see you later."

Idol: "Agreed. Take care. And stay out of trouble, Lisa."

Lisa: "Y-Yes sir."

(As Dior and Lisa walks toward the exit together, Idol watches them with suspicion. From the crowd, a pale-skinned female soldier with short, blond hair and blue eyes, wearing a red soldier uniform and beret, walks up to the group. The guardsmen salute her as she moves to Idol's side, offering a salute of her own.)

Female Soldier: "Sir!"

Idol: "You got all of that, Olivia?"

Olivia: "Yes, sir. Your orders?"

Idol: "Be prepared to accompany me at a moment's notice. Other than that, normal night duties as usual."

Olivia: "Sir, understood."

(Minutes later, Dior and Lisa take the forest path back home. As they walk, Lisa tightens her grip on the cake box, feeling a tension between them.)

Dior: "Who else did you tell about Lyone?"

Lisa: "The only other person was the owner of the tent for baked goods."

(Lisa lowers her head in shame, listening to Dior's frustrated sigh.)

Lisa: "I'm in trouble, aren't I?"

Dior: "You left home without permission, used the family prestige without permission, and outed Lyone's whereabouts. Yes, you are in trouble. But to be honest, we should have talked to you about this beforehand and included you in our strategy."

(From his window, Lyone catches sight of their arrival, noticing the shame on Lisa's face.)

Lisa: "I'm sorry, Dad."

Dior: "We'll discuss your punishment later. Come on, let's go inside. The bright side to this is that I still have time to cook and make a much better cake, ha ha."

(Lisa's shame is broken at the sound of Dior's comment. She walks back into the home, feeling better. However, Dior walks into the home, pondering the severity of their situation.

Later that evening, Lyone walks downstairs, led by the fresh smell of herbs and spices. He walks into the kitchen, noticing Jel and Dior deep in conversation. Dior continues to cook a hearty stew and Jel prepares to set the dinner table; neither aware of Lyone's presence.)

Dior: "I did not think you'd go there to be honest. Should we plan for a more serious punishment?"

Jel: "She'll thank me for it later in life. Besides, I'm not done with her punishment. Tonight, is just the prelude."

Dior: "This will be a test for her, then."

Jel: "She'll be fine. She has to learn to be more reserved and tactful, especially in the presence of high-ranking government and military officials. And since I invited General Idol over for dinner, this should be a perfect opportunity."

Dior: "So, you're sure having the general over is a good idea?"

Jel: "I have a hunch. Besides, he already knows about Lyone. If things play out like I believe they will, then we'll need some . . . insurance. Anyway, I already invited him so no going back now."

Dior: "True. Alright then, I leave this one up to you, dear."

(Jel turns to find Lyone standing by the kitchen entrance. With an inviting smile, she greets him, continuing her task.)

Jel: "Oh hey, Lyone. Would you like to help me set the dinner table, sweetheart?"

Lyone: "Um, sure Mrs. Kendric. But I don't know how."

Jel: "Now is a great time to learn, then. Also, remember you can just call me Jel."

Lyone: "Oh! Ok. I'll try to remember that."

(As the two set the table, Dior remains attentive, cheerfully watching over his shoulder.)

Jel: "Alright, just follow my lead. Setting the table is a fairly easy task once you're familiar with the utensils."

Lyone: "Ok."

(Minutes later, Dior finishes cooking, turning off the burners on the stove, allowing the food to simmer and cool.)

Dior: "Just about ready. Beef stew, mashed potatoes, and steamed vegetables. That should do it this time."

Lyone: "It smells sooo good!"

Jel: "And just in time. Table's ready. Thank you for the help, Lyone. Now, go and wash up. Our guest will be here soon, and dinner will be served shortly after."

Lyone: "Ok."

Lisa: "H-Hey guys."

(Everyone turns toward the kitchen entrance and find Lisa. Lisa shyly stands about, wearing a dark-blue dress along with black formal dress shoes. Her dark brown hair is naturally curled, flowing to her shoulders. Lisa's polished appearance stuns the room, causing her shyness to linger.)

Jel: "Wow, you look so beautiful, Lisa!"

Lisa: "Thanks, Mom."

Jel: "I have to take your picture!"

(Jel walks toward Lisa with a gleeful smile, coming to a sudden standstill with confusion.)

Dior: "Something wrong, dear?"

Jel: "I, um . . . I forgot where we keep the camera, ha ha."

Dior: "Don't you have a camera on your phone?

Jel: "Yes, but that's for work purposes."

Dior: "Ha ha, Alright then. I'll go get it, I think I know where it is. Dinner is almost ready, but watch the stove for me, dear."

Jel: "Ok. Thank you, dear."

(Lyone notes Lisa's discomfort as Dior leaves the kitchen.)

Lisa: "What?"

Lyone: "You look so . . . different."

Lisa: "Yeah, well, I hate wearing dresses."

(Lisa folds her arms in rebellion, earning Jel's scolding glare. Quickly taking notice, Lisa becomes intimidated, unfolding her arms, sighing.)

Lisa: "Thank you for the compliment, Lyone. I didn't mean to snap at you. Dresses just makes me uncomfortable."

Lyone: "Ha ha, gotcha."

(A sudden knock on the front door of the home captures everyone's attention.)

Jel: "Ah, that must be our guest! Dear, the guest is here!"

Dior: "Coming! I gotta get the charger for the camera!"

Jel: "I'm still watching the food! I can't get the door!"

(Lisa and Lyone look at each other with competitive smiles on their faces.)

Lyone: "Race?"

Lisa: "Let's go!"

Jel: "Wait! Hold on, you two!"

(They take off, playfully running.)

Lisa: "Don't worry, Mom! We got it!"

(Lisa beats Lyone to the front door, both bursting into laughter.)

Lisa: "Even in a dress I'm faster than you, Li'l L!"

Lyone: "Whatever! Just stop calling me that!"

(Lisa continues to laugh, opening the door. Then, they are almost instantly silenced by the mere presence of Idol, towering over them. The two stares at Idol with his formal dress and wireless earpiece. As they mutely stand about, he stares back at them, raising an eyebrow at the awkwardness.)

Idol: "So, am I invited in? Or should I just stand here?"

(Jel clumsily runs to the front door, greeting Idol with a salute. Idol salutes in return, both briefly maintaining eye contact and eases their stances.)

Jel: "General."

Idol: "Surgeon general."

(Jel directs Idol into their home with a hand gesture. As Idol walks into the house, Lisa watches Jel staring at the front porch, holding the door open.)

Lisa: "Something wrong, Mom?"

Jel: "Major Olivia Macy. You're more than welcome to join us for dinner."

Olivia: "Ma'am, I'll decline. I'm under orders."

Jel: "Alright then, major. Understood."

(As Jel closes the door, Lyone and Lisa look over to each other, puzzled.)

Lyone: "Who was that?"

Lisa: "I didn't even see anyone."

(Idol sniffs the air, smelling the food in the kitchen with an eager grin.)

Idol: "That smells wonderful!"

Jel: "Ha ha, yes. Dior's food is amazing."

Lyone: "Hey, who is watching the food?"

Jel: "Oh! I forgot to turn off the stove!"

(Jel runs for the kitchen, stopping at the sudden flash of a camera held by Dior.)

Dior: "Ha ha! Your face was priceless, dear. That's gonna make a funny—"

Jel: "Dear! The food! It's still cooking! I left it on the—"

Dior: "Don't worry. I turned it off already."

(As Jel sighs with relief, Lyone and Lisa chuckles amongst themselves.)

Dior: "Well, this is going to be an interesting night. Ha ha!"

(Later during dinner, Idol finishes his meal, sporting a satisfied grin.)

Idol: "Dior, I forgot how good your cooking is! It's been too long!"

Dior: "Ah, your approval is much appreciated, general, sir. Much better than eating on the battlefields of the past, eh?"

Idol: "Yes, I would agree. Although, to be fair, I miss those days at times. Great battles and honorable opponents."

Dior: "Indeed. It's too bad many of our fellow soldiers didn't make it."

Idol: "Mmmm."

(The two men momentarily remain silent, capturing Lisa's curiosity.)

Lisa: "Umm mister general, sir?"

Idol: "Yes, Lisa?"

Lisa: "Do you mind if I ask what battle you guys are talking about, sir?"

Idol: "Ah! So, it's a war story you'd like?"

(Lyone and Lisa are surprised by Idol's sudden enthusiasm. Jel takes a sip of her drink and Dior shakes his head; both nervously wearing light-hearted smirks.)

Dior: "Oh boy, here we go."

Jel: "And at the dinner table, no less."

Idol: "It was ninety-seven years ago, the dawn of the current Age of Exploration. Many great explorations of our world were taking place. Nation-states became emboldened to explore many zones that had previously remained uninhabitable due to the natural dangers of our planet. This is also a time where relations between nation-states were always on a thin thread, due to their competition for natural resources. During one great exploration in the central region of this continent, three exploration teams from three different nation-states all raced to explore the area. However, it quickly turned from an exploration to a skirmish battle, with all three sides fighting each other and fought the beasts that inhabited the area; along with the monsters that lived alongside them."

Lisa: "Wow! So, you were a part of that?"

Idol: "I wish! That would have been an amazing battle! But, no. That battle was merely the prelude to the three nation-states declaring war on each other, and then dragging each of their allies into the war after about thirty more years of fighting."

Dior: "A massive continental war. Thus, the name: Meiyon Continental War."

Idol: "Or at least that's what it was called before reinforcements from nation-states in the numerous continents across the world found themselves fighting in a sort of proxy war of their own in the middle of our war."

Lisa: "That sounds . . . scary."

Idol: "It was the first world war of the modern era. So, it was a lot of things besides just scary. Populations across the world were already reduced due to the limitations of medicine and technology, among other factors. So, in turn, nation-states could only spare the best of the best for war. My kind of battlefield. Dior and I were soldiers during the Meiyon Continental War. We fought against some of the strongest soldiers and monsters in the world! There was all kinds of crazy fighting techniques and abilities. But, the most notable thing, was to measure the sheer amount of loyalty our opponents had for their nation-state. Every single soldier fought tooth and nail to hold territory claimed by their nation-state. Many even made the ultimate sacrifice. It was a grand honor to be in the presence of legends."

Jel: "And on that note, how about we serve dessert?"

Dior: "Good call, dear. I believe I . . ."

(As Dior continues to speak, chatter from Idol's earpiece quickly catches his attention.)

Idol: "Excuse me, but are we expecting more company?"

Jel: "Not that I know of. Why?"

Idol: "Well, according to Olivia, an unknown person is heading toward the house. It seems our visitor is possibly one of the delivery men from the bakery tent at Wisden."

(Jel quickly ponders their situation, turning her attention to Lisa.)

Jel: "Lisa, did you use family prestige on anything else besides your gift?"

Lisa: "No."

Jel: "Hmm."

Dior: "Are you thinking what I'm thinking?"

Jel: "Yes I am."

Lisa: "What is it? What's going on?"

Jel: "Lisa, follow us. Lyone, you stay here."

Idol: "A word of advice: I wouldn't attempt to hide him at this point."

(Idol stares at Jel, gaining her sharp eyes in return; both suspicious of each other. A knock is heard at the door and Dior makes a quick decision.)

Dior: "He's right, Jel. Lyone, Lisa, come with us."

(The knocking at the door continues and the door cracks open. The delivery man is greeted by Dior.)

Dior: "Hello, can we help you, sir?"

Delivery Man: "Hello, Mr. Kendric. Honored to meet you. I have a birthday delivery for a person named 'Lyone' at this location."

Jel: "Who's there, dear?"

(Dior looks back into the home, opening the door wider to reveal Lisa, Jel, and Lyone being pushed in his wheelchair.)

Dior: "It's a delivery man. Says he has a package for Lyone."

Delivery Man: "That's right. It's for his birthday."

Jel: "Lisa, did you also pay for a gift?"

Lisa: "No. I have a receipt right here."

(Lisa holds the receipt in her hand. Then, everyone stares back at the delivery man, skeptically observing him. Unnerved by their stares, he replies, closely examining Lyone with his eyes.)

Delivery Man: "Well, this is a complimentary gift from the bakery tent owner."

Idol: "What's the holdup here?"

(The delivery man becomes visibly tense, hearing Idol's voice. As Idol steps up to the front door, everyone turns their attention to him.)

Jel: "Apparently, the bakery shop owner sent a special delivery to a restricted area."

Idol: "You are aware that this is a restricted area, right?"

(The delivery man remains silent, staring at Idol without moving a muscle.)

Idol: "Does your employer knows that this is a restricted area?"

Delivery Man: "Under Arbitrators Code three: Arbitrators are not obligated to disclose investigative details to Federal Union military personnel without a court order."

(Dior, Jel, and Idol reacts to his response, unsurprised in their body language.)

Idol: "Looks like I'll have to be more specific. This area is restricted by military law. You're out of your jurisdiction. Now, unless you wanna take everyone that's currently in Experimental Unit GH-10 to the Wyvern's

Den, I suggest waiting for publicly accessible information, on publicly accessible land. Understand?"

Delivery Man: "Understood."

Idol: "Good. Now, get out of here before I decide to take you to the Wyvern's Den instead."

(As Idol brandishes a challenging smirk, the delivery man briefly glare at the group, turning away and leaving the property. Dior closes the door, sighing with relief.)

Dior: "That was close."

Lyone: "Who was that?"

Jel: "That's not important, sweetheart. What's important is who he worked for."

Idol: "That man was a Federal Union Arbitrator in disguise. Pretty bold of them to trespass."

Jel: "It's over now. Let's get back to the dinner. Where were we?"

Lisa: "Dessert! And I have a surprise!"

(As Lisa runs into the kitchen, Lyone stands onto his feet and Jel takes away the wheelchair. Dior places a hand on Idol's shoulder, gaining his attention.)

Dior: "Dessert, general?"

Idol: "Right."

(Everyone gathers around the kitchen table once more. Lisa gleefully opens the refrigerator, taking out an unmarked box, placing it on the table in front of Lyone.)

Jel: "Ok, Lyone, go ahead and open it, sweetheart."

(Lyone looks over to Jel, observing her warmhearted smile of approval, curiously turning back to the box.)

Lyone: "What's in it?"

Lisa: "Open it and find out!"

(Taking Lisa's advice, Lyone opens the box, celebrated with a cake endowed by the words "Happy Birthday Lyone" written on it.)

Lisa, Dior, Jel, and Idol: "HAPPY BIRTHDAY, LYONE!"

(Lyone hesitates at their sudden excitement, staring at the cake with uncertainty.)

Lyone: "It's my birthday?"

Lisa: "Yeah! You said it yourself earlier, remember?"

(Noticing Lyone's uncertainty, Lisa becomes insecure, shyly placing her hands behind her back.)

Lisa: "It was on the porch earlier this morning. You said 'birthday.' I'm not sure if you were talking about yourself or not, but I know it's not my birthday. So, I wanted to get you a cake and surprise you, Lyone."

Lyone: "Yeah, I remember. It's just . . . everything's been happening so fast and I just . . . I just don't know what to say."

(Jel walks to his side, kneeling with her kind smile, placing her hand on his shoulder with care.)

Jel: "Hey, don't worry Lyone. We're all here for you. Our goal is to make sure you're safe and to help you find your parents. We're gonna make sure of it. Ok?"

(Idol listens closely to Jel's words, assessing the situation.)

Lyone: "Ok."

Lisa: "I didn't mean to make you sad, Lyone. I'm sorry."

(As Lisa lowers her head in shame, Lyone notices her feelings, reactively becoming remorseful.)

Lyone: "Hey, it's ok Lisa. This is a great present! Thank you."

(She looks up at Lyone, brightened with restored confidence.)

Lisa: "Really?"

(Lyone nods his head, mirroring Lisa's self-assurance, inquisitively turning back to the cake.)

Lyone: "So, um, what's this called again?"

Lisa: "It's a cake, silly! You eat it!"

Lyone: "Wait, I can eat this? All of it?"

Lisa: "Geez, Li'l L! Don't hog all of it! We have other people here too, you know!"

Jel: "Well, I don't mind taking a little piece."

Idol: "Same here! It looks delicious!"

(Lyone peers over to Dior, detecting his apathetic demeanor.)

Lyone: "Mr. Kendric, what about you?"

Dior: "I'll pass, Lyone. Thank you."

Lyone: "Huh? Something wrong?"

Lisa: "Don't worry, Dad is just mad he didn't make the cake."

(Dior turns his back, grumpy at Lisa's comment.)

Lisa: "Come on, Dad. If I had asked you to make it, it wouldn't have been a secret."

Dior: "I can make a cake ten times better."

(Sighing while rolling her eyes, she turns back to the table.)

Lisa: "Whatever, Dad. Stay mad. Anyway, cut the cake, Li'l L!"

Idol: "Wait, shouldn't we all sing the 'Happy Birthday Ni'Ador' song?"

Jel: "Ah, of course! And pictures! We need pictures!"

Idol: "Ha ha, let's have that song first. And since this is Lisa's surprise, how about you lead us, Lisa?"

(Lisa becomes nervous, blushing with an embarrassed smile.)

Lisa: "Um, do we have to?"

Jel: "Of course, Lisa. It's tradition. How else are we gonna wish Lyone a good year until his next birthday?"

Lisa: "By saying that and eating cake maybe?"

(Jel scowls at Lisa, causing Lisa to laugh nervously and comply.)

Lisa: "A-Alright! I'm just kidding! I got this!"

(As everyone awaits Lisa's cue, she briefly pauses, smiling with her eyes closed.)

Lisa: <singing>

Ni'Ador

from sea to shore

guided by our dreams and more

all year long we lived to say

Happy Birthday Lyone.

(Lyone is surprised by Lisa's charming singing voice. Then, everyone claps their hands, singing along with Lisa.)

Lisa, Dior, Jel, and Idol: <singing in harmony>

Ni'Ador

from sea to shore

guided by our dreams and more

all year long we lived to say

Happy Birthday

Lisa: "Li'l L!"

(Lisa's laughter spreads through the group, eventually drawing Lyone into laughter too. Later that night, Lyone and Lisa eat their cake, taking pictures with Dior behind the camera. Idol and Jel stands back, watching over the happy event.)

Idol: "Quite the beautiful family you have here, surgeon general."

Jel: "Thank you, general. Now, if only my other son would take some time off and come visit us, this would be perfect."

Idol: "I'm sure you know how important Christopher's duties are to our country."

Jel: "Yeah, I know."

Idol: "Mind if I talk to you in private, surgeon general?"

Jel: "Of course."

(Idol and Jel walk toward the living room to continue their conversation in privacy.)

Idol: "So, was this your plan all along?"

Jel: "Not sure what you mean, general."

Idol: "You know what I mean. Inviting me here to cover your butt with the Arbitrators, who have clearly launched an investigation into you and your family now."

(Jel gives a sly smirk with her arms crossed, comfortably leaning against a wall.)

Jel: "Well, my goal was to invite you here for dinner, so you could meet Lyone. We've been helping him heal at the request of his family. But Dior has been very curious about the boy's Energy Stream lately. Thought you might have some insight once you came into proximity."

Idol: "About the kid's family. I remembered you speaking as if they were missing before dessert. Now you're telling me they 'requested' him to be healed eh?"

(Jel remains silent, observing Idol's reaction to the situation.)

Idol: "Hmm, to be fair, the kid's Energy Stream does feel . . . different. I've felt something like it before. But his Energy Stream is unique in its oddness. It's difficult to explain. I've been trying to figure it out the entire night."

(Jel nods her head, agreeing with Idol's estimate.)

Jel: "Just like Dior. He has been perplexed by Lyone's Energy Stream since he arrived here."

Idol: "Alright, that's enough beating around the bush, Jel. It's quite obvious that you've gotten me involved in harboring an illegal immigrant. Now, I've made your life easier by shielding you from the first Arbitrators. But if you're expecting me not to pull the plug on this illegal operation, you'd better give me details, now."

(As Idol firmly stares, Jel stands at attention, posturing herself with confidence.)

Jel: "That's fair. Dior and Lisa found Lyone badly injured on a newly discovered mountain range during their exploration to the south. Once we nursed him back to health, we asked him the obvious questions. At the time, he couldn't recall the events prior to being injured. However, we eventually learned that he was injured during an explosion. He tells us that it happened in the Meriden Forest."

(Idol stands unconvinced at Jel's testimony, searching for deceit in her eyes, detecting her seriousness.)

Idol: "You're not kidding. But that's the other side of the continent. How is that even possible?"

Jel: "Your questions are our questions, general. According to the reports sent back by travelers and evacuees, The North-South Ryonian Conflict ended in some kind of massive explosion. His parents were also victims, but he knows nothing of their whereabouts now. For all we know, they could be dead."

Idol: "And yet the kid survived. So, how do you plan to verify this story of his?"

Jel: "Dior and I believe that if we bring him back to where we found him, it could help him remember what happened. So, Dior has been preparing for a long expedition back to that area."

Idol: "That does sound like a good plan. Still, this kid could be making up his experience."

(Jel remains silent with confidence, watching as Idol pace during his deliberation.)

Idol: "And you want me involved in this because . . .?"

Jel: "Well, we need you to continue covering us from Arbitrators and other military personnel. This is a . . . secret operation. Once we gain the information we're looking for, we'll report to you with details."

Idol: "And what's the time frame for this mission?"

Jel: "Dior has already been approved for an expedition beginning in a week and ending early spring."

Idol: "So about four months."

(Idol stops in front of Jel, giving her a stern gaze.)

Jel: "Do we have your support?"

(Idol doesn't reply, surprising Jel by stepping back into the kitchen, causing her to follow closely behind. The two wear their veneer of smiles, noticing Lyone with traces of cake on his face.)

Idol: "Looks like you're having fun with that cake, kid."

Lyone: "Yeah! This is pretty good!"

Idol: "So good that you decided to wear it on your face?"

(Lyone wipes his face as Lisa laughs.)

Lyone: "I didn't do that! Lisa wiped cake on my face."

Lisa: "Ha ha! You look so cute, Li'l L!"

Dior: "I still can make a better cake."

Idol: "Lyone, I hear that you're from the Meriden Forest?"

(Hearing Idol's question, Lyone looks over to him, warily shifting his attention back to his cake. Dior looks over to Jel, confirming approval when she nods. Afterwards, Dior walks closer to Lyone, placing a hand on his shoulder, reaffirming him.)

Dior: "It's ok, Lyone. You can answer."

Lyone: "Ok."

(With lingering caution, Lyone turns back toward Idol.)

Lyone: "I am from there."

Idol: "I see. Tell me about that explosion you witnessed."

Lyone: "Well, it was so big, everything was hit. I don't remember much after that. Before it happened, I think my parents tried to stop it, and my nanny and I tried to get away, but then . . ."

Idol: "Your parents and your nanny, what are their names?"

Lyone: "My dad is named Kai, my mom is Raine, my auntie is Rose, and my nanny is Lorelei. Are you gonna help me look for them, too?"

Idol: "Yes. But I won't lie to you, what happened in that area ended badly for a lot of people. You're a lucky kid to have made it out alive. I can't guarantee your family survived."

Lyone: "Don't say that!"

(Lyone's outburst silences Idol. Then, he quickly calms himself, taking a deep breath, lifting his head with a determined flare in his eyes.)

Lyone: "I know they're alive. My family spent a long time teaching me how to survive. If I made it out, I know they did as well. And I'll find them."

(Intrigued by Lyone's courageous attitude, Idol gives a reassuring smile.)

Idol: "That was a statement filled with resolve. You keep that up, and I'm sure you'll find them, one way or another. By the way kid, you missed a spot."

Lyone: "Huh?"

(Idol points onto his own face, causing Lyone to wipe his face as Lisa and Dior laugh.)

Idol: "It's time I've taken my leave. I'll make sure to keep in touch."

Dior: "Alright then, general. Until next time. Ni'Ador."

Idol: "Thank you for the dinner, Dior. Ni'Ador."

Lisa: "Ni'Ador, sir!"

Idol: "Ni'Ador, Lisa. Lyone, until next time. Ni'Ador."

Lyone: "Ni'Ador?"

Lisa: "It means 'Blessings from Ni!'"

Lyone: "Oh, ok then. Ni'Ador, I guess?"

Idol: "Ha ha! Thank you."

Lisa: "Now, back to cake!"

Dior: "How about we put this cake aside and I'll make a homemade cake from scratch?"

Lisa: "Can't hear you hating over there, Dad. Eating cake."

(As Lyone remains entertained by Dior and Lisa, Idol and Jel walks back into the living room.)

Idol: "I believe the kid. You have my support. I'll make an effort to try and find his parents."

Jel: "Thank you, general. I'll make sure they're on their way in a week."

Idol: "About that, surgeon general, this area is newly acquired and still under military possession. I'm only granting you three days' notice before the personnel restriction is lifted from this area. Understood?"

Jel: "Making sure you can prove your involvement is minimal, right, general?"

Idol: "You didn't answer my question."

(Idol glares sternly at Jel, causing her to respond by folding her arms.)

Jel: "Understood."

Idol: "Thank you, surgeon general."

Jel: "And what about your second-in-command?"

(Upon hearing Jel's question, he becomes irritated, hearing the suspicion in her tone.)

Idol: "You should know better than to question the loyalty of officers to their leaders. She'll follow my orders because it is what's best for her and her family's prestige."

(Jel maintains eye contact with Idol, unfazed by his objection.)

Jel: "General, with all due respect, people are only as loyal as your usefulness to them. It's the nature of our culture, after all. The snake with the deadliest venom wins the deadlock. You know the saying better than any of us. Ni'Ador, general."

(After briefly standing in silence, glaring at one another, Idol makes his way to the front door, leaving the home without responding. As Idol walks toward Wisden, Olivia jumps from the roof of the home, skillfully landing on the ground next to him. The two walks through the forest path together.)

Olivia: "Sir, I hope this kid is worth all of this trouble."

Idol: "After hearing what he has been through, I have a feeling we're onto something big. It's definitely a weird situation with him mysteriously ending up on the other side of the continent."

Olivia: "Sir, can we trust the surgeon general?"

Idol: "Jel is not a threat. Her prestige hinges upon her military position as one of the highest-ranking officers in the land. But her access to family prestige and business prestige is severely limited due to her self-exile. If she really wanted to, she could be one of the most influential people in the Federal Union."

Olivia: "But she chooses not to be. How curious."

Idol: "Don't underestimate her. She's still quite formidable as long as she remains a top-ranking military official. Once you get to know her, you'll begin to understand her. She knows that to be the best, you'll have to get dirty with the dogs. In the Southern Military Division, I'm the top dog of this military point. She'll need my help if she wants to keep her lifestyle and her head."

Olivia: "Her lifestyle? You mean Lisa and Dior?"

Idol: "Indeed. Those two foreigners are the reason she's doing what she does. It's only natural that she lends the same courtesy to the boy. If we have anything to fear about Jel, it's her soft heart for those foreigners. Which is why, if we're involved, we'll need insurance."

Olivia: "Your orders, sir?"

Idol: "Did you retrieve the data from the main terminal in their garage?"

Olivia: "Yes, sir. I've uploaded the info onto an external hard drive."

Idol: "Good. This gives us an out if we're questioned. Once our reports are turned in and the military restriction upon that area expires, you are to covertly monitor them. You are permitted to take overt action only when engaging hostiles. The main target, Lyone, is to remain safe. If he is in a compromising position, you are to recover and capture him. If recovery and capture isn't an option, you're to kill him and dispose of his remains."

Olivia: "Understood."

(Later in the night, Lisa yawns, walking from her room to the upstairs restroom. She comes to a sudden stop, passing in front of Lyone's room door, hearing Lyone humming a song. Then, she smiles, knocking on his door.)

Lyone: "O-Oh, um, come in."

(Lisa walks into Lyone's room, drowsily yawning.)

Lisa: "Still awake, huh? Must be from all the cake."

Lyone: "Heck yeah. That was great by the way. Thank you."

Lisa: "Anytime Li'l L."

Lyone: "By the way, that birthday song. You have a great voice! Wouldn't have guessed it!"

Lisa: "Thanks."

(Lyone pauses, watching Lisa's drifting gaze move toward the window.)

Lyone: "Something wrong?"

Lisa: "It's nothing Li'l L. Well, Its just . . ."

(Lisa stares at the family photo on the windowsill, directing Lyone to look in the same direction.)

Lisa: "I just wish my brother Chris was here."

Lyone: "So, that's who that is in the picture. Been wondering that for a while now."

Lisa: "He stayed here for a little while. This was his room."

(Lyone turns his attention back to Lisa, watching her take a seat in the chair at his bedside.)

Lisa: "You know, I'm actually adopted, Lyone."

Lyone: "Whoa, seriously?"

Lisa: "Yeah. My mom tells me that I was born in a nation-state called Guan; and also, that I was very lucky."

Lyone: "Wait, what's 'adopted' mean?"

(Lisa becomes annoyed, noticing Lyone's genuine curiosity.)

Lisa: "It means my mom and dad aren't the mom and dad I was born with, silly."

Lyone: "Oh, ok. Well, what happened to your other parents?"

Lisa: "I don't know. To be honest, I don't even remember how my first mom and dad even look. But, as I was saying, my mom said I was lucky."

Lyone: "But I thought you said you never met your first mom?"

(Irritated at Lyone's confusion, she shoves Lyone on the arm.)

Lisa: "Just shut up and listen. Anyway, my mom, *Jel*, told me that my big brother Chris saved me from a battle that took over sectors of my home nation-state. And when I was growing up, my big brother looked out for me all the time. Even when I got myself in trouble, he still helped me out, after he scolded me, anyway, ha ha. Then, we moved here, and he went away after we settled in."

Lyone: "Where is he now?"

Lisa: "He and the rest of his team are ambassadors for the Federal Union. So, they're always out of the nation-state on business. I haven't seen the idiot in years. And he said he'd be back."

Lyone: "You think he was lying?"

Lisa: "Of course not, silly. It's just that . . . I hope he's ok."

(Lisa hangs her head, troubled with uncertainty. Then, she hears a joyful chuckle, looking up toward Lyone's smile.)

Lyone: "You're too worried, Lisa. I think if your brother is as strong as your dad, then we shouldn't have too much to worry about."

Lisa: "Ha ha, silly. My brother isn't as strong as my dad. Heck, they don't even have the same training and fighting techniques. Plus, it all depends on . . ."

Lyone: "Lisa?"

(Lisa falls silent, interrupted by Lyone's confident tone.)

Lyone: "Like I said, you worry too much. He'll be ok. Just believe."

(After a thinking about Lyone's response, she sighs with relief.)

Lisa: "Yeah, you're right."

(She reflects Lyone's confident smile with one of her own, rising from the chair, making her way out of the room.)

Lisa: "Good night, Lyone. I gotta pee now."

Lyone: "Ha ha, good night."

(In the master bedroom, Dior and Jel relax together in their bed, strategizing about the situation with Idol.)

Jel: "And that's the gist of it."

Dior: "So, three days until Lyone can no longer be seen. Not even around our home. Seems we're going to have to go on that camping trip sooner rather than later."

Jel: "I also suspect that we're going to have more eyes on us than normal."

Dior: "Yes, that's a fair assumption. I'll speed up the plans to accommodate the time crunch. I'm sure Lyone is healthy enough to travel."

Jel: "What do you think will happen when you return to that mountain with Lyone?"

Dior: "I'm not sure. I'm certain he didn't get there by himself. I gotta admit, I'm anxious to solve this mystery."

Jel: "Of course you are, dear. Based on what we already know, Lyone may be involved in the North-South Ryonian Conflict. If that's true, he might travel back. And that will be a very dangerous trip back home."

Dior: "I've already planned to train him. Although I'm still planning certain exercises, I'll have four months to prepare him for whatever awaits in his future."

Jel: "Sounds like you have a handle on this. I'll leave it up to you."

(Dior smiles, smoothly leaning over to Jel, passionately sharing a kiss.)

Jel: "Love you, dear."

Dior: "Love you too, dear."

Jel: "Always?"

Dior: "Always."

(Suddenly, Dior pulls back the bedsheets, climbing out of his side of the bed. Jel laughs, watching him stand in a shirt and underwear.)

Jel: "Dear, what are you doing? The kids finally fell asleep."

Dior: "I know, I'm about to go to the kitchen and cook."

Jel: "Cook? What could you possibly be cooking at a time like this?"

Dior: "A birthday cake."

Jel: "A birthday cake? Don't tell me you're still mad about . . . wait, what am I saying? Of course you are."

Dior: "That's right. My honor as the best cook in my daughter's world is on the line. I'm going to bake my greatest birthday cake ever and win back her stomach!"

(Dior stands firmly in his underwear, determined for the challenge. Amused by his antics, Jel pulls the bedsheets over herself, chuckling.)

Jel: "Whatever, super nerd chef. Just make sure to put some pants on, ok?"

Dior: "Oh! Of course, dear! Ha ha."

(The next day, Lyone awakens to the smell of freshly-baked food, making his stomach growl with anticipation. He jumps out of bed, peeking out of his room, noticing Lisa walking towards the stairs.)

Lyone: "That smells great!"

Lisa: "Ha ha! Better hurry up Li'l L! I'm about to eat it all!"

(Lisa races down the stairs, causing Lyone to run out of his room after her.)

Lyone: "Hey, wait up!"

(The two reach the kitchen together, surprised by a towering decorative cake, frosted in vibrant colors, brought to life on the kitchen table. Dior proudly poses in front of it, standing heroically.)

Dior: "Happy Birthday, Lyone!"

Lisa and Lyone: "Wow!"

(A few minutes later, Jel comes to the kitchen, yawning and rubbing her eyes. She notices Lyone and Lisa, sitting at the table laughing together with a huge cake.)

Jel: "What's with all the noise, guys?"

(Dior walks up to Jel, kissing her on the cheek.)

Dior: "Good morning, dear! Want some of this masterpiece?"

Jel: "Dear, its not the place for that."

Dior: "I meant the cake! Wait, I should have let that one happened."

Lyone: "Jel, you have to try some of this cake! It's really good!"

Jel: "Maybe a small piece."

(Dior walks over to Lisa's side, eagerly awaiting her judgement.)

Dior: "So, Lisa, what do you think?"

(Standing with anxiousness, he watches Lisa take another bite. She nods her head, showing approval. Dior instantly pumps his fist in the air with a victorious smile.)

Dior: "Victory!"

(Everyone erupts with embarrassed laughter at Dior's antics.)

THE ODDS

(Later in the day, Lyone and Lisa sit in the office study room with Jel. The three review homeschooling material together.)

Jel: "Alright, Lyone, let's see if you remember the steps to solving a problem like this."

Lyone: "Um."

(Lyone takes a few seconds, studying the math equation written on the whiteboard. Lisa drowsily stares away from them, inattentive to the lesson.)

Jel: "You don't have to answer the whole question, remember. Just the first step."

Lyone: "Umm, do you simplify inside the parentheses?"

Jel: "Yes! Alright, Lyone! Good job."

(As Lyone smiles with pride, Lisa settles her blank stare upon the clock on the wall, watching the time change to the top of the hour.)

Lisa: "Alright, hour's up! Can we learn about something fun now? Like history?"

Jel: "Lisa, is there a particular part of history you want to learn about?"

Lisa: "Any part that has to do with fighting, of course."

Jel: "I should have known."

Lisa: "What? Nothing's wrong with that. At least it's more interesting."

Jel: "How are you going to learn about the intricacies of war if you can't even find the square root of seven?"

Lisa: "I know what the square root of seven is, Mom."

(Jel smiles, sternly folding her arms, examining Lisa with a glare.)

Jel: "Oh really? Well, how about you tell us the answer, Lisa."

Lisa: "The answer is three-point-five."

(As Jel's cynic glare endures, Lisa folds her arms with a confident smirk of her own.)

Jel: "You realize you're wrong, don't you sweetheart?"

Lisa: "Yeah, I know. But I'm confident enough to fool a fool."

Jel: "Alright, that settles it. More math for you."

(Lyone laughs as Lisa protests Jel's decision. Meanwhile, Dior stands outside the family home along with a group of three men and a large delivery truck. He talks to the lead worker, signing paperwork as the other two workers haul dry foods, supplies, and camping equipment from the truck and into the home.)

Dior: "Thank you. I really appreciate the swiftness of the additional order of equipment to this week's delivery."

Lead Deliverer: "Don't mention it. The surgeon general always pay our company good prestige. It's only natural that we return the favor."

(After signing the paperwork, Dior happily gives the clipboard back to the lead deliverer. He stands back, watching the crew finish unloading their truck.)

Dior: *"Good. It's gonna be a tough winter. Nice to have brand-new camping equipment."*

(Back in Jel's study room, Lisa struggles to keep her eyes open, listening to Jel's lecture. Suddenly, Jel's phone rings from her desk, demanding her attention.)

Jel: "O-Ok kids, break time."

Lisa: "Thank goodness!"

(As Jel walks over to her work phone, Lisa and Lyone hop out of their seats, playfully running toward the stairs.)

Jel: "Hey, be careful, you two!"

(She smiles at them, answering the phone call.)

Jel: "This is Jel speaking."

Idol: "It's Idol, surgeon general."

Jel: "General Idol? This is unexpected. Can I help you?"

Idol: "Are you near a television? Or a radio?"

Jel: "No, sir. This room is devoid of all forms of electronics besides this line and my work terminal, meeting the standards of the Federal Union Military privacy code—"

Idol: "Surgeon general, something very strange is happening as we speak. Please get to a radio or a television now. We'll talk afterward."

(Jel becomes increasingly concerned, hearing the urgency in Idol's tone.)

Jel: "Any channel or station in particular?"

Idol: "It won't matter."

Jel: "Ok then, general. I will call you back."

(Jel hangs up the phone, walking downstairs, avoiding the delivery team as they finish their task. As Lisa and Lyone play fight with each other, Jel ignores them, making her way to the television. Then, she turns it on, noticing a news report from a foreign place. The television screen shows a large arena filled with people, harboring numerous banners depicting a strange star constellation; a calm unsettling eye rest in the center of the banners. Attempting to change the channel, Jel quickly notices the same images on every station. As she stare at the images, the arena begins to look familiar to her, causing a nervous feeling in her stomach. Meanwhile, Dior stands outside, waving goodbye to the deliverers.)

Jel: "Honey! Please come quick! It's urgent!"

Dior: "Give me a second, dear!"

(Dior suddenly disappears in a burst of speed, collecting electronic devices at discreet places around the ground floor of their home, reappearing next to Jel with a handful of the items.)

Dior: "And here I thought Arbitrators would be more careful with espionage."

(After crushing the electronics in the palm of his hands, he sees the television, instantly becoming troubled . Images of crowds of people filled with furor, eclipsed by menacing flags, cycles on the television. But, most concerning of all, Dior senses a faint ominous aura spewing forth from the television itself.)

Dior: "What is this?"

Jel: "I-I don't know."

(As the sound of the roaring crowd fills the living room, Lisa walks into the space along with Lyone.)

Lisa: "Mom, is something wrong?"

(Lisa and Lyone become mesmerized at the sight of the television. The family becomes eerily silent.)

Dior: *"What the heck is this? Why can I feel an Energy Stream coming from an inanimate object? It's almost as if it's pulling me in."*

(Suddenly, the image changes to a large stage in the middle of the arena. The crowd erupts as a middle-aged man, wearing ceremonial robe fitted with armor walks onto the stage. Once Jel and Dior recognizes the man, they're shocked.)

Jel: "Isn't that Vaji of the Great Mountain Kingdom?"

Dior: "Yes, it is. And that arena is the Feasting Grounds. But those banners are not the flags of their nation-state."

Jel: "Wait, you don't think that—"

Vaji: "Ladies and Gentlemen! Citizens of Ni!"

(The image focuses on Vaji, commanding Jel and Dior's attention.)

Vaji: "I, Sir Vaji Valius of the Great Mountain Kingdom, have come to you today bearing good news, a declaration that will change the dynamics of our world as we know it. The Liberator has returned."

(Dior and Jel are perplexed, listening to the crowd erupt at Vaji's announcement.)

Jel: "What did he say?"

Vaji: "Rejoice! For the entity that has given us the Age of Sanctuary, bringing forth our current Age of Exploration, has finally reemerged as prophesied in the scriptures of Ti Grados Falivus. Our Liberator has come!"

(The crowd erupts once more as a large group of people, wearing dark masked and hooded robes, fitted with armor enter the arena in a synchronized fashion. The group gathers around the stage at the center of the arena, turning north at once, facing the grand balcony sitting high above. On each side of the balcony, stands two people, oddly dressed and easily identified. To the left, a youthful man with pale skin, long unkept black hair to his shoulders, and dark drowsy rings around his eyes. He stands slightly hunched, nonchalantly smoking a cigarette. However, attention is drawn to the single, strangely shaped horn, erected on the left side of his head. To the right, a young, peach-skinned woman with long hair; identical to her male counterpart. Each strand of her hair has distinctive, dark-purple coloring at the tips. Her hair easily sways in the wind, revealing her face one moment, and concealing it the next. She stares off into the distance, lost in her own world, blank-faced.

In unison, the dark-robed people at the center of the arena bow. The curtain in the back of the grand balcony parts, revealing a beautiful mature woman with skin as fair as snow. Her braided hair is wrapped with decorative ornaments that strangely interacts with the light around them. On her left hand, she wears a silver gauntlet with sharp pointed fingertips, sporting an odd oval jewel that rest below the knuckles; devouring the light around it. As the crowd cheers, the mysterious woman moves to the edge of the grand balcony, smiling softly, shifting her eyes amongst them.)

Vaji: "Since the dawn of civilization across the globe, we've been at the complete mercy of our mother, Ni, and the laws of her nature. It was our mother's reapers, that first kept our populations small through death and torment; locking us in a state of perpetual fear. Once those ferocious reapers were sealed away, the Monsters, the Beast, the Humanus, and the few oppressive forces that lived among the Humanoids rose to prominence, continuing the tradition of our destruction. Now, in this new Age of Exploration, comes the expansion of nation-states, technological advancement and population growth; bringing about many wondrous advancements in our evolution. And what do we do with our newly acquired prosperity? We practice barbaric tribalism, becoming the very fiends that we banished from our world centuries ago! But it isn't our fault. I see clearly what is at play; embedded in the very threading of our DNA. Within us, spews forth the nature of Ni; our mother and our warden. From birth, we have inherited the bloodlust and self-destruction that fuels the spiral of life and death; which grants Ni her strength at the expense of all other living organisms. Today marks the end of the slaughterhouse. No longer shall we be at the mercy of our mother! Welcome our savior: Astronamus, the final incarnation of the Liberator. Through the Goddess Liberator, we shall live and prosper as one!"

(At the sound of the cheering crowd, Dior clenches his fists, aggressively staring into the warped eyes of Vaji. Lisa and Lyone remain wrapped in silence and fear, feeling the mounting tension.)

Jel: "T-This isn't right. The citizens of the Great Mountain Kingdom aren't Liberator worshipers! This can't be right. Where is Garuda?"

Vaji: "This day marks the beginning of a new era. To all who wish to be saved from the jaws of Ni, come and be blessed by the grace of the Goddess Liberator. But to those who wish to experience the plague of death, what better way to die then by the sword of our savior? Make no mistake, this is indeed a declaration of war against Ni, and all of her reapers! No longer shall the harvest wait patiently for our end! It is time we take our destiny into our own hands!"

(As the crowd cheers once again, Vaji possessively scans them with his eyes, smiling with untamed confidence.)

Vaji: "To commemorate this day, this nation shall be cleansed of its past, and reborn anew! We will begin this revival with a sacrifice."

Jel and Dior: "Sacrifice?"

(The crowds stands in unison, and two more dark-robed people walk into the arena, dragging along a shackled elderly man. The elderly prisoner wears shining gold battle armor, fitted with a green cape depicting a sky dragon. Making their way to the stage, each row of dark-robed people rises to their feet, drawing their swords and posing. Once the captors arrive at center stage with the prisoner, they force him to kneel. Then, the television screen shows the prisoner's bruised face, alarming Dior and Jel.)

Dior: "King Garuda."

Jel: "This can't be happening."

Vaji: "King Garuda, you are all that is left of the Great Mountain Kingdom. A stain that must be washed away. You are granted last words, your Majesty."

(After hearing Vaji's mocking avowal of his kingship, everyone stares at a weakened Garuda, waiting for his reply.)

Garuda: "I'm sorry."

(Garuda lifts his head, drawing attention to the rage and sorrow in his gaze.)

Garuda: "My people, forgive me. My love for my countrymen is what led to my inaction. My refusal to bring an end to the rise of this fanatical cult. I'm sorry that you must now endure the burden of subjugation to this vile witch!"

(Vaji punches Garuda in the face, silencing him with a mouth full of bloodied teeth.)

Vaji: "Must you use your dying breath to curse our savior, uncle? I must admit, your boldness is the only thing I was fond of."

(Vaji slowly walks from Garuda's left to his right, dragging the blade of his long sword on the stage, positioning the blade at Garuda's neck. Jel urgently moves in front of Lyone and Lisa, trying to push them out of the room.)

Vaji: "Here lies the grave of a king and his kingdom."

Jel: "C-Come on now, children. Let's get out of here."

Lyone: "What's going to happen to him?"

Mysterious Voice: "Vaji."

(The family frightfully freezes, turning back to the television, spellbound by a sudden voice. Reacting to the voice, Vaji abruptly stops the swing of his blade inches away from the back of Garuda's neck. Afterwards, Vaji looks toward the grand balcony, blessed by Astronamus' pleasant smile.)

Astronamus: "Remove yourself from the stage. I have a better idea."

(As Vaji exits the stage on command, a spirit of dread befalls the Kendric home. They can hear Astronamus' voice, echoing throughout their home. Her soft voice whispers, bouncing from wall to wall, calling onto them in an unknown language, accompanied by the clearly identifiable words visibly verified on the television.)

Jel: "Dior, is it just me, or does it feel like she's here right now?"

(Dior stands motionless, his fists still clenched, his senses inundated by the enigmatic presence.)

Dior: *"Jel is unable to sense Energy Streams and even she can feel her presence? What the heck is this? How is it that I can sense her everywhere? How is this possible?"*

(Astronamus' turns her attention to the two henchmen standing at her sides.)

Astronamus: "Demosyn, Claire, take care of it."

(Demosyn remains uninterested, drawing Claire's attention.)

Demosyn: "It's your turn, sis. Have at it."

(Almost instantly, Claire turns to Garuda with glowing eyes and an eerily playful smile. She lifts her right hand, generating a ghastly dark-purple flame in her palm. In an instant, a massive burst of purple flames devours the entire stage. The sound of crackling fire and screams from Garuda fill the air, causing Lisa to fall onto her knees weeping in distress. Jel comforts her, sheltering Lisa in her arms. Dior and Lyone remain petrified after witnessing the execution. The dark-purple flames quickly disperses, leaving behind the stage and Garuda's corpse; both grayed and frozen in place as sculptures of sand. Lastly, Claire inhales deeply and exhales, blowing a strong torrent of wind, carrying the stage and Garuda's corpse away as dust in the wind tunnel. Astronamus turns to Vaji, noticing his bafflement at Claire's destructive might.)

Astronamus: "Wrap this up, Vaji."

(Upon hearing Astronamus, Vaji regains his poise.)

Vaji: "Y-Yes, Goddess Liberator."

(Vaji takes a final peek at the ground, littered with Garuda's petrified ashes. After composing himself, Vaji steps forth, regaining everyone's attention.)

Vaji: "Lastly, a message to those blessed champions of Ni of all species around the world: There shall be no salvation for those marked by the curse of our devourer. You are no more than instruments of death. No different than Ni's reapers. You have no place in paradise. And, as some of you may already be aware, we've taken the liberty of capturing the strongest of Ni's champions."

(Suddenly, the video on the television screen changes from the arena to a dark unknown location. Three people can be seen, floating into the air, suspended in three separate binding arrays of light, erected from floor to ceiling. As the image of the three becomes noticeable, Dior focuses on their faces, committing the image to memory.)

Dior: "Ni's strongest champions?"

(Jel looks at the television screen while holding a weeping Lisa. Suddenly, Lyone frantically runs to the television screen, tightly grappling at its corners, breathing heavily with tears in his eyes.)

Lyone: "Mom! Dad! Auntie!"

(Dior quickly grabs Lyone, desperately attempting to pull him away from the television screen. Lyone struggles, dragging the television a few inches before letting go.)

Lyone: "THAT'S MY FAMILY! LET ME GO! LET ME GO!"

Dior: "Calm yourself, Lyone!"

(As the image of Lyone's family remains on the television screen, Vaji concludes his speech, warning their opposition.)

Vaji: "The choice is yours, citizens of Ni: fight for damnation or conform to salvation."

(The television abruptly turns off, leaving everyone speechless. As Lyone helplessly relaxes, Dior notices the strange presence has disappeared.)

Dior: *"Was any of that even real?"*

(As Jel continues to comfort Lisa, Dior releases the seemingly calmed Lyone, dumbfounded by the situation.)

Jel: "It's over, sweetheart. It's over."

Lyone: <in Huadi> "Mom, Dad, Auntie Rose!"

(Lyone gradually becomes filled with rage at the thought of his family, being harmed by Astronamus and Vaji. Jel rises to her feet, walking over to comfort Lyone with a hug. But, when she touches his arm, she is instantly taken aback by the heat of his skin.)

Lyone: "AAARRRGGHHH!!!"

(Dior quickly senses a sudden preemptive surge in Lyone's Energy Stream, swiftly advancing forward, knocking Lyone unconscious with a speedy chop to Lyone's neck. Jel and Lisa are alarmed by Dior's action, watching Lyone fall onto the floor, motionless.)

Lisa: "Lyone!"

Jel: "Dior! What did you—"

(As Jel attempts to aid Lyone, Dior stops her with an arm in her path, sharply glaring at Jel over his shoulder with disapproval. After looking a Dior, she withdraws, noticing steam lifting from Lyone's body.

Later that day, Jel speaks to Idol on the phone, following up on the mysterious situation.)

Idol: "We're still waiting for a full analysis to figure out more details about the broadcast. But, we know enough to conclude that everything we saw was true."

Jel: "But how can that be? The Great Mountain Kingdom is not even at a technological level to broadcast in their own country! Yet they did so throughout the planet?"

Idol: "Although the Great Mountain Kingdom was our top trading partner in the Western Hemisphere, I can assure you, technology was not a part of the trading pact. And, even if it were, we've yet to reach that capability ourselves."

Jel: "Was that woman truly the last incarnation of the Liberator?"

(Both fall silent, feeling the tension of the situation. Then, Idol breaks the silence with an update from reports.)

Idol: "According to the holy book 'Ti Grados Falivus', the next and final incarnation of the Liberator will be born at the Peak of Incarnation; located at the top of the Libra Tower. Since the transmission, Saint Carnel Ronald Bernard himself addressed his nation and denounced this Astronamus person, declaring that she was never born at the Peak of Incarnation."

Jel: "I see. She is an imposter then?"

Idol: "Seems that way. And every other nation-state that officially follows the teachings of the late Liberator Ali Delibra through 'Ti Grados Falivus' have all denounced her as a pretender to godhood. Needless to say, they all want her head. But, as we were watching the broadcast, when that strange woman spoke . . ."

Jel: "You could feel her presence as if she was right next to you."

Idol: "You felt that as well?"

Jel: "Yes, I did. I never felt anything like it. Was that some kind of battle technique?"

Idol: "Amazing. Even a Huma without the active genetic trait to control their own Energy Stream could sense that woman's presence. And when I thought this couldn't get any weirder. I can't be sure, but, I suspect that this is more than just mere technological advancement, or even newly developed battle techniques."

Jel: "Do you think it's true? That Astronamus is the Liberator?"

Idol: "I don't know."

(Jel stressfully places her left hand on her forehead, eventually regaining her composure with an update of her own.)

Jel: "One last thing. Lyone said that his parents were the three captured Champions of Ni that were shown during the whole ordeal."

Idol: "Is that right? If that's true, it would mean we've found evidence of this Astronamus person being involved in the North-South Ryonian Conflict. If she's capable of bringing down three nation-states in less than a half of years' time, she could very well be a great threat to the planet."

Jel: "There is still pieces to this puzzle missing. We'll need to verify Lyone's involvement before we can draw a definitive conclusion."

Idol: "True. I'll leave the investigation up to Dior and yourself. If this is headed where I think it is, this situation is going to be one for the history books."

(Jel becomes concerned, judging the ambition in Idol's tone. Meanwhile, Lyone lies in his room, coming to consciousness as Dior and Lisa watches over him. He sits upright in his bed, wobbly holding his head.)

Lisa: "Lyone, are you ok?"

Lyone: "Urgh, w-what happened?"

Lisa: "Dad hit you hard. But Mom said you'll be ok."

(Dior stands by with his arms folded, staring cautiously at Lyone.)

Dior: "It's true. I knocked you out, Lyone. I believe it was for your own good."

Lisa: "His own good? Dad, you could have killed him!"

(Unremorseful, Dior ignores Lisa's accusation. Lyone focuses his eyes, adjusting to the light in the room.)

Lisa: "Hey, you're ok, right Lyone?"

Lyone: "Yeah, I think so."

(Lyone suddenly remembers the image of his family being held captive. Then, Dior abruptly places his hand in front of Lyone, preventing him from getting out of bed.)

Lyone: "Mr. Kendric? What are you—"

Dior: "Lyone, listen closely. Calm yourself before you rise to your feet."

Lyone: "How can I stay calm when my parents are in trouble? I have to save them!"

Dior: "And you believe that you can accomplish that right now?"

Lyone: "Yes, I can! Now let me go!"

(As silence captures the room, Dior watches Lyone carefully, taking a mental note of his determination. Afterwards, Dior decides to move out of the way.)

Dior: "Tell you what, I'll let you go. However, if you truly believe you have what it takes to save your parents, then show me."

(Lisa becomes surprised by Dior's challenge, nervously laughing.)

Lisa: "Ha ha, Dad, you can't be serious, right?"

Lyone: "Fine."

(Lisa becomes even more surprised, hearing Lyone's acceptance of the challenge.)

Dior: "Then follow me."

(Lyone jumps out of bed, following Dior out of the room. Lisa follows behind them, concerned by their seriousness.)

Lisa: "Wait, you guys are really serious?"

(Jel comes out of her study, noticing the three of them storming outside.)

Jel: "What's going on?"

(She follows everyone outside, watching as Lisa tries to stop Dior and Lyone.)

Lisa: "Lyone, you don't have to fight Dad! Don't be so thick headed!"

(Lyone doesn't respond to Lisa's plea, daringly staring at Dior. As Lisa turns her attention to Dior, he calmly stands with his back turned toward them.)

Lisa: "Dad, come on. Do you have to do this?"

Dior: "Lisa, remember when Chris would tell you to be careful touching roses?"

Lisa: "Yeah, but what does that have to do with this fighting?"

Dior: "Did you ever listen to him?"

Lisa: "Huh?"

(Lisa witnesses a deafening glare from Dior, gazing at her from over his shoulder, instantly becoming nervous, balling her fists to keep her composure.)

Dior: "Did you ever listen to Chris' advice?"

Lisa: "Um, well, of course not, Dad. You know that I came home one day with blood in my palm because of it."

Dior: "And that very lesson is the same one that Lyone must learn. But rose thorns are the least of his worries. This is an attempt to save his life."

Lyone: "I'm standing right here, you know! Are we fighting or what?"

(Dior shifts his eyes toward Lyone. In the surrounding forest, Olivia watches them with a set of high-tech binoculars, distributing sound from the target direction to a wireless earpiece.)

Dior: "We will not be fighting here, Lyone. Come. I'll take us to a suitable location."

Lyone: "Fine."

Lisa: "Wait, hold on one second! At least take me with you guys. I gotta see this, ha ha!"

(Jel walks up to Lisa from behind, gently placing her hand onto Lisa's shoulders, stopping Lisa from interfering. Then, she locks eyes with Dior, reading each other's body language.)

Dior: "We'll return soon enough, dear."

(Dior turns toward Lyone, noticing his lasting expression of confidence.)

Dior: *"Seems Olivia is preparing to follow me. I'm going to have to lose her. The last thing we need is spectators during this bout."*

Lyone: "Alright, I'm ready."

Dior: "Ok."

(Dior wraps his left arm around Lyone's torso, effortlessly picking him up, taking off in a burst of speed. Olivia follows suit, traveling in a burst of speed, shadowing them through the trees in the Yellow Shadow Forest. She eagerly tries to pursue in stealth, eventually coming to a stop, losing the signal of Dior's Energy Stream.)

Olivia: *"Darn, I lost him."*

(Without showing signs of fatigue, Olivia pauses in the shadows of the forest, contemplating the situation.)

Olivia: *"He was moving pretty fast for releasing so little energy from his Energy Stream. Not only could I not keep up, but I couldn't even keep a manual fix on him. No wonder so many look up to him."*

(As Olivia continues to ponder, one of the trees behind her opens a large eye with a triangular pupil. Its branches and roots slowly move toward her, attempting to constrict its prey. But, Olivia leaps high into the air, avoiding the monster's grasp, disappearing in a burst of speed once again.)

Olivia: *"Looks like I have no choice but to wait until they return."*

(Meanwhile, Dior appears in a small meadow within the Yellow Shadow Forest. The light from Yunyi shines, freely resting on the forest floor. As Dior releases Lyone from his grapple, Lyone looks around amazed at their speedy travel.)

Lyone: *"Holy crap that was fast."*

(Dior walks a few feet away from Lyone, sternly turning toward Lyone with his arms folded, granting him full attention.)

Dior: "Lyone, I would prefer not to waste too much time here."

(Burning with determination, Lyone briefly stretches, soon taking his fighting stance.)

Dior: "Come! If you truly wish to convince me that you have what it takes to fight, then show me!"

(Dior stands resolute, closely analyzing Lyone's every move, waiting for him to engage. Then, Lyone runs toward Dior and jumps, throwing a right punch. Dior blocks the attack with his left arm and the ground below them shakes from the impact. Lyone follows his attack with a right kick, striking Dior's left arm again. He then lands on the ground, executing a sweep. But, Lyone's leg hits Dior and doesn't inflict even the slightest sign of damage. Dior watches as Lyone flips a distance away, landing on his feet and entering a different stance. Lyone runs towards Dior once again, attacking him with a flurry of punches and kicks. Dior answers by dodging all of Lyone's attacks.)

Dior: "How do you expect to defeat anyone if this is the best you can do, Lyone?"

Lyone: "Shut up!"

(Dior stops dodging Lyone's attacks, allowing Lyone to strike him in the face. Lyone becomes surprised, watching Dior stand about unharmed by his attack. Then, Dior punches Lyone in the chest, sending him crashing to the ground a few feet away. Winded from the punch, Lyone slowly climbs to his feet, holding his chest.)

Dior: "How do you intend to defend anyone if you're unable to defend yourself, Lyone?"

(Lyone rushes towards Dior, intending to attack him once again. However, Dior catches Lyone's fist, squeezing it, causing Lyone to kneel in pain.)

Lyone: <in Huadi> "Ahhh! Let go!"

Dior: "How do you intend to save anyone when you can't even save yourself?"

(As Dior sustains his grip on Lyone's right-hand, tears fall from Lyone's eyes, unable to cope with the pain.)

Dior: "Who will save your family now, Lyone?"

(Suddenly, Lyone punches the ground with his left fist, causing a tremor, staggering Dior's balance. He pulls his right arm back, throwing Dior over his head. Dior lands on his feet a moderate distance away from Lyone, observing his fiery red aura. Lyone turns towards Dior, baring eyes full of anger, glowing red veins pulsing under his skin, and steam lifting from his body.)

Dior: *"It's as I thought."*

(Lyone launches himself toward Dior, attacking him with another punch. Dior dodges to the right with ease, countering with a kick. But, Dior kick strikes through an image of Lyone.)

Dior: *"His fighting capabilities has dramatically increased, along with a gradually increasing Energy Stream. Been a while since I fought one of these."*

(Dior patiently stands his ground as Lyone reappears above him with another punch. Dior catches Lyone's arm, throwing him through the air. Next, Dior runs forward in a burst of speed, catching up to Lyone, grabbing him by the neck, and slamming him into the ground, leaving a small crater upon impact. After the fight concludes, Dior lifts Lyone out of the hole, noticing Lyone now rendered unconscious and back to a normal state. Then, he walks to the middle of the meadow carrying Lyone.)

Dior: *"Darn it, Bhaja. The least you could have done was tell me what I was dealing with."*

(Dior places Lyone on the ground, walking a few feet away. He turns to the unconscious Lyone, pointing his right index finger toward him. Dior releases a narrow beam of energy, drawing three cryptic circles into the ground, connecting the circles by drawn lines with Lyone positioned in the center. Among the shadows in the surrounding forest, a ferocious black-and-yellow feathered, bipedal lizard-like monster watches in secret.)

Dior: *"Lyone, you'll have to forgive me."*

(After finishing the drawings, Dior retracts the energy beam, sitting at the edge of the symbols, entering a meditative stance. Then, he fills the symbols with energy, and a shadowy shroud blankets the area, restricting light. Disoriented in a cloak of darkness, Lyone awakens, climbing to his feet in slow-motion, listening to the sound of familiar faint voices.)

Faint Voice: "*. . . yone . . . sorr . . . son . . .*"

(Lyone's normal motion returns and the voice fades. He looks around, gazing into an endless void of darkness. He tries to speak, quickly realizing he cannot. Suddenly, letters slowly manifest before him, forming words:

"Speech has no existence here."

The strange words continue:

"Only actions know of this place. Step forward and overcome yourself."

The words suddenly scatter before him, turning into birds of light, flying off into the darkness. Lyone takes a step, suddenly finding himself at the top of a giant tower structure, connected to a twisting stairway that climbs to the top of another tower. He begins to walk up the stairway, cautiously surveying his surroundings.

Eventually, Lyone reaches the top of the next tower, taking a moment to survey the space. He stands alone, deciding to walk to the edge of the tower; once again greeted by the endless abyss of darkness. Suddenly, more letters begin to manifest, creating messages that captures his eyes:

"The door is locked. However, it can be opened with prowess and resilience."

Lyone stands in place, confused by the message of the words, deciding to look around. To his dismay, he finds the stairway leading back to where he came from, swallowed by the darkness along with the previous tower.

Then, the letters of the message condense into a stream of light, flowing to the other side of the tower, creating a shining door, capturing Lyone's attention. He proceeds towards the door and reaches for the doorknob. But, it becomes encased in an aura of darkness, barring his exit. Suddenly, a portal of darkness emerges before the door, and a clawed fiend with no face crawls out of the portal, causing Lyone to cautiously step backwards. The clawed fiend postures itself to fight, and Lyone realizes the danger. He takes his fighting stance as the fiend hunches its back. The fiend walks around Lyone, looking for an opening to attack.

Suddenly, the fiend rolls to the left and jumps towards Lyone with a slash from its right arm. Lyone ducks under the attack, moving to the fiend's back as it lands on the floor. Following its attack, the fiend swings its left claw. Lyone ducks under its swing, countering with a punch to its chest, causing it to explode in a burst of light. Lyone looks at his fist, surprised at his strength, nodding with approval.

Suddenly, four more portals of darkness appear, surrounding Lyone. Soon, he finds himself surrounded by four more clawed fiends. The first of the group charges toward Lyone, attempting to stab him with its right claw. Lyone avoids the strike, grabbing the assailant's arm, tossing it in the opposite direction. Unable to gain control, it remains on a collision course toward one of the other fiends. The intended target jumps into the air, avoiding the collision, and launches itself towards Lyone. The other two opponents charges toward Lyone from his sides, all ready to strike at once. Lyone backflips, dodging the synchronized attack from the three clawed fiends. Following, he charges forward, spin-kicking the middle fiend in the chest, causing it to explode in a burst of light.

He then sweeps another of his opponents off its feet, punching the fiend once its grounded, causing it to explode. Suddenly, the other two clawed fiends summon portals of darkness on the floor of the tower, jumping into them. The portals slither along the tower's floor to and from Lyone, causing confusion by their movements. One of the portals moves directly under Lyone. He jumps out of the way as the clawed fiend launches into the air, barely missing Lyone with its claws. Lyone rolls back onto his feet, unaware of the second portal parked behind him. The clawed fiend reaches out of the portal, slashing Lyone across the left leg.

Lyone quickly rolls forward to reposition himself, his face riddled with pain. He glances at the wound on his leg, noticing that his blood has been replaced with rays of light. Lyone steels himself as the two portals circle around him with sporadic movements. Then, one of the portals park itself under Lyone's feet. Anticipating an attack, Lyone jumps high in the air as the clawed fiend launches toward him with its claws positioned to impale. Lyone dodges the attack, grabbing the clawed fiend's legs, spinning it through the air, and throwing it into the tower floor, causing it to explode.

The last portal of darkness stops as Lyone lands on his feet. The fiend crawls out of the portal, preparing to meet Lyone head on. Running toward the fiend, Lyone strikes with punches and kicks. It dodges Lyone's attacks, countering with a slash once presented with an opening. But, Lyone skillfully parries its attack, hitting the clawed fiend's forearm with his wrist. Lastly, he hits the fiend with a spin kick to its chest, causing the final opponent to explode in a burst of light.

Lyone breathes a sigh of relief, inspecting the wound on his leg. Seconds later, his attention is drawn to the shining words, slowly appearing above him:

"If you lose too much of your light, you will be consumed by your darkness."

Suddenly, the tower shakes, causing Lyone to lose his footing. The words continue as Lyone looks around frantically:

"If you're reading this . . ."

Lyone quickly climbs to his feet, running to the edge of the tower. He nervously stares, witnessing a flood of clawed fiends climbing the tower from the dark abyss below. He backs away from the tower's edge, running to the center, overwhelmed with panic. Lyone closes his eyes, taking his fighting stance, controlling his breathing as the shining words above him continue:

"... he is trying his best ..."

As anticipated, clawed fiends from all edges of the tower swarm toward Lyone. Then, he reveals his eyes with a renewed sense of valor, prepared to defend himself. As Lyone valiantly fights off the horde of fiends, the shining words continue:

"... and if you lend him your faith ..."

Lyone is slashed by the claws of his opponents across the right arm and the back. However, he continues to fight despite the beams of light, piercing the surrounding darkness through his wounds. A group of his foes piles onto Lyone's body, taking him to the ground. The fiends mold together into a thick soup of darkness, attempting to devour Lyone whole. As he struggles to break free from the clutch of darkness, the shining words from above concludes:

"... then he may yet conquer that which is destined."

As Lyone refuses to surrender, the shining words burst into countless particles of light, occupying the space surrounding the tower. Lyone bursts from the grip of darkness, launching himself into the air, knocking many of his surrounding opponents onto the floor of the tower. As he ascends towards the sky, the particles of light quickly gather to Lyone's fist. Then, he plunges toward the center of the tower at a great velocity. He strikes the tower with his fist, filling the structure with light. Finally, the light blast away the clawed fiends in a spectacular display.

Lyone stands alone, assessing the space for any further danger. Once he is cleared of threats, he falls to his knees, breathing heavily with a relieved smile. After a few seconds, he stands onto his feet, refocusing his vision, noticing the magnificent shine of a light now beaming from the door. After a brief stare, he steps forward with assurance, opening the door, becoming engulfed by the tender embrace of the light.

Moments later, Lyone opens his eyes, finding himself standing in front of the hollowed tree of his inner world. He immediately begins to question the entire ordeal.)

Lyone: <in Huadi> "The heck was that?"

(Lyone looks down at his feet, noticing the red-and-black, puffy-tailed, cat-like creature growling and grooming itself. Afterwards, he turns his attention to the surroundings, realizing he stands within his inner world.)

Lyone: "I'm back in my inner world? But, I don't remember meditating."

(He looks behind himself, frightfully discovering an eerie standing manikin of the same height and stature as himself. Lyone becomes uneasy at the face of the manikin; a bizarrely clouded mirror.)

Lyone: "When did this get here?"

(After a careful inspection of the manikin, he stand about, scratching his head with confusion.)

Lyone: "That place where I was before. Was this thing responsible?"

(Lyone slowly walks toward the hollowed tree, checking his body, finding no signs of wounds.)

Lyone: "So strange."

(He sits on the ground with his legs folded, scratching his head, attempting to understand the strange turn of events.)

Lyone: "Floating words, shadows with claws, darkness everywhere . . . Oh wait! I was fighting with Dior before all of that happened!"

(Lyone frantically looks around the area once again, detecting the presence of no one. However, he notices the puffy-tailed creature, bouncing around on its tails, swatting at falling leaves.)

Lyone: "Maybe I should wake up, I guess."

(Lyone closes his eyes, focusing his mind, controlling his breathing. After a few seconds, he slowly opens his eyes, discovering himself resting in his bed at the Kendric family home. He sits upright, holding his head, still aching from his bout with Dior.)

Lyone: "Darn it."

Lisa: "This is going to be a normal thing for you, eh Li'l L?"

Lyone: "Huh?"

(Lyone looks to his bedside, noticing Lisa placing food on the desk next to his bed. Lyone lays back onto his bed, sighing in frustration with his hand on his head.)

Lisa: "You ok?"

Lyone: "No."

Lisa: "Is it your head? Let me see."

Lyone: "It's not that, Lisa."

(Lisa pauses with a smile, shaking her head at Lyone's stubbornness.)

Lyone: "Ok, it is that. But, this is nothing compared to what my family is going through."

(Lyone stares up at the ceiling of his room, contemplating his next course of action.)

Lyone: "I'm leaving tomorrow."

(As Lisa sighs from Lyone's persistence, they're suddenly interrupted by a knock on the door.)

Lisa: "Oh, um, come in."

(Dior and Jel walks into the room, both visibly concerned about Lyone's situation.)

Jel: "Sorry to interrupt you two. But, there is something we must discuss with Lyone."

Lisa: "Oh no, go right ahead, Mom."

(Jel walks up to Lisa, comfortably placing her arms around her.)

Dior: "Lyone."

(Lyone looks away toward the window, ignoring Dior.)

Dior: "Your opponents are, more than likely, much stronger than even me."

Lyone: "I don't care. Nothing is going to stop me from saving them! I'm going to save my family no matter what."

Dior: "Then allow us to aid you."

(Despite his defensiveness, Lyone turns his attention to Dior, curiously listening to his offer.)

Dior: "In your current physical, mental, and Energy Stream condition, the best you can do is deal with a small, select group of opponents. But with the right training, you can be a great fighter, Lyone. Let me train you for the duration of the winter and teach you the basics. Foundation is the key to success."

(Lyone and Dior stares at one another, gauging each other's resolve.)

Lyone: "Fine."

Lisa: "Wait a minute. Dad, just the basics?"

Dior: "Lisa."

(Jel wraps her arms tighter around Lisa, gaining her attention.)

Jel: "Don't worry, Lisa. We'll handle this."

(Once Lisa is assured, Jel turns her attention to Lyone.)

Jel: "Lyone, believe it or not, we developed a plan to help you some time ago. But, I have to be honest with you, we've been given an ultimatum to escort you from our home or face charges."

Lyone: "Ulti-what? Charges?"

Jel: "It means we have to get you out of here or suffer consequences."

Lyone: "Fine with me. I've stayed long enough."

Dior: "Glad to hear you're eager to travel. We'll be camping for most of the winter—"

Lisa: "Can I come, too?"

(Lisa wears a confident smile, drawing everyone's attention.)

Dior: "Actually, yes Lisa. I would like you to come with us."

Lisa: "Yes! So, when do we leave?"

Dior: "We leave tomorrow. Understood?"

Lisa: "Got it!"

Lyone: "Perfect."

Dior: "Good. But, before we wrap this conversation up, I'd like to talk to Lyone privately, please."

Jel: "Oh? Alright then. Lisa?"

Lisa: "Umm, yeah. Sure."

(Jel and Lisa leaves the room together, closing the door behind them.)

Lyone: "Hey, by the way, Dior, I had this weird dream—"

(Before he can finish, the room becomes engulfed in a black aura. Outside of the door, Jel and Lisa speaks to each other, unaware of the strange darkness surrounding Lyone's room.)

Lyone: "What the . . ."

Dior: "Calm yourself, Lyone. What you see around us is a technique I control. You have questions for me, do you not?"

Lyone: "Umm, yeah. I guess I do."

Dior: "Then how about we make a deal. You ask me your questions, and I'll ask you my questions after. Sound fair?"

Lyone: "Alright. So, what's going on with this aura? I felt something like it when I was in my inner world not too long ago."

Dior: "The power you see around you is from a very ancient technique. You may have experienced a strange event in your inner world, accompanied by a manikin with the face of a mirror. That was also a technique I used on you while you were unconscious after our bout. It bridges the gap between the essence of your being and your consciousness. If you survive the trials it presents, you are rewarded with better mental stability, mental control, and increased access to the essence of your being."

Lyone: "I'm not sure what any of that means. But, what if I fail?"

Dior: "Your essence consumes your mind. And what is the body or Energy Stream without the mind?"

(Lyone remains confused, sensing a grimness in Dior's tone.)

Dior: "You'll die if you lose, Lyone."

Lyone: "W-What?! I can die? Why would you do that to me?"

Dior: "Because in this world, the chance of you dying without this technique is greater. The technique will only affect you when you're having a near-death experience. And considering what you are, this should help you have better control of yourself."

Lyone: "Wait, 'what I am?'"

Dior: "During our bout, you transformed when you experienced a great deal of anger. And it was no minor transformation, considering the amount of training it would take to learn a transformation with that level of physical metamorphosis."

Lyone: *"That word again."*

Dior: "Truth be known, Lyone, if I was any other person on the planet, with the exception of a small few, I'd be hard pressed to deduce that you're a Renzido."

(Becoming nervous and defensive at Dior's words, Lyone keeps his eyes fixed on him, responding with a threatening tone.)

Lyone: "So now what? You're gonna kill me?"

Dior: "Fortunately for you, I'm one of those exceptions. No, I'm not going to kill you, Lyone. I merely want to confirm my suspicions. But you are on the correct path."

Lyone: "What do you mean?"

Dior: "I've been told by Jel about how you avoid conversation when discussing your race and species. I assume your parents were the ones who told you to hide what you are from the world. Well, they were right. Revealing what you are would only attract the wrong kind of attention."

Lyone: "Yeah, they told me the same thing."

(Dior examines Lyon closely, watching his growing concern.)

Dior: "Tell me, did your parents ever explain your situation as a living Renzido?"

(Lyone shakes his head, acknowledging his lack of clarity.)

Dior: "There may be a reason why they never told you. But I believe you're mature enough to know the truth. It's because your race is considered extinct by most nation-states around the world."

Lyone: "Extinct?"

Dior: "It means your people died off. There is a chance that there are more Renzido hiding in the world. But, more than likely, you and your family are what's left of your people."

Lyone: "What? But how?"

Dior: "They were hunted down by every other race and species on the planet. Even other Humanus species joined the hunt. The reasons behind this have many different factors; but it makes you a target regardless. Meaning, if you keep what you are to yourself, you might be able to avoid such conflict."

(Lyone pauses briefly, bombarded by his own thoughts.)

Narrator: "During that time, I couldn't describe this feeling I had in my gut. But thinking back on it now, I know exactly what it was: loneliness. Just the thought of being the only person left in the world like me was overwhelming. Although, if anything, it gave me another reason to get my parents back. And in an instant, my sorrow turned to anger."

(Lyone balls his fists, alarming Dior to his rising anger.)

Dior: "Lyone!"

(After Dior's sudden outburst, Lyon snaps out of his trance, turning his attention to him.)

Dior: "Your anger is what causes your transformation. Be aware that you have little to no control when you've transformed; which makes you dangerous while in that state. So, this is a fair warning: don't make me have to knock you out again."

(Lyone calms himself, taking heed to Dior's warning.)

Lyone: "Ok, sorry."

Dior: "Hopefully my technique aids you accordingly. Although you can learn to better control your emotions without it, this technique will help you reach that goal faster."

Lyone: "The name of the technique. What is it?"

Dior: "The Trial of Inner Reflection. I'm bound by oath, so I'll say no more. But, I owe you that much."

Lyone: "One last question then. I saw words of light floating in that dark place. Were you guiding me?"

Dior: "The Trial of Inner Reflection manifest itself according to its host. Once I enacted the technique upon you, I can no longer control or intervene. Those words were a part of your essence."

(Lyone falls silent, watching Dior walk toward the door to his room. Dior opens the door, causing the black aura to dissipate. Then, he is greeted by the smiles of Jel and Lisa.)

Jel: "Is everything ok?"

Dior: "Yes, everything is fine now that we're all on the same page."

Lisa: "You sure, Dad? We were standing here the whole time and never heard a word."

(Dior closes Lyone's door, stepping closer to Jel and Lisa with a confident smile.)

Dior: "Don't worry so much, Lisa. There are some things that speak for themselves."

Lisa: "Yeah, ok, Dad. Whatever. I just wanna know one thing, though."

(Lisa folds her arms, giving Dior sass.)

Lisa: "Why did you tell Lyone we'll only teach him the basics? We all know that freeing his parents is going to take years of training!"

Dior: "What I aim to do is give Lyone a choice, Lisa. It's the least any of us can do for him considering his situation."

Lisa: <whispering> "More like the illusion of choice."

Jel: "Did you say something, dear?"

Lisa: "Yeah! I said I can't wait until tomorrow! I'm pumped to train!"

(Lisa throws punches at the air and Dior chuckles.)

PARTY OF THREE

(The next day, Lisa and Lyone inspects their camping equipment, working through a checklist of items.)

Lyone: "Alright, the medical supplies are good."

Lisa: "Good, I'll mark it."

(Lisa marks the checklist with a pen, curiously peeking at Lyone, continuing the inspection.)

Lisa: "So, are you nervous?"

Lyone: "Huh? Nervous? Why would I be nervous?"

Lisa: "Well, we are going back to where we found you. You're not nervous to find out what's there?"

Lyone: "Nope. I'm looking forward to it."

Lisa: "What do you expect to find there?"

Lyone: "Won't know until we get there, right? Only one way to find out."

(Meanwhile, in Jel's private office, Jel and Dior deliberates over a recently delivered briefing document; both concerned by its content.)

Dior: "So, the war has already begun. This is very surreal."

Jel: "Looks like the Great Mountain Kingdom has begun their march toward neighboring nation-states south of their location. And what's worse is that they are not being slowed down by the vast number of uninhabitable zones in their way."

Dior: "Meaning, they're killing monsters and beasts along the way. Does the report mention anything about the Grand Shine of Centre and Daafir? Surely those two nation-states have stopped their conflict, considering the threat at their doorstep."

(Jel turns her attention to the briefing document, reading its content out loud.)

Jel: "'The nation-states of Daafir and the Grand Shine of Centre are well-prepared for another long-term military engagement due to the ceasefire; which lasted a decade. However, there has been no effort from either nation-state to intercept the Salvation Battlefront.'"

Dior: "The Salvation Battlefront? Is that what they're calling their military operation now?"

Jel: "Looks that way. The nation-state even changed its name to 'Allhaven' according to this document. It goes on to say, 'There has also been no effort from the two nation-states to postpone their conflict and form an alliance against the enemy's fast-approaching onslaught.'"

Dior: "What the heck are Centre and Daafir thinking? They must have gotten word of the declaration of war by now."

(Jel places the document in her desk, locking it with a key. Afterwards, she walks to the front of the desk, sitting on its edge, musing over the events.)

Jel: "Hmm, knowing the history of Daafir and the Grand Shine of Centre, I'd bet they are each waiting to see what the other does first before making a move of their own. Which puts them both at a disadvantage to Allhaven's aggression. The report doesn't state the amount of time left until contact is made between the three nation-states. But it's safe to assume that it won't be long now."

(Troubled by the situation, Dior paces, ingesting Jel's assessment.)

Dior: "You're right. This is indicative of their history. But if they wait too long, there will be no chance to properly position themselves for a defense."

Jel: "Maybe they won't need to."

Dior: "Hmm, how so?"

Jel: "Maybe they both worked out a plan ahead of time for cases like this. They may have been at each other's throats for thousands of years, but both cultures are rooted in the principle of honor. I don't see a reason why the two wouldn't have already worked out an agreement in case an invader attacked one or the other during their own personal conflict."

Dior: "I hope you're right on that part of your analysis, dear."

(Jel stands with a confident smile.)

Jel: "You shouldn't trouble yourself too much. You have a task to accomplish, right?"

(Dior pauses his pacing with a burdened sigh, turning toward Jel with a smile of his own.)

Dior: "Yes, of course. All the equipment is ready, and the preparations have been completed."

Jel: "Then one last thing."

(Jel reaches into the pocket of her lab coat, taking out a smartphone.)

Jel: "Here, this smartphone holds a secure line directly to my work phone. We can keep in touch this way and I'll inform you about any updates."

Dior: "I see. Promise you won't forget?"

Jel: "Ha ha, of course not, dear!"

(Jel laughs nervously, handing over the smartphone to Dior.)

Dior: "Thank you. But, you forgot something."

Jel: "Oh? What?"

(Dior pulls Jel closer, intimately sharing a kiss.)

Jel: "Take care of the kids, ok?"

Dior: "That's a promise."

(He places the smartphone in his pocket and the two leave Jel's study together. Later in the day, Jel stands on the porch of their home, serenely observing Lisa help Lyone adjust the equipment strapped onto his backpack.)

Lisa: "Alright, all set. Will you be ok like this?"

Lyone: "Yeah, I'll be fine."

(Jel steps off the porch, walking up to the kids, giving them both hugs and kisses.)

Jel: "Be careful out there, you two. Ok?"

Lisa: "Don't worry, Mom! Besides, Li'l L has his big sis with him! I'll make sure he's fine!"

Lyone: "Yeah, yeah, whatever. Mrs. Kendr . . . ehh, Jel, thanks for everything."

Jel: "Ha ha, no problem Lyone. You're going to be a great man one day."

(Jel turns her smile towards Lisa, noticing her embarrassed blush.)

Jel: "And you're going to be a great woman yourself dear."

Lisa: "Stop it mom. That's embarrassing ha ha."

Jel: "Ok, ok, ha ha. I love you dear."

Lisa: "Always?"

Jel: "Always."

(As Jel turns her passionate gaze toward Dior, the kids stand by, watching their shared moment. Jel hugs Dior, sharing a brief kiss. Lisa continues to blush with a smile, standing with lingering embarrassment. Then, Lisa notices Lyone, staring with genuine curiosity, pushing him out of his trance.)

Lyone: "Hey!"

Lisa: "Stop staring."

(Jel and Dior release their embrace. Next, Jel takes a step back, proudly observing the three-party members.)

Jel: "Ni'Ador everyone."

Lisa and Dior: "Ni'Ador!"

Lyone: "Oh, umm, Ni'Ador ha ha!"

(Once Jel bows to the three, they return the gesture, bowing with respect. Afterwards, the party proceeds toward the Yellow Shadow Forest.

Meanwhile, hidden in the surrounding trees, Olivia watches the departure of the trio through binoculars. She puts her equipment away, jumping onto the ground, dashing after them in a burst of speed.

Later that day, Lisa, Lyone, and Dior traverse through the Yellow Shadow Forest, heading south toward their destination.)

Lyone: "So if I remember correctly, once we travel through this forest, there's a desert, and then a valley we have to go through before we reach the mountain where you guys found me, right?"

Dior: "Yes. At our current pace, we could be there in two to three days."

Lyone: "But, why?"

Lisa: "Huh? What do you mean?"

Lyone: "I've seen Dior move so fast that I didn't realize we moved until we stopped. Why couldn't we just do that again?"

Lisa: "That's because it takes a lot out of your Energy Stream and your body to sustain that level of travel at long distances. Not to mention the fact that you'd be drawing the attention of every living thing in the area. By the time you stop, you'd be so tired from all of it."

Lyone: "And probably followed by something that wants to eat you for dinner."

Lisa: "Yup! Always be aware of your limits and your environment."

(As the conversation continues, Dior comes to a sudden halt. Failing to pay attention, Lisa walks into him, falling onto the ground.)

Lisa: "Hey! Dad, why did you do that!"

Lyone: <imitating Lisa> "'Always be aware of your limits and your environment.' Ha ha!"

Lisa: "Shut up, Lyone! You're such a hater!"

(Lyone continues to laugh, helping Lisa onto her feet.)

Dior: "You're partially right, Lisa."

Lisa and Lyone: "Huh?"

(Dior turns around with a smile on his face.)

Dior: "There does exist techniques that can mask your Energy Stream during large expenditures of energy."

Lyone: "Ex-pen-da . . .?"

Lisa: "Dad means using a lot of energy a once."

Lyone: "Ahh, ok."

Dior: "Yes. Also, there are techniques that aid in cutting Energy Stream expenditure. All are advanced and take time to master. But, traveling at a much faster pace shouldn't be too hard once you've learned them."

Lisa: "Well then, now I have to ask, what's the point in traveling on foot if you can do that, Dad?"

(Lisa and Lyone remain curious, watching Dior turns his attention to the forest floor.)

Dior: "Lyone, look."

(Dior directs Lyone and Lisa's attention, examining the toadstools peppered throughout the forest.)

Dior: "Tell me, are those edible?"

Lyone: "Edible?"

Dior: "Meaning, can you eat them?"

Lisa: "Oh, that's an easy—"

Dior: "Lisa, I want to hear Lyone's answer."

(Lisa catches Dior's intent, covering her own mouth, gleefully awaiting Lyone's answer.)

Lyone: "No."

Dior: "Why not?"

Lyone: "Because they're poisonous."

Dior: "Oh? How can you tell?"

Lyone: "You can tell by the coloring around the rim. The lighter the coloring, the quicker you die. It's the norm with most toadstools that grow in dark places, except for a few. You have to make sure it has no signs of light coloring around the rim."

Lisa: "Wow, nice job, Li'l L! How'd you know that?"

Lyone: "My family taught me. Whenever my dad, Auntie Rose, and I would camp, they would teach me about the nature of Ni, the many different environments, how to gather food, how to build shelter from raw materials, hunting, and other stuff about the wild."

Dior: "Wilderness survival. Sounds like your family trained you well."

(Lyone nods, agreeing, uttering a statement in Huadi.)

Lyon: "Lef na dea stra Ni. Stra pe gro thro ki."

Lisa: "Um, what?"

Lyone: "It's a saying my aunt taught me. It means 'Ni finds life from death. But, the strong finds blessings through their offspring.'"

Dior: "Interesting. And what does that mean to you?"

Lyone: "To me, it means we were born to die. But, we were also born to grow stronger than our parents. If my parents are Ni's greatest champions, then I'll be the strongest ever!"

(Dior smiles, inspecting the determined flare in Lyone's eyes. Suddenly, Lisa flicks her fingers, hitting Lyone on the back of his neck.)

Lyone: "Ouch! What was that for?"

Lisa: "Ha ha! Strongest ever, eh? How're you gonna be that if you didn't see that coming, Li'l L?"

Lyone: "That's because you sneak-attacked me!"

Lisa: "No excuses!"

(Dior laughs, turning around, continuing to lead the way along their path. Nearby, Olivia skillfully jumps from tree to tree, following them from a distance, harboring a burdensome pant.)

Olivia: *"I knew Dior was strong, but this is just annoying."*

Dior: "Tell me Lyone, have you noticed anything strange about traveling through this forest?"

Lyone: "Hmm."

(As he follows Dior, Lyone looks around, listening closely to his surroundings.)

Lyone: "Yeah, a few things."

Dior: "Like what?"

Lyone: "Well, for starters, it's too quiet. In a forest like this, you'd expect all kinds of different monsters. But we haven't heard or seen even one."

Dior: "This is true. Many types of monster call this forest home, and they aren't around for some reason."

Lyone: "But it gets weirder."

Dior: "How so?"

Lyone: "It's pretty dark in this forest all the time."

Dior: "That's a natural occurrence because of the trees."

Lyone: "Yeah, but, every now and then, daylight breaks through the gaps between the trees. In a place like this, any smart person would stay out of the light. It'll make you a target for predators. But, we've walked through the light numerous times, and nothing."

Dior: "Interesting. What do you believe could be the cause of this?"

Lisa: "I know what—"

Dior: "Lisa, let Lyone figure it out, please."

Lisa: *"I knew it. Dad's testing Lyone again. This whole hiking trip is just one big test."*

Lyone: "Hmm, well, if I had to guess what's going on, something must be really delicious on the other side of the forest and it's drawing attention. Or something is scaring them off. Hmm, should we be worried?"

(Dior claps his hands, confusing Lyone with his response.)

Dior: "Good job, Lyone. You used your deductive reasoning to build a theory of what is happening around you; using only the information from environmental factors. That's quite impressive for a young mind."

Lyone: "Umm, I-I don't understand."

Lisa: "What Dad is trying to say, is that he is the one that's pushing away all of the monsters from the area using his imperial force."

Dior: "That's right. You can be at ease, Lyone. This is all my doing. Well, that and there probably is something tasty on the other side of the forest ha ha!"

Lyone: "So, you're doing this? With 'Imperial Force'? What is that?"

Dior: "Do you remember what an 'Energy Stream' is?"

Lyone: "Um . . . a little bit."

Dior: "Either you know, or you don't. Which is it Lyone?"

Lyone: "Ok, I don't know. What is it again?"

Dior: "An Energy Stream is the part of your body that constantly interacts with energy in any given environment. Energy Streams are faint auras that inhales and exhales energy to and from the environment. Much like how your lungs interact with oxygen. With enough training, you can proactively manipulate your Energy Stream and combine its influence with many different types of techniques and transformations to accomplish some pretty amazing things."

Lisa: "Like moving super-fast, or become super strong, or using energy as a weapon-."

Lyone: "Or warding off threats. I see. I remember now."

Dior: "Good. Now, Imperial Force is a very elementary technique. When you have the ability to control your Energy Stream-"

(Dior's body suddenly becomes engulfed in his signature black aura, bringing amazement to Lyone's eyes.)

Dior: "You can horde energy from the environment, into your Energy Stream. This causes it to illuminate around your body. Two things happen: One, you deprive the Energy Streams of other, weaker, living organisms from the energy available in the surrounding environment, creating a great amount of strain on them; causing the organisms that can't take the pressure to run away. Two, your Energy Stream emits an identifying signature throughout the affected area, causing you to become detectable by other organisms that can control their own Energy Stream."

Lyone: "Wow, that's so cool!"

Dior: "Ha ha, it works the other way around as well. I can also draw living organisms to this location by exhaling energy into the environment. But, that takes a lot more control and capacity."

Lyone: "Wait a minute, if your Imperial Force can ward off monsters like this, then how come Lisa and I don't feel it? And why wasn't your Energy Stream showing until you made it show? Am I missing something?"

(Dior cleverly grins at Lyone's questioning, converting his Energy Stream back into an undetectable form.)

Dior: "Good questions. Let's just say, when you've mastered the full control of your own Energy Stream, like me, you've accomplished what is known as 'Ebb and Flow'. Combine that with other techniques, I am able to hide my Energy Stream from physical detection while using Imperial Force at the same time. I can also selectively impose or exclude organisms from the influence of my Imperial Force. Ok, let's leave it there for now. We'll have a chance to get more in depth with these topics later."

Lyone: "Oh, I-I see. Thanks for telling me all of this. It's all new to me."

Lisa: "Hmm, didn't you say you were trained by your family? They didn't teach you that?"

Lyone: "No, we didn't get far with Energy Streams and Imperial Force. I just learned a lot about surviving in the wilderness, and a little bit about martial arts. Is that a bad thing?"

Dior: "Of course not. It's as your quote from earlier says: 'Ni finds life from death.' It's only natural to learn about one of your greatest adversaries and turn it into one of your greatest allies. So, don't worry. I can help you learn the rest of what you need to know."

(Lisa looks ahead along their path and notices a great amount of light at the end.)

Lisa: "Hey, look! That's the end of the forest!"

Dior: "You're right, Lisa. And perfect timing as well. Looks like Yunyi is setting along the horizon. It's best we set up camp at the edge of the forest and not in the open desert if we can help it."

Lyone: "The desert? We're there already?"

Lisa: "Yup. It gets really cold at night out there."

Lyone: "Yeah, that makes sense. The trees should provide a bit more shelter from the wind, right?"

Dior: "Exactly. We'll sleep here tonight and continue tomorrow."

(As Dior and Lisa begin to take off their equipment, Lyone cautiously surveys the forest with his eyes.)

Lyone: "What about the monsters?"

Lisa: "What about them? Don't tell us you're afraid of the dark, Li'l L. Ha ha!"

Lyone: "I'm serious, Lisa. We don't wanna become food, right? You guys do have a plan, right?"

Dior: "In fact, we do. We'll use a technique called Scarecrow."

Lyone: "Scarecrow? What's that?"

Dior: "It's a technique that uses energy to create an intimidating apparition. The apparition is harmless, but it's very useful when warding off monsters and possibly even certain species of beasts."

(After his explanation, Dior smiles, noticing Lyone's clueless stare.)

Dior: "Ha ha, maybe it's best if I show you."

(Dior briefly steps away from Lyone and Lisa, drawing their attention. Next, he closes his eyes, summoning his black energy stream. The black aura splinters off from his body, forming a large figure in front of him. The figure shapeshifts into a giant, three-headed boar-like creature with hair trailing down its spine, and flames expelling from its nostrils when it snorts. The kids are frightened by the fierce-looking apparition, hugging each other in fear.)

Lyone: <in Huadi> "W-What the heck is that?"

Dior: "You see what I mean now, Lyone?"

Lyone: "I-Is that thing a Scarecrow?"

Dior: "Yup. Scary, isn't it? Lisa don't tell me you're scared as well. You've seen this one before."

Lisa: "Yeah, well, that doesn't make it any less scary when I see it!"

(Dior laughs at them, cheerfully turning back to the apparition.)

Dior: "Come now, you two, it's harmless. I even gave it a name. I call it Tri-Bacon!"

(Lyone and Lisa become embarrassed by the apparition's name, expelling their fear.)

Lisa: "You can't be serious, Dad."

Dior: "What's there not to love about a giant, fire-breathing, three-headed ghost pig named Tri-Bacon? Besides, I was gonna call it 'Pop the Mother Pork King Beast,' but that's a bit too flashy of a name, don't you think?"

(He looks back toward Lyone and Lisa, noting their embarrassed body language.)

Dior: "Yup, I was right. Tri-Bacon it is. So, this is the Scarecrow technique. Its purpose is to ward off monsters or beasts that come too close to camp. And, as vicious as it looks, it's actually quite harmless."

(After listening to Dior's claim, the kids share the same expression of doubt, causing him to laugh nervously.)

Dior: "Ha ha, ok, ok! My Scarecrows may know a thing or two about playing advanced cat and mouse because of experience. But, most Scarecrows are wards and are not used for combat. Generally speaking, of course."

(Tri-Bacon snorts, shooting flames from its nostrils, gaining everyone's attention.)

Lyone: "Alright, I get the whole scaring-off-a-predator part. But, how are we supposed to sleep with this giant, three-headed ham sandwich snorting all over the place like that?"

Dior: "Don't worry, I'll show you."

(Dior focuses his mind, causing Tri-Bacon to convert into a transparent ball of floating energy. Next, it reverts to its previous form, crashing to the ground, causing a small tremor, catching Lyone by surprise.)

Lyone: "Wow! You made it do that?"

Dior: "That's right! You see, Scarecrows are made of energy. And most of the time, they're transparent and controlled using your mind. To do advanced things with your Scarecrow, such as materializing, it takes a great deal of skill and training. Just like any other energy-based technique."

Lyone: "Wait, now let me make sure I understand what exactly happens. So, the ham sandwich is going to be quietly floating around in its transparent form, watching over the camp. And when it comes across a monster or something--"

(Interrupting Lyone, Lisa dramatically grabs his shoulders, attempting to scare him.)

Lisa: "BOO!"

(Lyone calmly looks back at Lisa in disappointment.)

Lyone: "Really?"

(Lisa sticks out her tongue at Lyone, playfully mocking him and his attitude with sass of her own.)

Dior: "Ha ha! You'd be correct in your assessment, Lyone."

Lyone: "So, question, what if the Scarecrow comes across something that it can't get rid of?"

Dior: "Very good question. Scarecrows are tethered to the Energy Stream of the user. Meaning if something happens to it, you'll feel it."

Lyone: "Even when you're asleep?"

Dior: "Yup. Unless you're drugged or something."

Lyone: "Ok, then, another question."

(Lisa punches Lyone on the arm, interrupting him with a smirk on her face.)

Lyone: "Ouch! What was that for?"

Lisa: "Too many questions! If you have to talk, the least you can do is help set up camp before Yunyi sets."

Lyone: "Alright! Alright! Geez!"

Dior: "Ha ha, don't worry, Lyone. We'll have plenty of time to answer your questions. But Lisa's right, we should get moving."

Lyone: "Well, if it gets the job done, that's all that matters, right?"

Dior: "Agreed! Now, watch this. Tri-Bacon roll over!"

(Tri-Bacon rolls on its right side, mowing down a tree in the process. As Dior nervously laughs, Lisa shakes her head, shrugging at his awkward clumsiness.)

Lisa: "Ok, Dad. We get it. The giant pig is as clumsy as you are."

(Later that night, the party sits around their campfire while bundled in separate blankets, eating food and drinking hot tea. As the cold wind brushes through the surrounding trees, Lyone periodically shifts his sight to the forest, ensuring their safety. Lisa notices his uneasiness, poking him with her elbow.)

Lyone: "Huh? Something wrong?"

Lisa: "I was gonna ask you that question, Li'l L."

Lyone: "Oh, don't mind me. Just looking around, you know."

Lisa: "Really now?"

Lyone: "Yeah. Remember what I said early in the day about the light coming through the trees and how monsters in this forest use it to hunt? Well, I have a feeling that being here at night is even worse."

(Lisa sighs at Lyone's caution, picking up a stick from the ground, poking at the campfire.)

Lisa: "There is a monster from the insectoid species called Nydala. It was recently discovered by a group of Federal Union scouts as they were exploring the area around the new settlement, Wisden. Only one of them came back to give details about the nydala. What it does is roam the Yellow Shadow Forest at night, giving off this bright white light from its butt. And, what really stood out, was the sound of its wings as it hovered over the forest floor. They crackled and buzzed with electric element, sparking through the night. Enough to make your skin crawl with every movement of its hypersonic wings. You wanna know what happened to that crew of scouts?"

(Captivated by Lisa's story, Lyone swallows and nods with curiosity. Lisa fascinates him with a grin, lowering her voice, drawing Lyone closer with every word.)

Lisa: "Well, the crew saw the white light as it floated through the darkness and heard the menacing sounds of the monster. Even though they didn't want to encounter it, they needed evidence of exploring the area for the rights to name the place. And once they reached the light, they were greeted with the sight of the horrible Nydala. They tried to fight the monster, so they can kill it and return it to the military camp. But then, the battle took a turn for the worst. The light on its butt began to glow yellow, paralyzing those who gazed upon it. All but one of the crew members fell victim to paralysis as he took cover behind a tree. The yellow light went away, but the last standing member was so petrified with fear, he couldn't move a muscle. After working up the courage, he peeked at the monster from behind cover, as it hovered over each of the paralyzed crewmen and sucked all of the fluids out of their bodies by penetrating the back of their necks with its needle-like nose."

Lyone: <in Huadi> "What the heck?"

Lisa: "Once they were sucked dry of fluids, the nydala injected its larvae inside of the corpse, making it fill up like a balloon. The surviving crew member could do nothing to save them. So, he fled with the sound of those creepy, crackling wings fading behind him."

(Lyone quietly sits, fearfully swallowing his saliva after the end of Lisa's story.)

Lyone: "Y-Yeah, so, question. We're kids, right?"

Lisa: "Yeah, so?"

Lyone: "Why the heck are we here? Can we get out of this forest?"

(Lisa and Dior chuckles at Lyone's discomfort, leaving Lyone confused. He remains puzzled, watching Dior pour another round of hot tea.)

Lyone: "Wait, so was what you said true or not, Lisa?"

Lisa: "Oh, everything I said was totally true."

(At a loss for words, Lyon stares as Lisa and Dior peacefully drink their tea.)

Lyone: "Wait, so are you joking or?"

Lisa: "Ha ha, Li'l L, listen. I'm completely serious. There is actually a monster in this forest exactly like I said."

Lyone: "Then why are you not scared? That thing could easily kill both of us!"

Lisa: "Because of dad."

(Lyone pauses, noticing Lisa's comfortable smile.)

Lisa: "Come on, Li'l L, where did you think I learned that story? Why do you think I'm confident that we'll be fine? Dad told us that we'll be safe, and I trust him. I've seen him in action. Probably not at his best, but he's pretty strong. So, don't worry. And if Dad's not here to protect you, I've got your back!"

(As Lisa raises her fist with great confidence, Lyone glances over at Dior, noting his comfort while drinking tea. Noticing their nonchalant attitudes, Lyone takes a sip of his own tea, staring off into the distance, dumbfounded.)

Faint Voice: <in Huadi> *"Still scary, though."*

Lyone: <in Huadi> "Really, though."

Lisa: "There's that language again."

Lyone: "Huh? Did one of you say something just now?"

Lisa: "Of course not, Lyone! What? You're hearing things now? Are you that scared?"

Lyone: <in Huadi> "Shut up!"

(While Lisa chuckles, Lyone takes another sip of his tea, thinking to himself.)

Lyone: *"It must have been those voices again. Where are they coming from?"*

Lisa: "Ok, Li'l L, so I know I asked you this before, but I seriously wanna know. What language is that?"

(After hearing Lisa's question, Dior quietly watches, closely listening to Lyon's response.)

Lyone: "It's really not that important, you know. I can speak Aio like this."

Lisa: "Yeah, but you speak the other language every now and then, too. How come you won't tell me what it is?"

Lyone: "Because it's not really that important. Let's drop it, ok?"

(Lisa notices Lyone's sudden avoidance, making her slightly agitated in response. Dior looks away from the two, sipping the last bit of his tea. Afterwards, he stands to his feet, capturing Lisa and Lyone's attention.)

Dior: "Alright you two, let's call it a night. We have a long way to travel through the desert tomorrow."

(Lisa stands onto her feet, tiredly stretching while Lyone looks through his bag, preparing for bed.)

Lyone: "So, anything we should look out for tomorrow?"

Dior: "It's a desert. So be mindful of your water supply. Luckily for us, Lisa and I scouted out this desert long before this trip. We should be fine."

Lyone: "Got it."

(Lisa grabs her bag, casually walking over to her tent.)

Lisa: "Goodnight."

Lyon: "Goodnight Lisa."

Dior: "Goodnight."

(Lyone and Dior watches, waiting for Lisa to enter her tent alone.)

Lyone: <whispering> "Hey, Mr. Kendric, you think we should tell her about me?"

Dior: <whispering> "Don't worry. She'll be fine. She won't press the matter unless it's serious."

Lyone: <whispering> "Ok."

(As Lyone and Dior bow, bidding each other goodnight, Olivia watches from a distance with her binoculars, discreetly kneeling on a tree branch high above the forest floor.)

Olivia: *"Good, I can get some sleep now."*

(Suddenly, Olivia notices Dior's Scarecrow, floating about the area as a small ball of gaseous light. As Olivia remains calm, the Scarecrow briefly stops near her, eventually moving on through the forest.)

Olivia: *"Scarecrows can't find you if you're Energy Stream is hidden. Still, more obstacles. Following these guys is such a pain. I'll just use remote-control surveillance."*

(Olivia searches through her bag of equipment, retrieving a small four-legged drone fitted with a camera. After placing it onto the tree branch, she uses a wrist controller to operate the drone. The video feed appears as a hologram, beaming from her high-tech bracelet.)

Olivia: *"This should work."*

(After some adjustments to the drone, Olivia watches with her binoculars, noticing Lyone and Dior retire for the night in their separate tents.

Later in the night, Olivia sleeps in her tent at her own camp. She awakens to check the video feed of the drone, cynically noticing the video is unavailable.)

Olivia: "Great. Can't wait to find out what happened to it."

(Olivia quickly dresses herself with her military-grade protective vest, camouflage pants, and boots. Next, she carefully arms herself, retrieving a handgun and a long-range rifle. After checking the equipment, she grabs her backpack, drawing her sidearm, silently leaving her tent. Once clearing the area, she safely places the handgun into its holster on her belt. With her rifle strapped around her torso, she runs through the forest, vanishing in a burst of speed.

A minute later, Olivia appears near the camp, carefully moving about with her sidearm drawn, walking to the tree where the surveillance drone lies. At the sight of Dior's scarecrow, she comes to a stop, lowering her weapon and calming herself. Once the Scarecrow passes, Olivia momentarily clears the area. Next, she effortlessly jumps from the ground, nimbly landing onto the tree branch beside the drone.

As she assesses the status of the drone, she glances towards the camp, noticing three figures creep through the night heading toward the edge of the forest. She quickly places her surveillance drone in her backpack, following them with caution.

Meanwhile, Lisa carefully sticks her head out of her tent, hearing suspicious noises.)

Lisa: *"Huh? I know I heard something."*

(Lisa slowly walks out of her tent, tiptoeing toward Lyone's tent. She peeks inside, finding him fast asleep, snoring and scratching himself. Lisa rolls her eyes, leaving him to rest.)

Lisa: *"Figures."*

(Next, she tiptoes over to Dior's tent, peeking her head inside, becoming concern once she finds its empty.)

Lisa: "Dad?"

(Lisa steps away from Dior's tent, carefully looking around the area. Noticing Dior's scarecrow, she continues the search, finding no trace of his whereabouts.)

Lisa: *"Where did he go?"*

(Suddenly, Lisa feels an Energy Stream, rapidly fading nearby, silently deciding to move toward it with caution.

A few minutes later, near the edge of the Yellow Shadow Forest, Lisa finds the source of the departed Energy Stream; the corpse of a native six-legged wildcat.)

Lisa: *"Did dad do this? But why is he so far away from the camp?"*

(Lisa's thoughts are suddenly broken by the sound of speech nearby. She carefully moves closer to the voices, keeping cover behind the surrounding trees and bushes, getting close enough to hear the conversation clearly. To her surprise, Dior speaks in another language; one unknown to her. Peeking her head from behind the tree, she spots Dior, standing along with six other people wearing dark-colored clothing. The clothes are marked with three circles in a triangular formation with a fourth, larger circle encompassing the smaller three. Four of the six people wear silver masks that seem to float through the darkness of the night, reflecting light from the three moons above. The remaining two group members, an elderly man and woman, standing before Dior. The duo's faces remain visible, with their distinctive daemon lord masks positioned behind their heads. As Lisa eavesdrops behind cover, Dior engages in conversation with the two leaders.)

Dior: <translated> "The least you could have done was tell me the child is a Renzido. Well? Is there an explanation Znanos? Bhaja?"

(The two stands silently, giving Dior judgmental stares, stalling the answer to his questions. The elderly man steps forward.)

Dior: <translated> "Speak, Znanos. I demand answers!"

Znanos: <translated> "Calm yourself. We knew nothing of this."

(Dior analyzes their body language, observing with a lingering suspicion.)

Dior: <translated> "So none of you knew."

(Dior briefly turns away, rubbing the back of his neck with concern, deliberating details about the situation.)

Dior: <translation> "Lyone went through a Renzido Age Transitioning during his stay. He also nearly transformed into his Blood Flow. He could've killed my family multiple times over if not for my swift actions!"

Bhaja: <translated> "Lucky for them, they're in the care of the Third."

Dior: <translated> "Bhaja, it was you and that strange lady with wings who brought Lyone to my doorstep. I suspect you know more than you're telling us."

(Hearing Dior voice his suspicion, Znanos turns to Bhaja, closely listening to her response.)

Bhaja: <translated> "I was instructed to not disclose anything."

Dior: <translated> "By who? That woman? And who was she to give such an order to the Second?"

Bhaja: <translated> "It was our Holy Mother, Ni, that gave the order not to disclose specific details during the Cradle's recovery."

(Dior's skepticism quickly fades at Bhaja's answer, thinking carefully about the situation.)

Bhaja: <translated> "As much as I dislike this situation, it's quite obvious what Ni's priorities are regarding your family."

Dior: <translated> "And what would those be?"

Bhaja: <translated> "The survival of the Cradle is of greater importance, to put it simply. Even if the Cradle is a—Renzido."

(Dior turns, slowly walking closer to Bhaja, glaring with fury. She stares back, standing unwavered by Dior's intimidation.)

Bhaja: <translated> "Is there a problem?"

Dior: "I do not appreciate your manner of speech regarding my family."

(Lisa becomes more attentive, hearing Dior speak in Aio. Hidden in the surrounding trees, Olivia watches closely as well, listening through her high-tech binoculars.)

Bhaja: "Your family is a fabrication. You know this as well as any of us. The task of overseeing and protecting the Cradle is of the highest priority, regardless of your original assignment, as ordained by our Holy Mother. Do you understand?"

(Znanos and Bhaja watches Dior closely, standing with stern glares. Dior firmly folds his arms behind his back, calming himself.)

Dior: "Understood."

Bhaja: "Good."

Znanos: "I understand your frustration with being given limited information, especially considering a Humanus Renzido fiend is our Holy Mother's chosen vessel. This is throwing me off, as well."

(Znanos holds his composure, attempting to hide his irritation.)

Dior: "Before the Age of Sanctuary, and the following Age of Exploration, Ni's blessings were given to the strongest of organisms in preparation for the Raadaiema. In this age, she has decided to reduce blessings due to the change in environment; manually picking those worthy. I know that Lyone is apparently the son of modern-day Champions of Ni; all of which are

Renzido, and blessed by our Holy Mother. Now, the question is, just how much of Ni's blessing did his family receive?"

Olivia: *"That boy is a Renzido?"*

Lisa: *"Renzido? Whats that?"*

(Dior and Znanos focuses on Bhaja once again, waiting for her response.)

Bhaja: "The blood relatives of the Cradle received ten percent each. the Cradle has twenty percent."

(Dior, Znanos, and the surrounding members of the congregation are stunned. Also stunned by the revelation, Olivia removes her binoculars, consumed by her thoughts.)

Olivia: *"Ten and twenty percent of Ni's blessing? And these guys are serious. Who are they?"*

Dior: "Why would our Holy Mother give them such an unprecedented amount of Her blessing?"

Znanos: "And to members of our enemy ranks no less?"

Bhaja: "Is it not obvious? It is to birth something even more unprecedented."

(The congregation falls silent, anxiously awaiting an answer to an obvious question.)

Dior: "What is being nursed within the Cradle?"

Bhaja: <translated> "The first ever Humanus-born Reaper."

(The congregation is rendered speechless, peaking Olivia and Lisa's curiosity.)

Olivia: *"Weird. I thought I heard the word 'Reaper.'"*

Dior: <translated> "We all knew this day would come. But, this honor is given to a Renzido? Aren't the Humanus our enemies?"

(Znanos sternly folds his arms with his eyes closed, hanging his head with growing resentment.)

Bhaja: <translated> "Those questions are irrelevant now. We're here with your new orders: You are only permitted to teach the boy the basics of combat. You're not to interfere with tests administered by the Lunon Ecliptical. Once the boy's training is complete, you are to release him from your custody to one of our clansmen. You are not to accompany the boy after his training comes to an end. That is all."

Dior: <translated> "Are these orders directly from our Holy Mother?"

Bhaja: <translated> "These are collective orders from our Holy Mother, the Lunon Ecliptical, and the lady that visited Lyone at your home during his healing process."

Dior: <translated> "I see. That lady with the wings. Correct?"

Bhaja: <translated> "Yes."

Dior: <translated> "Whats her name?"

Bhaja: <translated> "Unimportant. Just be aware that she has as much authority over the Cradle as Ni has proclaimed. Although, she wanted to tell you that she apologizes for her long periods of silence. Healing the boy's mind was her top priority; which required focus."

(Dior folds his arms, retreating into his thoughts of Lyone's past recovery period, hearing him groaning in pain periodically, waiting for results of his recovery in the kitchen with Jel as she complains about the situation. The strange lady meditates at Lyone's bedside, sitting on the floor of the room with her legs folded. Her light brown skin is infused with hardened black scales, displayed on certain parts of her body. Her shiny hair is slicked to the back, easily reaching the floor as she sits. Her ribbon like cape rest upon her body from her shoulders. And her lizard-like tail curls around her slim waist, resting into her lap.

Lisa quietly opens the door, peeking into Lyone's room, gawking at the strange lady. Then, the strange lady abruptly opens her left eye, peering back towards Lisa, sticking out her long forked tongue. Lisa gasps, quickly closing the door and runs away. The strange lady chuckles to herself, resuming the meditation at Lyone's bedside. In the kitchen, Dior firmly stands with his arms folded, listening to Jel's concerns.)

Jel: "And I'm not mad at the child resting and being nursed here, but when I can't even attempt an assessment of the situation because of some strange woman in my house, I have a problem with that!"

Dior: "I understand, dear."

Jel: "And you know that both the Federal Union and my family will have my head if they find out we're hoarding unknown people in an experimental military home!"

Dior: "I understand, dear."

Jel: "Do you, Dior? We have a half-dead child alone in a bedroom with a lady with wings and a tail, who apparently thinks that meditating about the last time she washed her butt is more important than assessing the child's physical condition!"

(As Jel irately paces about, Dior nods his head with his eyes closed, responding.)

Dior: "I understand, dear."

Lisa: "Moooommm!"

(Lisa anxiously runs downstairs, stopping into the kitchen, teeming with words to say.)

Jel: "Not now, honey."

Lisa: "But mom, I was peeking into the guest room, and was watching that weird lady, and she peeked at me, and then stuck her tongue out, and it was long and narrow, and weird looking, and it was split at the front!"

(Jel glares at Dior; more annoyed than before.)

Jel: "The strange lady also has the tongue of a serpent, Dior."

Dior: "I understand, dear."

(As Dior clears his throat, Jel remains infuriated, unhappily shaking her head. Later that night, as the commotion finally dies down, Dior walks outside to the front porch of their home, taking a deep breath of fresh air, easing his tension.)

Dior: <translated> *"Bhaja, I appreciate you remaining hidden. Otherwise, I would probably be in a bed unconscious myself."*

(Suddenly, Bhaja casually appears next to Dior shrouded in black smoke, electrified with energy. They continue their conversation in an unknown language, speaking with each other through telepathy.)

Bhaja: <translated> *"Indeed. No need to place your original mission in further peril."*

Dior: <translated> *"From the looks of things, this situation won't be ending anytime in the next day or so."*

Bhaja: <translated> *"You're right. This seems as if it's going to take a substantial amount of time."*

Dior: <translated> *"Give me an estimate."*

Bhaja: <translated> *"Unclear. The child's injuries are affecting all levels of his being; physical, mental, and the Energy Stream. If I had to guess, it'll take weeks, months maybe."*

(Dior sighs in frustration, listening to Bhaja's assessment.)

Bhaja: <translated> *"You must forgive us, Dior. This situation is a work in progress. But, I assure you, I and your visitor will figure this out. We'll take care of this. We only ask that you shelter us in your division."*

Dior: <translation> *"Although we're pushing the limits, my clan members are already in place. However, what are you planning to do about my wife and my daughter? Surely you don't intend for them to remember these events? And if you and that weird lady are staying for more than a week, that's too big of a time lapse in their memory."*

Bhaja: <translated> *"Do not worry. Your assignment will not be compromised. We will deal with the process of removing their memories."*

Dior: <translated> *"I hope you know what you're doing."*

(Dior commandingly turns to Bhaja, watching her nod with eyes of confidence. Then, she slowly walks backward, fading into the shadows.

As Dior's memory comes to an end, he shifts attention back toward Znanos and Bhaja, continuing their conversation, hiding within the Yellow Shadow Forest. As they proceed, Lisa slyly remains hidden behind a tree, eavesdropping. Olivia eavesdrops as well, positioning herself in a distant tree with her high-tech binoculars.)

Dior: <translated> "I wonder why Ni has given this lady the authority she has over the Cradle."

Bhaja: <translated> "None of that is of our concern. You have your new orders. You are expected to abide by them."

(While Dior briefly falls silent, Znanos and Bhaja observes him, firmly waiting on his reply.)

Dior: <translated> "Understood."

Znanos: <translated> "Good. Now that it's settled, it seems we have guests to attend to."

Dior: <translated> "Yes. How unfortunate."

(Listening closely to their conversation, Lisa attempts to silence her breaths from the cold temperature, trying to hear a word she can recognize. Suddenly, she hears a finger snap, gaining her attention. However, she is unaware of the cloud of smoke forming behind her. One of the members of the congregation appears from the smoke, grabbing Lisa and taking her captive. As she struggles, the congregation member restrains her, covering her mouth, carrying her to the group. Meanwhile, Olivia watches with surprise, identifying Lisa being carried to the group's circle.)

Olivia: *"Wait, that's Dior's daughter. What are they doing?"*

(As Olivia watches, everyone in the congregation eerily turns their heads in her direction, gazing with mystique. Noticing their stares, she becomes overwhelmed by uneasiness, hastily putting her binoculars away and attempts to jump off the tree branch. But, before she can flee, a dark light envelopes the tree from an insignia drawn on the ground around it, voiding her of all senses, teleporting her to the middle of another insignia located in the center of the group. Once her senses return, Olivia wearily kneels on the ground, lifting her head, finding herself surrounded by the swords of the silver masked members of the congregation.)

Olivia: *"Great. Just my luck."*

(While Lisa continues to struggle, she notices Dior, leering at him with resentment, calming herself.)

Znanos: "I'll take care of this."

Dior: "Wait. You are guest in my division. This is my duty."

Znanos: "Very well."

(Dior steps forward, preparing to carry out his task. However, he is stopped by the sudden sound of Bhaja's voice.)

Bhaja: "One more thing. We are aware that you utilized the Uidon Yu; breaking our covenant to the Lunon Ecliptical."

Znanos: "I hope you weren't expecting us not to find out."

(After feeling a sudden rush of tension, Dior calms himself, closing his eyes, lowering his head, accepting his conviction.)

Znanos: "As the Third, you are already aware that this violation is unredeemable. We will be commandeering your division until a new Third has been proclaimed. We will also prepare your Tiishado."

Dior: "I see. Should I surrender now?"

Bhaja: "No. You're to continue as normal for the time being. However, once we have reached the point of success for this mission, we expect you to uphold the rest of your oath, Yoasis."

Dior: "Understood."

(Znanos and Bhaja departs, walking into the darkness of the night, leaving Dior to ruminate his condemnation. Dior stands with his head hung, desperately confining within the overwhelming feeling of dread, standing in front of Lisa. She resentfully glares, watching Dior walk closer with his face concealed by the night. Then, the moonlight reveals Dior's teary eyes, invoking a flood of sympathy within Lisa.)

Dior: "*This will not hurt, Lisa. But still, forgive me. Forgive me for now, and for what is bound to come.*"

Lisa: "*Dad?*"

(With Olivia watching closely, Dior's body becomes engulfed in an aura of darkness. Dior places his right hand on Lisa's head, instantly rendering her unconscious. As one of the masked congregation members carry Lisa, Dior turns his remorseless gaze to Olivia.)

Olivia: "You plan to do the same to me?"

Dior: "Indeed I do, major."

(Dior steps to her front, summoning his brimming aura once more.)

Olivia: "How long did you know I was—"

Dior: "Don't bother. When you wake up, you won't remember this night happened."

Olivia: "I see. A technique that erases memories. And to use something like that on your own daughter? Pretty sinister, Dior. Didn't think you had it in you."

Dior: "You have no idea, major."

(As Olivia fearlessly stares at Dior, he places his hand on her head, instantly rendering her unconscious. Next, he searches her belongings, discovering the binoculars and the surveillance drone. He takes the binoculars out of her bag, tosses them into the air, and destroys them with a burst of energy from his hand.

Dior leaves the surveillance drone in the bag, turning his attention to the remaining three congregation members.)

Dior: "You two, return the major to her camp. Also, place everything she possesses exactly as they were during your infiltration assignments before this meeting."

(The two congregation members carries Olivia away, leaving the last member and Dior with Lisa. Dior steps forward, taking Lisa into his arms, dismissing the final member with a nod. Carrying Lisa with him, Dior makes his way back to their camp.

Once Dior reaches camp, he walks into Lisa's tent, placing her inside of her sleeping bag. Before leaving, he places his hand on Lisa's shoulder as she rests, soundlessly praying. Afterwards, he makes his way to his own tent, pausing to apprehensively glance toward Lyone's tent. Finally, he walks away, retiring for the night.

In the morning, Olivia awakens in her tent, yawning and stretching. However, she instantly feels an odd sense of urgency, quickly moving out of her sleeping bag. She puts on her clothing, protective gear, loads her sidearm with a clip of bullets, and cautiously proceeds out of her tent. Once outside, she looks around, checking her surroundings, confirming no signs of threats, adding to her discomfort. A few minutes later, Olivia wears a communication device around her ear, discussing her situation with Idol.)

Olivia: "Sir, it's as I've said, although no signs of threats or intrusion have been found in the area, my binoculars are missing. They held audio and visual recordings."

Idol: "And you don't remember waking up even for a second last night?"

Olivia: "Sir, that's correct. And what's even weirder is that I woke up feeling calm and relaxed. I've never slept like that on the field. I'm beginning to think I was drugged. Perhaps in my sleep?"

Idol: "Hmm, do you have any marks on your body? Or side effects, like a headache or nausea?"

Olivia: "Sir, that's a negative. No signs of any form of physical trauma."

Idol: "I see. Doesn't seem like you were drugged then. Is there any other evidence suggesting your camp was infiltrated?"

(Olivia momentarily gathers her thoughts, remembering her surveillance drone recording the camp of Lyone's party.)

Olivia: "Sir, I set up a surveillance drone near the target's camp. It should have recorded everything moving to and from the camp during the night."

Idol: "Then that should give us all the information we need. Why didn't you mention this sooner?"

Olivia: "Sir, I-I don't know."

Idol: "Hmm, yes. Now I'm also starting to feel uneasy. Get back to me once you've gathered more information. Something strange is going on."

Olivia: "Yes sir!"

Idol: "And one more thing, major. I've managed to free up three of our squad members to help in this operation: Private Aksana Blancher, a tech operator, Private Joshua Tailor, a survival tactician, and Private William Dawson, a fitness and wellness advisor. They will be your supports for the remainder of this mission."

Olivia: "Can they hear me now?"

William, Aksana, Joshua: "Yes ma'am!"

Olivia: "It's been a while since I've had drills with you three. Thanks for the help."

William: "Anytime, major! Just let us know if you need anything and we'll help as best as we can."

Aksana: "Major, just to let you know, I've already secured extra equipment to replace your missing equipment, along with new experimental gear that'll help you in the field."

Olivia: "Thank you, Aksana. I appreciate it. You mentioned experimental equipment? Like what?"

Aksana: "Remember those experimental-grade monitoring pills?"

Olivia: "Those are ready for field testing now?"

William: "Yup! With those, I'm gonna be able to get instant information concerning your physical and Energy Stream condition. That way, I'll give the team the best information possible. Don't worry, I'll watch ya' back!"

Joshua: "Hehe, while Will is watching your back, and everything else that's behind you . . ."

William: "Hey!"

Joshua: ". . . be sure to let me know details about your environment; even take a pic with your smartphone if possible. I'll strategize with you about ways of getting around safe and undetected."

Olivia: "Sounds like a plan, Joshua. Thank you. I'm fortunate to have you all on the mission. Let's make this happen."

William, Aksana, Joshua: "Yes ma'am!"

Idol: "Alright, Olivia, make sure to give us a call if you need help with anything."

Olivia: "Yes sir!"

(Olivia walks back into her tent, turning off her communicator. She retrieves the remote-control bracelet from her bag, bringing up the holographic video feed. Once the video feed shows as unavailable, she quickly packs up her camping equipment, eventually leaving camp to recover the surveillance drone.

Later in the morning, Olivia slowly advances toward the tree concealing the surveillance equipment. Once she reaches her destination, she jumps into the tree, examining the surveillance drone, finding no evidence of tampering.)

Olivia: *"Hmm, I may be able to look over the recorded footage to figure out when the video went down."*

(Looking toward Lyone's campsite, Olivia notices Lisa exercising and Dior cooking food for breakfast. She draws her high-powered rifle, using the scope to gain a closer look at the camp's activities.)

Olivia: *"As much as I dislike aiming at something I don't intend to kill, I have little choice at this point."*

(Lyone joyfully awakens to the smell of breakfast, climbing out of his sleeping bag, changing into his travel clothing. As Lisa prepares to eat, Dior uses a glove to lift a long flatstone from the embers of the campfire, carefully standing it next to a tree. He takes off the glove, wiping sweat from his face, focusing energy into his right hand. Suddenly, Lisa interrupts his process.)

Lisa: "Hey, Dad!"

Dior: "Hmm?"

(As Lisa calls out to him, Dior loses his concentration, dispersing the gathered energy. She directs his attention toward the forest and he discovers a large, lizard-like monster, standing on its hindlegs, brandishing razor sharp talons on its feet, a long tail, sharp teeth, and a distinctive black-and-yellow feathered coat covering its body.)

Lisa: "Never seen a monster like that before."

Dior: "I have."

(The black-and-yellow feathered monster glares at Lisa, mesmerizing her into its eyes. Dior abruptly steps in front of Lisa, breaking the spell. Lyone walks out of his tent fully dressed, loudly yawning, oblivious to the situation. The monster quickly notices Lyone, briefly shifting attention to Dior. Finally, it runs off in a burst of speed covered by the darkness of the Yellow Shadow Forest.)

Lyone: "Hey guys, what's for breakfast?"

Lisa: "What was that?"

Lyone: "Huh? What was what?"

Dior: "It was a Black-and-Yellow Feathered Seifer. Vicious scavengers and hunters. Usually they move in packs, but that one seems to be alone. Strange."

(As Dior turns to Lisa, Lyone guardedly search for monsters, scratching his head to no signs of threats.)

Lisa: "Its eyes were weird."

Dior: "It marked you."

Lisa: "What? Marked me?"

Dior: "Usually, the alpha of the pack marks the prey. Then, the pack stealthily surrounds them while the alpha continues to hypnotize the prey by staring into its eyes. The prey is usually so intimidated, it can't look away. And, before you know it, three of them jump on you, stabbing and ripping your flesh apart with those talons of theirs."

(Lyone stomach growls loudly, humorously gaining their attention.)

Lyone: "Yeah, that's stomach talk. It means, you guys keep talking while I go ahead and eat this food, man."

(As Lyon walks over to the campfire, Lisa and Dior turns to each other, comically shrugging their shoulders. They join Lyone, taking their seats near the fire, eating breakfast together.)

Dior: "Hope you two enjoy breakfast."

Lyone: "This soup is just what I needed!"

Dior: "Thank you, Lyone. The meat in it is a bit overcooked. But, it came out well in the end."

Lyone: "Thanks, Mr. Kendric. All we need now is a shower and we're good."

Lisa: "Seriously."

Dior: "Ha ha, don't worry. You two will get used to going days without bathing."

Lisa: "Yeah, no. As much as I like camping, I'll never get used to not bathing."

Lyone: "Why would you want to is the real question. Ha ha!"

Lisa: "I know right? Like, wash your butt for real though!"

(Dior watches with a smile, listening to the two joke with each other.)

Dior: *"Good. She doesn't remember a thing. And Lyone, a Renzido that is the Cradle of a Reaper. He has no idea what's in stored for him."*

(Dior stares into his cup of tea, wandering into his mind amidst the reflection of his face within the cup, drifting into a memory of the night before Lyone regained consciousness at the Kendric family home. He tempers his impatience, standing alone on his front porch, leaning over the rail. Bhaja unexpectedly walks out of his home, stopping beside him, briefly alarming Dior at the sight of her casualness.)

Dior: <translated> "Why are you walking out of my home in plain sight, Bhaja? You want to jeopardize my mission?"

Bhaja: <translated> "Don't worry. The area is cleared, and your family is asleep."

(Sensing no threats, Dior calms himself.)

Dior: <translated> "Fine. So, have you figured out how we're going to handle this without breaking the covenant to the Lunon Ecliptical?"

Bhaja: <translated> "It's done."

(He immediately turns toward her, riddled with skepticism.)

Dior: <translated> "What? But how? Surely you didn't break the covenant!"

Bhaja: <translated> "As I said, worry not."

(Suddenly, the strange lady appears in front of the home, gaining their attention. As she stretches various parts of her body, her ribbon like cape spreads apart, revealing them as massive wings. Bhaja turns back to Dior, firmly resuming their conversation.)

Bhaja: "Listen closely. Memories were both erased and replaced for both members of your family."

Dior: "What? You can implant memories? When did you learn a technique like that?"

Bhaja: "I didn't. The origin of the ability resides with our visitor. Now, I will inform you of what you should expect from your family members to maintain consistency. . ."

(As their conversation continues, the strange lady flies off into the night, peaking Dior's criticism.)

Dior: "That's enough Bhaja! I've been patient enough with you and that lady, invading my division and impeding my priorities. I demand answers!"

Bhaja: "As much as I would like to disclose details, I cannot."

Dior: "And why is that?"

Bhaja: "It is because I have limited access to this information as well. At the moment, I am aware that the boy is the Cradle."

(Dior becomes distraught upon the revelation, keenly focusing his attention.)

Dior: "I see. And, he was gravely injured. A direct assault upon one of the keys to our salvation. This means that our Holy Mother and the Lunon Ecliptical are directly involved."

Bhaja: "Indeed. You must focus on the information I have to give you. Keeping consistency among the events that currently resides in the minds of your family is vital for the success of our new mission."

Dior: "New mission?"

Bhaja: "Yes. Our Holy Mother has commanded an audience with all three of the Eyes of the Saedowhui."

(Sensing the urgency, Dior concurs with the request.)

Dior: "Yes. We shouldn't wait another moment."

(As Dior's memory comes to an end, he takes a sip of his tea, listening to Lyone and Lisa laughing and joking; they remain oblivious to their roles in a grand scheme. Afterwards, Dior calmly stands unto his feet, capturing their attention.)

Dior: "Alright, it's about time we start packing and travel."

Lisa: "Gotcha. Lyone, I'll gather all the camping equipment. Mind taking care of all the trash and waste?"

Lyone: "Got it!"

(As Olivia stalks from a distance, the party rise to their feet, casually cleaning the camp. While Lyone collects trash with a bag, a gust of wind blows some of the garbage about. Once the garbage lands onto the ground, he hears Lisa, chuckling at his misfortune.)

Lyone: "Hey, that's not funny!"

Lisa: "Ha ha, now you know why I gave you the trash."

Lyone: "Whatever, you're doing this next time."

(Lyone walks near the cooking flatstone, bending to collect trash. However, he leans his right hand against the flatstone, haphazardly burning himself. Hearing Lyone's painful grunting, Lisa and Dior urgently run to his aid.)

Dior: "Lyone, are you ok?"

Lyone: <in pain> "I burned myself on that rock."

(When they turn to the flatstone, Dior recognizes it, instantly feeling guilty. Lisa moves to aid Lyone, carefully standing next to him.)

Lisa: "Let me see it."

(Once Lisa inspects the burn, she smiles with relief, noticing the burn isn't too severe.)

Lisa: "Alright, it's not that bad, thank Ni. Stay here, I'll go get the med kit."

(Lisa runs over to her bags, attempting to retrieve her first aid kit. Suddenly, she feels a massive surge of energy, quickly turning around, noticing Lyone angerly balling his fists with a rising Energy Stream. Dior instinctively moves in, knocking Lyone unconscious with a strike to the neck. As Dior catches Lyone from crashing to the ground, Lisa runs back to them, furiously protesting Dior's actions.)

Lisa: "Dad, what the heck? Stop hitting him!"

(Lisa grabs Lyone from Dior, carefully lowering Lyone onto the ground, urgently assessing his condition.)

Lisa: "Was that really necessary, Dad? Why do you keep knocking him out?"

Dior: "Don't worry, Lisa-"

Lisa: "No! You keep hitting him and knocking him out every time his Energy Stream goes crazy! What's going on?"

(As Dior maintains his silence and stern demeanor, Lisa suspiciously glares at him, sensing something elusive afoot.)

Lisa: "You're hiding something, aren't you?"

Dior: "Lisa, there is no need for an interrogation. We should focus on healing Lyone's wounds."

Lisa: "Which one, the burn or the headache? Both caused by you, Dad."

(Enduring Lisa's suspicions, Dior sighs, walking up to Lyone. Then, he lifts Lyone from the ground, placing him over his shoulder. As Lisa scornfully observes, Dior carries Lyone into his tent. Meanwhile, Olivia turns away from the scope of her rifle, thinking over the situation.)

Olivia: *"Hearing their conversation was much better than reading lips."*

(A while later, Lyone lies on top of his sleeping bag with his hand wrapped in bandages. Dior sits in a chair outside Lyone's tent, calmly drinking hot tea. Lisa concentrates on her exercises, ignoring Dior with an air of resentment about her. Olivia spies on the party from a distance, eating military rations at the base of a surrounding tree.)

Dior: *"Lyone is such a sensitive kid. Even just a mild sense of anger sets him off. It's to be expected with Renzido. But, at this rate, I may have to subject him to another forbidden technique from the Uidon Yu; despite the consequences."*

(Drawing Dior's attention, Lisa takes a break, quietly drinking tea alone near the campfire.)

Dior: *"I'd better call Jel."*

(He stands to his feet, casually walking over to his tent, feeling Lisa's gaze of suspicion following him.)

Dior: "Lisa, watch over Lyone, please."

Lisa: "Sure."

(As Dior proceeds into his tent, Lisa walks over to the chair in front of Lyone's tent, irritably folding her arms, taking a seat. Olivia decides to move, positioning herself behind bushes near Dior's tent, eavesdropping on his conversation.

Back at the Kendric Family home, scientists and military officials gather for an event, loudly conversing throughout the residence with orchestral music playing. The phone in Jel's study rings, remaining unheard due to the commotion. After a few seconds, Dior hangs up, placing the phone away.)

Dior: *"She must be working."*

(Dior walks out of his tent, meeting Lisa in front of Lyone's tent. As he stands next to her, she tries to ignore him, both keeping their silence.)

Lisa: "Stop it, Dad."

Dior: "Stop what?"

Lisa: "The thing you're doing."

Dior: "What am I doing?"

Lisa: "I'm serious."

(Dior chuckles, walking away toward the campfire.)

Dior: <imitating Lisa> "Ok then, stay mad."

(Lisa fights off the sensation to laugh, hanging her head low with her lips curled.)

Lisa: "*Such a brat.*"

(Later that evening, Lisa sits in the chair outside of Lyone's tent, meditating in silence. Dior sits near the campfire, preparing to roast food for the camp. To their surprise, Lyone walks out of his tent, woozily holding his head.)

Lisa: "Lyone! Are you ok?"

Lyone: "Mr. Kendric, can you stop hitting me?"

Lisa: "I told him the same thing!"

(Dior stands to his feet, firmly walking over to Lyon.)

Dior: "How's your hand?"

Lyone: "I can feel a slight sting, but I'll be ok."

Lisa: "Dad, don't change the subject. You keep hitting him!"

(After Lisa voices her concern, Dior bows to Lyone, sincerely apologizing.)

Dior: "Sorry for everything, Lyone. I should have been more attentive with the cooking materials. I'll also try not to hit you again. No promises though."

Lisa: "No promises?"

Lyone: "Don't worry about it."

Lisa: "What?"

(As Lisa lingers in confusion, Lyone offers Dior his right hand, gesturing an acceptance of his apology.)

Lyone: "I understand."

Dior: "Good. Now, you may wanna shake with the other hand, Lyone."

Lyone: "Oh!"

(Lyone laughs, quickly offering his left, shaking hands with Dior. Afterwards, Lyone looks near the campfire, noticing meat being prepared.)

Lyone: "You're about to cook?"

Dior: "Yup! Caught some Forest Gum while you were out. Prepare to be amazed!"

Lyone: "Heck yeah! Lisa, did you hear that?"

(Lyone turns around towards Lisa, noticing her seated in the chair outside of his tent with her arms folded.)

Lyone: "Lisa? Something wrong?"

Lisa: "Not talking to you right now."

Lyone: "Oh. Ok then, I guess."

(As Lyone turns away puzzled, Dior concentrates on preparing dinner, using his energy to heat up the large flatstone. Later that night, the trio silently sits around the campfire, eating their food, keeping warm from a howling wind. Olivia watches the party, setting up her surveillance drone in one of the surrounding trees. She receives a sudden call on her earpiece, pressing onto it during her task.)

Olivia: "Sir!"

Idol: "Major, your report."

Olivia: "Sir, I'm currently watching the targets at their camp in the forest to the southeast."

Idol: "Forest to the southeast? Are they still in the forest with the yellow leaves?"

Olivia: "Yes, sir. Apparently, Lyone injured himself and they took a day to let him recover. I don't know too much about what they were saying at the time, but the target seemed to have something strange happen to him."

Idol: "Strange, you say?"

Olivia: "Yes, sir. Briefly, after the injury, the target's Energy Stream seemed to have rapidly increased before Dior knocked him out."

Idol: "That is weird. William, any thoughts?"

William: "Hmm, he injured himself, then his Energy Stream started to increase as a response? There exist techniques that give results like that. But, I wouldn't know if the target has learned that kind of technique. I'll need more information about the target before we can determine what happened."

Olivia: "I see. In that case, don't worry about it. Things returned to normal after that."

Idol: "Understood. Make sure to keep an eye on the target's condition should it change in the future."

Olivia: "Yes, sir."

Idol: "So did you figure out what happened to your equipment?"

Olivia: "Sir, the surveillance video proved to be inconclusive. The video feed failed to continue after midnight. Also, there were no signs of tampering."

Idol: "Now this is getting strange. You mean to tell me that there was no point in the night where you awakened to check the video feed?"

Olivia: "Sir, my thoughts exactly. Aksana, do you mind running an analysis on the feed?"

Aksana: "Of course, major. I'll make sure to get the analysis to you ASAP."

Olivia: "Thank you, Aksana. I know there is something here. We just can't pin it down. The missing surveillance video doesn't explains the missing binoculars. If anything, it gives us more of a reason to suspect that Dior is responsible for these occurrences."

Idol: "Yes, it could be Dior. Or it could be someone or something else."

(Olivia pauses briefly to consider Idol's suggestion. Afterwards, she cautiously surveys the area, scanning the surroundings with her eyes.)

Idol: "Have you seen or heard anything suspicious since we last talked?"

Olivia: "No, sir. And the fact that it's nighttime in a light-sapping forest doesn't help much."

Idol: "Well, if in fact you've been compromised, we can safely say they won't kill you—yet."

Olivia: "Sir, thanks for the assurance. Now, I'm sure I won't be sleeping tonight."

(Olivia remains hyperaware of the area, noticing Dior moving into his tent alone.)

Olivia: "Sir, Dior's on the move. I'm moving to intercept."

Idol: "Watch your back out there, Olivia."

Olivia: "Yes, sir."

(Olivia quickly places her rifle's strap around her chest, jumping into the air, disappearing in a burst of speed, reappearing on the ground. She stands a few feet away from the back of Dior's tent, eavesdropping on his conversation.)

Dior: "Hey, dear, how are things at home?"

Jel: "Things are fine, dear. Thank you for asking. So, I've been given word that new housing for our family is nearly complete inside of Wisden. I've been ordered to prepare to move sometime after the winter is over."

Dior: "Pretty unfortunate timing considering Lisa and I will be camping for the duration of the winter. We won't be able to join you and help prepare. She has to increase resistance to the elements if she plans on being a better adventurer than me, ha ha!"

(Dior notices a snuffle sound being made by Jel.)

Dior: "Getting sick, dear?"

Jel: "Sick? I don't think I am. My last checkup suggested my health is relatively fine. Can't say the same for the people around me, though."

(Jel snuffles again, rubbing her nose, cautiously looking around her study. On the outside of the home, hidden in the surrounding forest, mysterious people secretly record their conversation, listening with wireless earpieces, watching Jel from video feed broadcasted on their wrist controllers.)

Dior: "Hmm. Maybe you should get that checked, just to be safe, dear."

Jel: "Yeah, maybe you're right. I could have picked up a bug somewhere."

Dior: "Yup. It's important we stay healthy at our age. *A bug, huh? As I thought.*"

Jel: "But enough about me, how's Lisa holding up?"

Dior: "She's still as tough as nails, of course. Although, not too long ago, she was injured a bit."

Jel: "Oh! What happened?"

Dior: "She burned herself while we were cooking. But, don't worry. She has healed up since then. Everything should be fine now."

Jel: "A-Alright. You two should be more careful."

Dior: "Agreed."

(Recognizing the code words, Olivia stares sharply at Dior's tent, listening carefully to his speech.)

Dior: "So have there been any new developments with the war in the west?"

Jel: "No, not yet. Umm, just the same thing off and on TV. *I can't tell him about the reports while they're listening.*"

Dior: "Alright then, hopefully, things aren't getting out of control."

Jel: "I don't know. Something tells me, it's going to get worse before it gets better."

Dior: "Yeah. I'll make sure Lisa is prepared for anything."

Jel: "Thank you. Well, I have to leave. I'll talk to you later, dear."

Dior: "Ok. Love you."

Jel: "Love you, too."

Dior: "Always?"

Jel: "Ha ha! Always."

(Dior hangs up his smartphone, putting it away into his bag. Next, he walks outside, noticing Lyone and Lisa quietly eating their food, rejoining them at the campfire.)

Lisa: "Thanks for the food, Dad."

Dior: "You're welcome."

Lisa: "I'll help clean up before bed."

Lyone: "I'll help to."

Dior: "Lyon, wait. You should get some more rest. We'll need you as best as we can get you for traveling the desert tomorrow."

Lyone: "Oh, um, ok. I guess I'll get ready for bed, then. Good night guys."

Dior: "Good night."

(As Lyone retires for the night, Dior closes his eyes and folds his arms, holding back his irritation as Lisa nonchalantly cleans the camp.

Later in the night, Olivia meditates a few yards away from Lyone's campsite, controlling her breaths, hiding her Energy Stream. During her meditation, a large serpent monster emerges from the surrounding forest with spotted scales that subtly glow through the night's shadows.

The serpent monster slowly slithers toward Olivia, targeting her as its prey. But, before it strikes, Dior's scarecrow Tri-Bacon falls from the sky, snorting flames from its nostrils, creating a fiery tremor upon landing. The serpent monster becomes immediately intimidated, fleeing back into the forest. Then, Tri-Bacon reverts into its floating energy state once the threat is gone moving elsewhere.

Late into the night at the campsite, Lisa lies in her sleeping bag, staring at the top of her tent, assessing her recent interactions with Lyone and Dior.)

Lisa: "*What are they hiding?*"

Voice: "Lisa."

(Lisa looks towards the entrance to her tent to find Dior, holding her tent open.)

Dior: "Come."

(Dior walks away, closing Lisa's tent. She sighs with frustration, crawling out of her sleeping bag. She puts on shoes and a jacket, following Dior's lead outside of the camp. Once they move to a secluded space within the forest, Lisa stands with her arms folded, shielding herself from the cold wind and Dior's scolding glare.)

Dior: "Look at me, Lisa."

(Upon request, Lisa shifts her eyes from the ground to Dior's harsh gaze.)

Dior: "Lisa, the way you conducted yourself tonight after dinner was very disrespectful. You know better than to ignore a guest humbling themselves. Do you have anything to say for yourself?"

Lisa: "I wasn't listening at the time."

Dior: "Listening to what?"

Lisa: "To Lyone, saying good—night."

(Caught in a lie, Lisa turns her eyes towards the ground again, tightening her lips.)

Dior: "You're lying to me now, Lisa?"

(She remains silent, avoiding Dior's question.)

Dior: "Answer me, Lisa."

Lisa: "Well, aren't you lying to me?"

(As Lisa rebelliously stares at Dior with her head lowered, he becomes angered. Following, the pupils of his eyes emit a sudden glow of black light, instantly bringing Lisa to her hands and knees under a massive amount of weight on her Energy Stream.)

Dior: "Then, in that case, I'm only going to say this once. If you keep this attitude up, I'm going to start making your life miserable for the remainder of the winter. No more excuses. Understand?"

Lisa <struggling> "Really, Dad?"

Dior: "I'm sorry, I didn't hear you say you understood me."

(He increases the weight upon her Energy Stream, causing her to bend her elbows, sweating and panting.)

Dior: "No more excuses. You do what I tell you to do or we will have a problem. Now, do you understand?"

Lisa: <struggling> "Y-Yeah! I got it! I understand!"

Dior: "Good. Now, five pushups as punishment."

Lisa: <struggling> "B-But I can barely move!"

Dior: "I promise you, Lisa, I can keep you like this all night. So, the faster you do those pushups, the faster I let you go."

(While Dior towers over Lisa, she proceeds with her pushups, burdened by his Energy Stream. Ten minutes later, Lisa lies on the ground, fainted. With his Energy Stream withdrawn, Dior picks her up, carrying her in his arms, walking back to camp. Afterwards, he carries Lisa into her tent, helping her into a sleeping bag. Lastly, he walks to his own tent, stopping to view the three moons shining above their camp.)

Dior: *"She'll understand someday."*

(In the morning before dawn, Lisa walks out of her tent, dizzily holding her head. Dior sits on top of a large blanket spread in front of his tent, preparing breakfast for the party. As Dior follows her with his stern gaze, Lisa silently takes a seat by the campfire.)

Dior: "Lisa."

(Lisa turns towards Dior, noticing a prepared plate of fruit and vegetables with dipping sauce. She walks over to receive the food, gratefully bowing.)

Lisa: "Thank you, Dad."

(After receiving her food, she quietly walks back to the campfire. As Dior continues preparing meals, Lyone walks out of his tent, cheerfully yawning and stretching.)

Lyone: "Good morning!"

Lisa: "Good morning, Lyone."

Dior: "Good morning, and good timing, Lyone! This morning, I'm preparing semi seku fruit and sliced kungou. Both are very good for the brain."

Lyone: "This isn't because I burned myself, right?"

(Lyone laughs, embarrassedly rubbing the back of his head, spreading laughter amongst the party.)

Dior: "Let's just say this is coincidental, eh? Ha!"

(Lyone walks over to Dior, collecting a plate of food. Then, he walks to the campfire, sitting shoulder to shoulder with Lisa.)

Lisa: "Why are you sitting so close to me?"

Lyone: "Why are you so quiet this morning?"

Lisa: "Why are you so annoying this morning?"

Lyone: "Why didn't you brush your teeth this morning?"

Lisa: "You're supposed to brush after you eat food."

Lyone: "So, you admit you have bad breath, then?"

(As Lyone victoriously grins, Lisa irritably roll her eyes, standing onto her feet, and moving to the opposite side of the campfire.)

Lyone: "Come on, Lisa! I'm just messing with you. You do the same to me all the time!"

Lisa: "Not in the mood."

(As the two argue with each other, Dior eats his own plate of food, sitting in front of his tent.)

Dior: *Sometimes I forget they're just kids.*

(Meanwhile, Olivia sits on one of the surrounding tree branches, collecting her surveillance equipment while keeping an eye on the camp. She reviews last night's recordings, noting the part involving Dior and Lisa.)

Olivia: "Hmm."

(Later that morning, The party stands together with their equipment packed and campsite cleared.)

Dior: "Ok, looks like we're all set."

Lyone: "Yup! Off to the desert!"

(Lyone begins to march toward the desert, brimming with confidence.)

Dior: "Ha ha! Nice to see that you're eager to walk on sand."

Lyone: "I've never been in a desert before! It should be fun! Right, Lisa?"

(Lyone turns towards Lisa, immediately becoming concern. Dior also turns to Lisa, noticing her standing away from the party with her head hung.)

Lyone: "Lisa, is something wrong?"

Lisa: "I-I'm going back home."

(She avoids looking directly at them, once again feeling the tension of Dior scolding gaze.)

Lyone: "Going back home? What are you talking about? You know we can't go back."

Lisa: "I'll go back by myself."

(Lyone walks up to Lisa with playful naïveté.)

Lyone: "Come on, Lisa, you expect us to believe that? You don't want to get eaten by the nydala, right? Ha ha!"

Lisa: "I DON'T CARE!"

(While Lyone stands surprised at Lisa's sudden outburst, Olivia spies behind a nearby tree, listening to their conversation, waiting for their move to the desert.)

Lisa: "It's obvious that you guys are hiding something from me! I don't know what it is, but I know it's bad enough for Dad to make me shut up about it! And if that's how it's gonna be, then I don't wanna be here anymore!"

Dior: "Lisa, that's enough!"

(As Dior marches toward Lisa, she stand strong despite her fear.)

Dior: "What you don't know is for your own good! If you continue to be rebellious, I will not hesitant to make you do as I say! Understand?"

Lyone: "Wait, Mr. Kendric."

(Upon hearing Lyone's voice, they fall silent, turning their attention to him.)

Lyone: "I'll tell her."

Dior: "Lyone, I really don't think that's necessary."

Lyone: "Maybe you're right. But I think Lisa's right about one thing. If we're gonna be traveling together, she should know. Especially if something happens to you or me, right?"

Dior: "Lyone, I understand what you're saying, but I've told you before. If this isn't kept a secret, there are people in this world that will seek to harm or kill you."

(Lisa becomes visibly worried upon hearing Dior's words. At the same time, Olivia becomes greatly interested in their conversation.)

Lyone: "I trust her, Mr. Kendric."

(As Lyone stands with an unwavering stare, Dior looks into his eyes, eventually shaking his head with a smile, reaching a conclusion.)

Dior: "You two are such a hassle. Fine, I won't stop you from telling her. But, before you do . . ."

(Dior focuses his mind, summoning his black Energy Stream, bizarrely warping the space around himself.)

Dior: "Alright you two, come closer."

(Mystified by Dior's power, Lyone and Lisa steps closer to him. Olivia remains in cover, peeking at the odd surge of energy around Dior.)

Olivia: "*What is he doing?*"

(Suddenly, Dior's aura swallows the trio in a shroud of energy, making them disappear.)

Olivia: *"What the heck? Where did they go?"*

(Olivia focuses her mind, attempting to pinpoint their location.)

Olivia: *"They're still there. Amazing how well camouflaged the aura is. What kind of technique is that?"*

(Inside the invisible shroud of energy, Lyone and Lisa gawks around in amazement. They find themselves in the middle of a strange barren wasteland, floating in a void, shrouded by black fog at the edges. The two observe each other, noticing their bodies and clothing are void of color.)

Lisa: *"Where are we?"*

Voice: *"Over here."*

(Lisa and Lyone turns around, spotting Dior walking towards them, noting the somber gray coloring of his person. Once Dior reaches them, Lyone turns his attention toward the sky, noticing Yunyi shining high above them. However, the warmth from Yunyi's rays of daylight are replaced with a grayed dispassionate melancholy shine.)

Lyone: *"What a weird place. Is this the same place Mr. Kendric brought me before?"*

Dior: *"No, this is a different technique."*

(To Lisa's surprise, she cannot speak despite moving her lips.)

Lisa: *"I can't talk!"*

Dior: *"Inside this technique, your mind speaks."*

Lisa: *"Whoa, that's weird. Dad just talked without moving his mouth."*

Dior: *"Yes, I know that. That's what I just said."*

Lisa: *"What the heck? Hey Dad, can you hear me?"*

Dior: *"Yes, I can hear you, Lisa."*

Lisa: *"Wow! You can hear my thoughts! Hey Lyone, can you hear me?"*

(As Lisa turns to Lyone, he stands about, scratching his head, lingering in confusion. Then, he attempts to speak, learning he is unable to do so.)

Lisa: *"Haven't you been listening, silly? We talk with our thoughts."*

Lyone: *"Well this is strange. I'm still trying to figure out where we are."*

Dior: *"This place is the manifestation of a technique I used. We're still where we've always been, physically speaking. Just know that this is the safest place to tell Lisa what's going on. Now, Lyone . . ."*

Lyone: *"Mr. Kendric really needs to cut his nose hairs."*

(As Lisa soundlessly chuckles, Dior awkwardly covers his nose with his hand.)

Lisa: *"We can hear your thoughts, Li'l L! Ha ha!"*

Lyone: *"Oh crap! I mean, shoot! Sorry!"*

Dior: *"Try not to get distracted, Lyone. I can only hold this technique for a limited amount of time, so let's make this quick and inform Lisa about the situation."*

Lyone: *"Got it, ha ha!"*

(Lyone turns his attention to Lisa, taking a serious tone and demeanor, procuring a moment to gather himself.)

Lyone: *"Lisa, I'm a Renzido."*

Lisa: *"Oh, ok."*

(Lisa stares at Lyone, waiting for him to elaborate.)

Lyone: *"You don't know what that is, do you?"*

Lisa: *"I have no idea what that is."*

Dior: *"Well, to make this short, Lyone is a member of an ancient group of people who supposedly went extinct hundreds of thousands of years ago by way of genocide."*

Lisa: *"Genocide?"*

Dior: *"That means that other people killed them off."*

Lisa: *"What? But why?"*

Dior: *"I don't know. It could have been for many reasons. I do know that Renzido were some of the greatest fighters of their time, which made them dangerous to many. But, in a world like this, that alone doesn't explain why it happened. Just understand, Lisa, that if people in this world finds out that Lyone is a Renzido, there's a great chance he could be hunted down and killed. That is why we must keep this a secret. And that means no talking about this. Ok?"*

Lisa: *"Ok, I understand. But I do have another question."*

Lyone: *"What is it?"*

Lisa: *"Dad keeps knocking you out for some reason. Does that have to do with you being a Renzido?"*

Dior: *"Yes. Renzidos are identified by the many Lineage Transformations available to them. However, Renzidos are best identified by a specific Lineage*

Transformation linked to a genetic trait called Blood Flow. When a Renzido experiences a rush of an emotion that is tied to the Blood Flow gene, they undergo the transformation of Blood Flow. It's a state in which they have little to no control of themselves, attacking any and everything around them. Blood Flow transformations and the emotion to triggers the Blood Flow gene differs depending upon the individual's genetic makeup. In Lyone's case, the emotion that is connected to his Blood Flow gene is anger."

(Lisa remembers the numerous times Lyone was rendered unconscious, noting the anger he experienced during each occasion.)

Lisa: *"I see. Yeah, that makes sense now. Li'l L definitely has a short temper!"*

Lyone: *"Hey, don't talk about me like that while I'm standing right here! And stop calling me Li'l L!"*

Lisa: *"See? There goes that temper. Ok, don't worry guys. I'll try not to make Li'l L mad, and I'll keep this a secret. You can count on me!"*

Dior: *"Alright then, are we all on the same page now?"*

Lisa: *"Yup!"*

Lyone: *"Sounds like it."*

Dior: *"Good. And remember, no discussing this."*

(After the party agrees, Dior closes his eyes, focusing his Energy Stream, dispersing the mysterious realm before their eyes. After the trio returns to the normal space within the Yellow Shadow Forest, Olivia remains hidden behind a tree, perplexed by their sudden appearance.)

Dior: "Ok you two, before we leave for the desert, quick announcement."

Lyone: "We can talk like normal again!"

Lisa: "Yeah, that was weird. Feels like I was holding my breath."

Lyone: "I know right?"

Dior: "Hey! Focus, you two!"

Lyone and Lisa: "Oh!"

(As the three casually have their conversation, Olivia secretly glares at them with suspicion.)

Olivia: *"They're acting as if nothing happened. Definitely hiding something. I have to figure this out."*

Dior: "So, for the remainder of our travels, I won't be using my imperial force to repel monsters. More than likely, we'll come across many different types of monster species and probably even some beast species. Prepare to defend yourselves if necessary. Understand?"

Lisa: "Alright, Dad."

Lyone: "Got it."

(Dior gives them a confident smile, proudly noting their eagerness to proceed. After the party checks their equipment, they stand together, ready to move onward.)

Dior: "Ok, looks like we're all set."

Lyone: "Alright then! Let's roll!"

(Lyone runs towards the south with excitement, leading Lisa and Dior into the desert.)

Lisa: "Wait up, Li'l L!"

Narrator: "Even at a young age, I knew that building trust with others was important. Luckily for me, good allies weren't so hard to find, at least in those days."

(A few hours later, the party joyfully travels through the desert with light winds blowing around them, and the rays of Yunyi shining upon them from above. As Dior fills up one of the party's canteens with water generated from an orb of energy held in his hand, Lyone looks around the desert, spotting many small huddles of cacti grouped together around the golden-brown desert sand.)

Lyone: "Hey, Mr. Kendric, does this desert have a name?"

Dior: "Although we've submitted names, nothing has been ratified yet."

Lyone: "Hm, I wonder how that process works?"

Dior: "Well, Lyone, as an independent explorer contracted by the Federal Union Adventurer's Guild, I hold the right to name any territory I've officially scouted by bringing back documented proof and evidence from within said territory. This desert, the valley further south, and the mountain where Lisa and I found you are all under my contract."

Lyone: "Um?"

Lisa: "He means we were here first, so we get to name the place!"

Lyone: "Oh, ok. Well, who named the Yellow Shadow Forest?"

Dior: "That's being disputed considering a Federal Union scout returned from the forest describing features and organisms seen during a pursuit of the beasts that were expelled from the land; which is now Wisden. So, technically, the 'Yellow Shadow Forest' doesn't really bare that name. Unless, of course, the Federal Union decides to select that name suggestion."

Lyone: "So, the Federal Union scout was there first and they get to name it?"

Dior: "Yes and no. Those scouts were employed by the Federal Union's Southern Division Forces. Since they were employed by the military, the military gets to name the place. People can submit suggestions. But they have the final word in that case."

(Lyone ponders Dior's explanation, turning his attention back towards the schools of cacti across the desert.)

Lyone: "So, since you guys were here first, all you have to do is report about some features and things that live in this environment?"

Dior: "And the biggest thing that stands out here are those schools of cacti."

Lyone: "Yeah, I was about to ask about those."

Dior: "Well, they're called kipi. They're members of the cactus monster species. They live in schools and are usually peaceful unless you bother them. They're also the most common cactus monster in many deserts across Ni; with slight variations between populations of course."

Lisa: "Which is why I suggested the 'Kipi Family Desert' as the name for this place! You know, I asked Dad if I can have one, but he said they'll just shoot needles at me. Ha ha!"

Lyone: "So, we shouldn't eat them, or . . .?"

Dior: "Thinking with your stomach again, I see! Ha ha!"

Lyone: "Hmmm. By the way, I've heard you speak about monsters and beasts before. What's the difference?"

Dior: "Good question. Monsters, apart from a small percentage of the population, are lesser organisms driven by primitive directives like survival and reproduction. They can roam in packs and coordinate but are unable to do the thing that beast can."

Lyone: "I think I understand. Whats the thing beast can do that monsters can't do?"

Dior: "Beast are the evolution of monsters that have developed advance culture and reasoning capabilities. Making them able to communicate between Beast of other family lineages, Beast of other kinds, build structures, cultivate their own social norms, and even learn advanced Energy Stream techniques like Humanoid Species and Humanus Species can."

(Lyone thinks carefully about Dior's explanation, identifying another question to ask.)

Lyone: "…like Humanoid Species and Humanus Species can. You make it sound like we could be members of the Beast Species, but you mention those two other species separately. What makes us different then Beast?"

Dior: "Another good question. Truth is, we're not exactly sure. What we do know is there exist different Humanoid and Humanus Species across the planet; all distinctive in certain evolutionary traits such as bipedalism, nearly bare skin, two distinct sexes, and other traits. However, no one has figured out the exact point in time which the Humanoid and Humanus Species came into being. Some believe we're merely the next stage of evolution from a distant Beast ancestor. Some believe we were created as special categories by Ni. Some believe were created from other divine entities. Truth is, we've yet to figure it out."

Lisa: "Which is why dad's job is so important!"

Lyone: "Oh? Why do you say that?"

Lisa: "Because dad is helping to make uninhabitable zones habitable, so we can investigate the world for the truth of who and what we are!"

Dior: "Thus the term for our current 'Age of Exploration'. I, and many other explorers, are at the forefront to travel through perilous environments, fill with danger and mystery to find spaces where people can exist with the smallest amount of environmental danger. This gives nation-states the ability to setup a bulwark, expand, and learn about Humanoid, Humanus, and Ni in the process."

Lyone: "I see. That makes sense. My only question now is, what makes Humanoid Species and Humanus Species different from each other?"

Dior: "Oh that's simple. They can't reproduce."

Lyone: "Hmmmm…re-pro-duce."

Lisa: "Oh! Oh! I know this one--"

(Dior loudly laughs, nervously cutting the conversation short.)

Dior: "L-Let's, ummm, save that topic for another time, shall we?"

(As the three continue through the desert, a tall skinny dog-like monster emerges from under a large rock formation in the distance. With its long bushy haired tail positioned over the monster's body, it detects the trio, barking three times, echoing its voice throughout the land, alerting the party. Once the party recognizes the threat, three more dog-like monsters emerge from the rock formation.)

Lisa: "Looks like we got company."

Lyone: "Wouldn't it be the other way around? I mean, they're the ones that live here."

Lisa: "Not the time to be a smart a-"

(As Dior looks over his shoulder at Lisa, she quickly covers her mouth, laughing nervously.)

Lisa: "Sorry! I meant 'smart butt!' Ha ha!"

(The pack of wild dog-like monsters jump from the rock formation, dashing toward the party. Everyone places their equipment onto the sand, preparing themselves for combat.)

Dior: "These are dust devils. Should be good practice. Ready, you two?"

(Lyone and Lisa agrees with a nod, confidently standing their ground, watching pack of dust devils posturing themselves a few of yards away.

Meanwhile, as Olivia watches the pending bout through the scope of her rifle, four small black cylinder devices are setup in a square formation, surrounding the space where Olivia lays on her stomach. Within the space, she remains visible. Outside the space, herself and her weapon appears distorted, blending into the sand, providing cover.)

Olivia: *"This should be interesting."*

(As the dust devils attempt to surround the party, Lyone and the others back away slowly, preventing the monsters from positioning around them. The lead dust devil in the center barks, causing the other three to charge forward and attack.

A dust devil pounces toward Lyone and he rolls to the right, avoiding the attack. While two of the dust devils run pass him, Dior stands his ground with his arms folded behind his back, confidently smiling at the leader of the pack. As the other two dust devils pounce toward Lisa, a light blue aura resonates from her body, quickly unleashing a hot mist that conceals her. The dust devils jump through the mist, missing their attack, unable to locate her. Suddenly, she attacks one of the monsters, kicking it in the stomach from its right, launching it a few feet away, following with a swift punch to the snout of the other dust devil and a roundhouse kick to its face.

Meanwhile, Dior patiently smiles at the leader of the pack. It stares back, brandishing its sharp teeth, growling fiercely. Then, the leader pounces towards Dior, gliding through an image of his body. The lead dust devil turn back to Dior, noticing he is nowhere to be found. Suddenly, Dior appears at the monster's right with a magnifying glass, examining the monster's bushy tail.)

Dior: "Hmm, so the hairs on the tail acts like an umbrella of shade. Interesting evolutionary trait."

(The lead dust devil tries to bite Dior's face, slamming its jaws together, missing him completely. Next, Dior takes off at a blinding speed, continuously disappearing and reappearing around the lead dust devil, confusing the monster with sporadic movements. Meanwhile, one of the dust devils stands in opposition to Lisa with a bloodied snout. The monster pounces toward her. She evades by moving left, skillfully grappling the tail of the monster. Next, she spins the monster around, throwing it onto the sand dazed and unable to fight.)

Lisa: "That was easy."

(Suddenly, one of their foes lunges toward Lisa from behind. To her surprise, she hears a loud thump, accompanied by a canine's whimper. She quickly turns around, locating the other dust devil knocked out on the sand. Afterwards, Lisa turns towards Dior, watching him oppose the lead dust devil with a sly grin.)

Lisa: *"Figures."*

Lyone: "Get off, you big idiot!"

Lisa: "Huh?"

(Lisa quickly looks at Lyone's direction, noticing one of the dust devils on top of him, struggling to hold it off. Firmly gripping under its neck, Lyone repeatedly punches the monster in the body. In the distance, Olivia gently places her finger onto the trigger of her rifle, targeting at the dust devil attacking Lyone. However, Lyone quickly looks around, spotting a school of kipi.

Then, Lyone uses his legs to flip the dust devil overhead, slamming the monster onto the kipi. Agitated, the kipi instantly launch their barbs into the dust devil's body.

Lisa runs over, helping Lyone onto his feet. The two observe the once-ferocious beast; now reduced to a whimpering pup, struggling to rid itself of the five-inch barbs sticking out of its body. Finally, the dust devil faints from the exhaustion and pain.)

Lisa: "Hate to be that guy."

Lyone: <in Huadi> "That mutt almost killed me."

(Olivia smiles, easing her finger away from the trigger, continuing to watch.

Lisa and Lyone unexpectedly feel a small tremor under their feet. Suddenly, the two are knocked aside by a monster, erupting from under the sand. They quickly look up to the sight of a large, hairy, blubbery worm-like monster, towering over them. As the duo quickly attempt to regain their footing, the monster screeches from its bulky armored beak, forcing them to cover their ears from the debilitating sound.)

Lyone: <in Huadi> "The heck is that thing?"

(The worm-like monster stops its screech, beginning to regurgitate fluid. Olivia sighs, placing her finger back onto the trigger of her rifle, targeting the new monster.)

Dior: "Lisa! Lyone! Move!"

(As Lisa and Lyone frantically jump out of the way, the worm-like monster showers acidic fluid from its beak onto the sand, narrowly missing its targets. Afterwards, it dives back underground, circling around the area.)

Lisa: "Dad! What is that thing?"

Dior: "Both of you! Don't move!"

(Lisa and Lyone follow Dior's lead, tensely stopping any movements. Dior's attention remains focused on the lead dust devil, observing the dust devil restricting its movements on purpose.)

Dior: *"Smart pup. It knows that the desert gyrm can only find us by vibrations."*

(Dior confidently grins, stomping onto the ground, causing the lead dust devil to flinch. Then, Dior jumps high into the air moments before the desert gyrm erupts from the sands below. Next, he dives toward the gyrm, emitting a strong aura of energy into his right arm. Finally, in the blink of an eye, he appears on the ground behind the gyrm, heroically posing with his right arm reaching out, slicing the gyrm's body in half. The corpse of the monster falls on top of the sand in parts, oozing acidic body fluids. Olivia spies on the party's celebration, easing her finger away from the trigger once again, sarcastically smiling.)

Dior: "You two ok?"

Lyone: "Heck yeah! That was so cool how you finished off that thing!"

Lisa: "What was that thing anyway?"

Dior: "A desert gyrm. They burrow under the sands waiting for prey. Our fight must have attracted it."

Lisa: "It almost got us good."

Dior: "The both of you did a good job at making the right decisions on the battlefield."

Lisa: "Hear that, Li'l L?"

(Lyone stares off into the distance, focusing his eyes away from the party.)

Lisa: "Something wrong?"

Lyone: "Look."

(He points his finger toward the lead dust devil, carrying two of its comrades. The fourth dust devil slowly walks behind the leader, limping on one of its hind legs.)

Lyone: "Guess that does it."

Lisa: "They picked the wrong prey."

(As the party watches the dust devil's retreat, shade covers the desert in their immediate area. Olivia observe from a distance, detecting something directly over their party, blocking Yunyi.)

Olivia: "What is that?"

(Lyone looks toward the sky, spotting an obscure shadow blocking Yunyi.)

Lyone: "Strange, I don't see any clouds—"

(Dior swiftly steps in front of Lyone and Lisa, creating a dark barrier of energy and a sudden explosion of black flames engulfs the sand around them. Once the flames crashes into Diors barrier, Lisa and Lyone ducks for cover, holding their ears. As the smoke from the explosion clears, Lisa and Lyone rise to their feet with caution, noticing a great black bird, brandishing jade-colored talons and eyes, feasting on the charred corpses of the four dust devils.)

Lisa: "What the . . .?"

(The giant avian monster notices the party, petrifying Lyone and Lisa with fear. The monster summons a powerful green Energy Stream, drawing forth Dior's Energy Stream with its imperial force. Lisa and Lyone become wary and weakened in the presence of the battling Energy Streams, forcing Dior to direct his imperial force to defensively safeguard the party.)

Great Avian Monster: *"Impressive. I can tell you're not one to be taken lightly."*

(Dior becomes increasingly cautious, hearing the monster speak to him through telepathy.)

Dior: *"Telepathy in another language is a learned trait. You must be an elder valzu."*

Elder Valzu: *"Be at ease. Today, you're not my prey."*

(The elder valzu collects the corpses of the dust devils in its beak, opens its enormous wings, and flies off into the air, sending a massive gust of wind in all directions. The flap of its wings causes a sandstorm, forcing the party to shield themselves, burying them under the sand.

As the dust settles, Dior lifts himself from under the sand with Lyone and Lisa in his arms. After placing them onto their feet, they take a moment to shake off their fatigue.)

Lyone: <in Huadi> "That giant—THING—came out of nowhere! I thought we were going to die."

(As he fuses about their near-death experience, Lyone hears the sudden sound of laughter. Then, he takes notice of Dior and Lisa, hysterically sharing laughter together.)

Faint Voice: <in Huadi> *"These two are out of their minds."*

Lyone: <in Huadi> *"Seriously. Wait, what the . . .?"*

(More confused than ever, Lyone scans the desert, searching for the source of that voice. Lisa and Dior slowly regain their composure.)

Lisa: "Dad, be honest. We would have died, huh?"

Dior: "You guys would have lived for about half a minute at the start. Considering if I would be crazy enough to fight it with you and Lyone to worry about ha ha!"

Lisa: "Figures. Any idea what that monster was?"

Dior: "That was definitely an elder valzu."

Lisa: "A valzu? They grow THAT big?"

Dior: "Normally, no. But, there is a rule in combat upon Ni. The older the opponent, the deadlier they potentially are. I'm guessing it managed to live long enough to realize the potential it was born with. Evolution in the works. I'd hate to fight that valzu's children in a hundred years, ha ha!"

Lisa: "I'm just glad that it flew off, even though it buried us in sand. Still pretty exciting!"

Lyone: "Hey guys."

Lisa: "Something wrong?"

Lyone: "Did you guys hear a voice just a few minutes ago speaking my native language?"

Dior: "I didn't hear anything of the sort."

Lisa: "Me neither."

(As Lyone retreats into his thoughts, Lisa steps next to him, mockingly smiling.)

Lisa: "You're probably tired from all the fighting, Li'l L. Maybe we should find a place to take a break?"

Dior: "No, we have to keep moving to reach the oasis before nightfall. The last thing we need is to be out in the open at night in this desert."

Lyone: "That makes sense. You can always expect a desert to be very active at night."

Lisa: "Alright then, if that's the plan, we better get going."

(Everyone in the party picks up their equipment from the sand, checking for missing items before they're ready to continue. After confirming no more threats, Olivia sighs in relief. While Lisa helps Dior checks his equipment, Lyone looks over to the large rock formation where the dust devils dwelled, noticing eyes looking at them from under the rocks.)

Lyone: "Hey guys, what's that?"

Dior: "Hmm?"

(Lyone directs their attention to the rock formation. As the party takes a closer look, they notice three dust devil pups, cautiously staring back at them.)

Dior: "Looks like the pups of the pack of dust devils that were just killed."

Lyone: "They're not going to last long out here. What should we do? We could make their deaths easier by killing them quickly. Then, we could use their corpses as bait for bigger game."

Lisa: "Yeah, but that feels kinda wrong, doesn't it? I mean, they're defenseless."

Lyone: "They're going to die anyway."

Lisa: "I guess so. But, do we have to kill all three of them?"

Lyone: "That's true. We only need one of them as bait. Maybe we shouldn't waste time and energy on the other two?"

Dior: "I agree. One of them is good enough."

Lyone: "Are you gonna need help?"

(Dior takes mental note of Lyone's willingness to participate, turning his attention back toward the pups.)

Dior: "Not to worry. I'll take care of it."

(Lisa folds her arms with discomfort, Lyone sits onto the sand watching, and Dior walks over to the rock formation, prepared to finish the deed.

Later that night, the party rests at a small desert oasis, surrounded by sheltering trees and rocks. As a chilly breeze rolls through the area, Lisa moves closer to the campfire, hungrily eating a large piece of cooked meat. Then, Lisa feels a hand on her shoulders, covering her from the cold with a blanket. She turns around, watching Dior walk away with his arms folded behind his back. He walks until he reaches the edge of the oasis, coming to a stop, staring at the planet's moons floating above them. As Lyone continues eating, Lisa glows with a loving smile, standing onto her feet, walking over to Dior.)

Lisa: "You're not freezing, Dad?"

Dior: "I've trained in harsher weather than this."

Lisa: "Yeah, I should have known you'd say something like that."

(As Dior continues gazing at the night's sky, Lisa sits on the sand with her blanket and smile.)

Lisa: "I have a question, Dad."

Dior: "Oh? What's that?"

Lisa: "The elder valzu from earlier today, was it strong enough to kill you?"

Dior: "To be honest, I don't know. It seems to have naturally learned techniques that are leagues ahead of even most Humanoids and Humanus."

Lisa: "Like what?"

(Lisa listens carefully, watching Dior close his eyes, hearing his analysis of the situation.)

Dior: "Let's see: It was hiding the bulk of its Energy Stream even after it dive-bombed the dust devils, it could condense energy into element, it used its imperial force to draw out my Energy Stream while attempting to kill you and Lyone through inflicting Energy Stream Death, it could speak to me using telepathy and accurately sync languages, and could create a local sandstorm with a flap of its wings. And, I'm betting that's not even half of its capabilities considering how flawlessly all the mentioned abilities were executed. That elder valzu was a thing of beauty."

(Shocked at the picture painted by Dior, Lisa briefly remains silent, shifting through her swarming thoughts.)

Lisa: "O-Ok. So, like, that was a really bad situation, wasn't it?"

Dior: "Nah, I probably could have won."

(Dior looks down at Lisa with a confident smile, abruptly erupting in laughter together.)

Lisa: "Ha ha! Probably, huh?"

Dior: "Probably."

(Dior takes a seat onto the sands next to Lisa, gently wrapping his arm around her, keeping her warm as they stare at Ni's moons.)

Dior: "Lisa."

Lisa: "Yeah, Dad?"

Dior: "I'm sorry."

Lisa: "Sorry? For?"

Dior: "For not trusting you about Lyone. I can only hope you understand that I was merely trying to protect him."

Lisa: "No, I understand."

Dior: "Do you?"

Lisa: "Of course. Lyone is like family to us. Keeping him alive is top priority, even if that means lying to other family members. Right?"

Dior: "Well, when you put it that way, it's hard to disagree."

(Dior turns back towards the sky, calmly retreating into his thoughts.)

Dior: *"At least she knows the importance of why I did what I did. Even if she doesn't acknowledge her big mouth."*

Lisa: "Plus, I talk too much sometimes. But, don't worry, I'll keep a lid on the secret, ok?"

(Lisa captures Dior's attention once more, voicing the thoughts in his head while displaying a confident smile similar to his own. He laughs, pulling Lisa closer to him, giving her a hug.)

Dior: "Ha ha! I believe you, Lisa."

Lisa: "Thanks, Dad. Love you."

Dior: "Love you too, sweetheart."

Lisa: "Always?"

Dior: "Ha ha! Always! Now, I'm going to get more food. Lyone has the right idea!"

Lisa: "Ha ha, ok!"

(As Dior walks over to the campfire, Lisa turns her head, catching a brief glimpse of a feathered monster with sharp talons stepping behind a large rock formation in the distance. She curiously peers at the large rock formation, making her way back to the campfire.)

Dior: "Lyone, you seem to be enjoying yourself, ha ha!"

Lyone: "Baiting that giant serpent was a good idea! I wouldn't have guessed that it tastes so good."

(Dior walks over to a round, makeshift rock table and takes some food.)

Lisa: "Geez. Li'l L, you ever think about breathing when you eat?"

Lyone: <mouth full of food> "Breathing is for the weak!"

Dior: "He has a point, Lisa. Dead people are pretty weak, ha ha!"

(Surprised by Dior's joke, Lyone swallows his food, flippantly turning toward him in protest.)

Lyone: "Hey, I didn't mean that!"

Dior: "Oh really? Ha ha!"

Lyone: "If I die, it's not gonna be by way of food. Or maybe, food is to die for? Ha ha!"

Lisa: "I can definitely see you dead with a smile in a puddle of gravy!"

Lyone: "Shut up, ha ha!"

(As Dior eats, he remains entertained, listening to them laugh and joke around the campfire.)

Dior: *"Good. We made it this far without any major accidents. And I'm starting to get a better picture of Lyone's character. As much as they get along, the differences between their upbringings are drastic. And for good reason. Lyone didn't hesitant to exploit his options to survive in the wild; which was expected. But his sense of empathy seems to be lacking."*

(From a rock formation in the distance, Olivia spies on the party through her scope of her rifle, remaining in camouflage by four black cylinder devices. Then, the subtle sound of a call on her earpiece alerts her. She taps onto her earpiece with her right hand, keeping an eye on the party.)

Idol: "Major."

Olivia: "Sir!"

Idol: "Your report."

Olivia: "Yes, sir. Currently, the party is resting at an oasis in the middle of the desert southwest of Wisden. It's the same desert recently discovered and reported on during Dior's explorations of the terrains in the unexplored south."

Idol: "Has the target made contact with any other Adventurer's Guild personnel that are currently in that territory?"

Olivia: "No, sir. There seems to be very few Adventurer's Guild members in this area. I suspect it's due to the geography. Anyone would be hard pressed to stay in this desert for a long period of time. Well, anyone except—"

Idol: "Dior Kendric himself. I take it you had the pleasure of seeing him in action?"

(Olivia momentarily remains silent, gathering her thoughts with a menacing glare, placing her sights on Dior.)

Olivia: "Sir, I believe my presence on this mission is compromised."

Idol: "I see. You've found definitive evidence this time?"

Olivia: "Sir, before we arrived in the desert, the party got into some kind of argument. They didn't specify exactly what they were arguing about, but it was important enough for Dior to use this strange technique to shroud the entire party. I didn't know what happened at first, but once I searched the area using my own Energy Stream, I noticed they were still in the same spot. They were just—concealed."

Idol: "What happened next?"

Olivia: "Sir, after some time passed, the strange energy that concealed them dispersed and they were back to normal."

Idol: "That's it? Just like that, back to normal?"

Olivia: "Exactly. Seems like they aired out their grievances under the cloak of that technique. Question is, why would you use such a technique merely to hold a conversation unless you knew someone was watching you?"

Idol: "Reasonable observation. At this point, it's pretty safe to assume that Dior knows you're watching."

(Olivia briefly pauses, curiously deciphering Idol's tone, quickly arriving at a realization.)

Olivia: "Sir, you don't sound surprised."

Idol: "Of course not. Dior is the most likely culprit behind your string of bad luck."

Olivia: "Sir, even I can admit that I'm not a hundred percent sure."

Idol: "Major, I've had the opportunity to serve my country in a party filled with some of the strongest fighters from around the world; all of whom were chosen for their fighting capabilities. Dior wasn't our leader, nor was he the strongest, but he was certainly the most skilled. There was no location on those battlefields he couldn't infiltrate, no neck that could run from his blade. It was as if he was one with the shadows. So, rest assured, he knew you were following him before this mission ever began."

Olivia: "Well then, sir, why don't I just go over there and have dinner with them?"

(As Idol laughs at her sarcasm, Olivia irritably glares at Dior through her scope, pointing her middle finger at him.)

Idol: "Ha ha, I'm sure you understand that at this point, your goal is not to hide from Dior, but to hide from the target and anything else that could identify you. I trust the camouflage zone tech has been helpful?"

Olivia: "Sir, it is. I'm glad these things weren't taken from me at least. How is that care package coming, Aksana?"

Aksana: "Already inbound. It should reach your location by dawn."

Olivia: "Thank you. I must admit, these new technologies are amazing. Even the carrier drone shows impressive results in its efficiency."

Idol: "Agreed. We owe a great deal to our science and research department. But that's just one department our military is ramping up. Believe me, you haven't seen anything yet."

Olivia: "Sir, I can only imagine. Thanks for everything, guys. You've all been a big help thus far."

Joshua: "Hey Major, by the way, you may already know this. But, better safe than sorry. So, water supply is very important in a desert climate. But, if you're planning to take a drink by condensing the little amount of hydro energy in your environment to water element, be wary of your Energy Stream giving off your signature in the process. That could make your presence known to other organisms around you."

Olivia: "Thank you for the heads-up Joshua."

William: "Speaking of drinks, maybe we can all get a round of Isu's Brew after this, ha ha!"

Joshua: "Is that your way of asking the major out for a drink?"

William: "What? No! I specifically said, 'all of us!'"

Joshua: "Sure, that's exactly what you meant, ha ha!"

Aksana: "Either way, I'll pass."

William: "But why?"

Aksana: "The last time we drank too much Isu's Brew, we all woke up on the roof of the bar with a few dozen chickens. The back pain I had after sleeping on that roof was horrid. So, I'm out."

Joshua: "Well, if my girl is out, so am I."

William: "Aww, come on, you guys!"

(As Olivia hears laughter on her earpiece, she shakes her head with disapproval. Then, Olivia notices the party, preparing for sleep.)

Olivia: "Sir, looks like they're about to call it a night."

Idol: "Alright then, I'll contact you once again in—"

(When Idol abruptly stops mid-sentence, Olivia feels a sudden rush of energy, massively spewing into the environment, sending a chill down her spine. She takes her eyes away from the scope of her rifle, urgently searching around the surrounding area.)

Olivia: *"That rush of energy. Where's it coming from?"*

Idol: "What the heck?"

Olivia: "Sir? You feel that as well?"

Idol: "Yeah. Feels like . . ."

(Dior quickly stands on his feet, turning his eyes to the horizon, feeling the tumultuous change in the environment's energy.)

Dior: "A Chaos Maelstrom."

(Lyone and Lisa urgently look around, trying to detect the cause of the disturbance.)

Lyone: "W-What is that?"

Dior: "It's what happens when too much energy floods or collides within an environment. It could drastically destabilize the environment and anything inside of it. It could even kill us!"

Lisa: "Well, I don't see anything out of the norm in this desert."

(Similar to Lisa, Dior and Lyone are unable to notice anything out of place in the desert. Dior acts swiftly, closing his eyes, focusing on the energy signatures, searching for the point of origin. Olivia suddenly opens her eyes, discovering the origin of the chaos maelstrom.)

Olivia: "Sir, that energy signal is coming from the other side of the planet!"

Idol: "Yes, I feel it as well. Could that be the same region of the world where Daafir and the Grand Shine of Centre are?"

Olivia: "Whatever the case, that amount of energy could easily destroy the planet."

(As a bright light rises over the desert's horizon, Olivia braces herself, desperately attempting to hide her fear. The light engulfs the night, bringing visibility to the desert, drawing the attention of all the living organisms. Moments later, the light quickly recedes back over the horizon, revealing Lyone and Lisa, fearfully hugging each other. Dior tensely stares at the light, tracing it with his mind until the Energy Streams producing it also fades away.)

Dior: "It's over."

Lisa: "Are we dead?"

Dior: "Congrats, you two. You escape death once again."

(They both open their eyes, sighing with relief at the return of normality, releasing each other from their fearful embrace.)

Lyone: <in Huadi> "I'm too young for this crap."

Lisa: "I really thought we were going to die that time."

Dior: "Although we're still alive, something did die this night."

(Later that night, Lyone stares at the roof of his tent, restlessly thinking about recent events. He sits upright within his sleeping bag, remembering the cruel feeling of being swallowed by light.)

Voice: <whispering> "Hey, Lyone! Are you awake?"

(Lyone turns his eyes to the entrance of his tent, hearing Lisa's voice from outside.)

Lyone: "Huh? Yeah, I am. Need something?"

Lisa: <whispering> "Can I come in?"

Lyone: "Yeah, it's ok."

(Lisa walks into his tent, sitting across from him with her legs folded.)

Lisa: <whispering> "Can't sleep, huh?"

Lyone: <whispering> "Nah."

Lisa: <whispering> "Yeah, me neither."

Lyone: <whispering> "I understand. But hey, I have a question, why are we whispering?"

Lisa: <whispering> "Because I don't wanna wake up Dad."

Lyone: "As if he ever sleeps, ha ha."

Lisa: "Yeah, yeah. You're right. He's probably eavesdropping on us right now."

(As the two briefly fall silent, they can both hear Dior snoring from his tent, bringing smiles to their faces.)

Lyone: "Hey, can I ask you a question?"

Lisa: "Yeah."

Lyone: "Are you, umm, scared of dying?"

(As he awaits an answer, Lisa gazes into Lyone's eyes, seriously contemplating in silence. Then, she unexpectedly bursts into laughter, puzzling Lyone.)

Lyone: "Hey, what's so funny?"

Lisa: "Your face, Li'l L! You should have seen it! Ha ha!"

Lyone: "Whatever, you're crazy."

(Lyone disengages from the conversation, folding his arms, laying back into his sleeping bag.)

Lisa: "The answer is an obvious 'yes', Li'l L. I mean, who walks around on Ni thinking, 'today is a good day to die?'"

Lyone: "I was just asking a question. You didn't have to laugh at me."

Lisa: "Aww, come on. I was just teasing you, Li'l L."

Lyone: "I know. It's just that . . ."

Lisa: "Go on, Lyone. I'm listening."

Lyone: "There are so many things in this world that can kill us. Even this evening, that flash of light from that chaos mal-storm thing, I thought we were done for. It scares me to know just how powerless we really are, you know?"

Lisa: "Yeah, I understand how you feel, Lyone. But, I have to admit, you're being a bit disingenuous."

Lyone: "Umm, dis-in-gen-us?"

Lisa: "Ha ha, disingenuous. It means you're being misleading."

(Noticing his continued confusion, Lisa takes a moment, considering of a more creative way to communicate.)

Lisa: "Alright, I'll explain it to you this way. Remember those three dust devil puppies we saw earlier? We killed one of them and used its body as bait to catch that giant serpent we ate. Tell me, were you thinking about how powerless the puppy we killed was? Or whether it was scared as it was moments away from dying?"

(Lyone briefly thinks about the two situations, indifferently scratching his head.)

Lyone: "I mean, I wasn't. But that was a different situation. Those pups were going to die anyway. We were going to die because of some idiots that refuse to control themselves."

Lisa: "Really though? Think about it. We chose to take the life of that pup. And, although we don't know who was responsible or the circumstances behind that chaos maelstrom, we do know that we're not dead; however, not by our own choice."

Lyone: "Come on, Lisa, it's not the same. When we're out in the middle of nowhere and have no idea where our food is coming from, we have to do what we can to survive."

Lisa: "You're right. Which is why I didn't put up a fuss when it was decided."

Lyone: "Then why are we arguing?"

Lisa: "Because we had other options. Need I remind you that my Dad is leagues ahead of the two of us in many things? If he wanted to, he could catch any monster in this desert with ease and without the use of bait."

Lyone: "And what if your Dad is not with us?"

Lisa: "Then we do what we gotta do."

Lyone: "Alright then, looks like I win."

(Lyone bigheadedly smirks, laying back into his sleeping bag.)

Lisa: "Look, all I'm trying to say is, remember to extend the same feelings you have to others and explore your options, before you make a decision you'd regret."

(Lyone sits upright once again, giving Lisa a sarcastic smile.)

Lyone: "Yeah, until I get strong enough to have choices. I'll try to keep that in mind when my stomach growls."

Lisa: "Cool, Li'l L, I understand. And when you get strong enough, try not to blow up the planet. Little people like us gotta eat, too."

(Lyone rolls his eyes, falling back on his sleeping bag.)

Lyone: "Yeah, yeah, whatever! Time for sleep."

Lisa: "Yup."

(As Lisa leaves Lyone's tent, he sleepily yawns, tucking himself inside his sleeping bag.)

Lyone: *"Blow up the planet. What does she think I am? Some kind of world-killing fool? I live here too you know!"*

(Suddenly, he hears someone walking into his tent, dragging with them something else along the ground. He looks up to find Lisa, walking back into his tent with her sleeping bag.)

Lyone: "H-Hey, what are you doing?"

Lisa: "What's it look like I'm doing? I'm sleeping here."

Lyone: "What about your tent?"

Lisa: "Weren't you the one that was talking about how you're so scared to die? Don't worry, I've got ya back, Li'l L! I'll sleep right here and make sure that trouble doesn't find you."

(As Lyone stares at Lisa with suspicion, she slyly smiles, rolling her eyes at him.)

Lisa: "Don't worry! You're not going to wake up with a bug on your face or something like that! I promise!"

(Once Lisa finishes settling within his tent, he decides to ignore her, flopping back into his sleeping bag.)

Lyone: "Whatever."

(Lisa crawls into her sleeping bag, trying to fall asleep. Subsequently, a silence settles across the night.)

Lyone: "Lisa."

Lisa: "What?"

Lyone: "You asleep?"

Lisa: "No. I'm not. Why?"

Lyone: "Just checking."

(Silence settles once again.)

Lyone: "Lisa."

Lisa: "What?"

Lyone: "Got a question."

Lisa: "What is it?"

Lyone: "What do you want to do before you die?"

Lisa: "Really Lyone? Creepy much?"

(Silence settles once again.)

Lisa: "I wanna get stronger than Dad."

Lyone: "Why?"

Lisa "To protect my family once he's gone."

(Silence settles once again.)

Lisa: "What about you?"

Lyone: "Same."

Lisa: "Copycat."

Lyone: "Shut up."

(The two quietly laugh at each other. Silence settles once again.)

Lyone: <drowsy> "Lisa."

Lisa: <drowsy> "What?"

Lyone: <drowsy> "You asleep?"

Lisa: <drowsy> "Yes, I'm asleep, Li'l L."

Lyone: <drowsy> "Ok then. Goodnight."

Lisa: <drowsy> "Goodnight."

(As the two finally fall asleep, a calm wind blows against their tent.)

Narrator: "My parents always taught me that death was natural. But they never really taught me about the fear of death. Fear came to me in many different forms, but the fear of death was always something that was present. I understood why. Death is a natural occurrence that happens every day. Its just how Ni works. But to be in the presence of monsters that want to eat you alive? Or to know that they are people out there that can kill us all if they wanted to? It's frightening. However, If I had let that stop me, I'd never have found the strength to defend myself and the people I love. Even if that meant gaining power that could destroy the world; becoming one of the feared. Fear is always there. But the courage to overcome fear needs to be constantly maintained. That's the difference between predator and prey. I woke up as the prey the next morning. Guess who had a bug on his face?"

Lyone: "Ahhhh! LISA!"

(Lisa and Dior listens to Lyone's wail, causing her to chuckle, sitting together eating breakfast near the campfire at dawn.)

Dior: "He's not getting better at this, is he?"

Lisa: "Not in the slightest! Ha ha!"

CHAPTER

NATURE OF THE MOTHER

(Later that morning, the party stands together at the desert oasis, checking their equipment before their departure.)

Lisa: "I don't know about you guys, but that bath in the oasis is just what I needed."

Lyone: "It was pretty cold. The wind didn't do me any favors either."

Dior: "As long as neither of you overused soap, I think we'll be fine."

Lisa: "Don't worry, Dad. We know that we don't have a lot of soap. We'll be careful with how much we use."

Dior: "It's not just about usage, Lisa. It's also about pollution."

(While Lyone kneels checking the equipment in his bag, he looks up towards Dior, carefully listening to his words.)

Dior: "We're not the only ones that use this oasis. So, we should preserve the environment. If not for Ni, for those who may come after us. Ni'Ador?"

Lisa: "Ahh, ok. Ni'Ador."

211

Lyone: "But why should any of that matter? I mean, I understand preserving it for others. But Ni doesn't care about us. Ni is hostile because that's just the way the planet is. So, we have to take every advantage we can to survive. Right?"

Dior: "*The irony of that statement.*"

(He looks towards Lyon, noting his curiosity.)

Dior: "That's true to an extent, Lyone. How about we talk about this as we keep moving forward?"

Lyone: "Alright then."

Dior: "Has everyone completed the equipment check?"

Lisa: "Yup! Good to go!"

Lyone: "Yeah, I'm ready."

Dior: "Alright, let's go."

(As Dior leads the party toward their next destination, Olivia observes and listens from a distance, using a new set of high-tech binoculars.)

Olivia: "*Much better.*"

Lyone: "So, what did you mean when you said, 'to an extent?' It's not like Ni purposely interferes with life, right?"

Dior: "Actually, Ni does interfere with our lives directly. In fact, we wouldn't have had the Age of Sanctuary without the direct involvement of our Holy Mother."

Lisa: "Oh! Dad, can I tell it? This is like, one of the only topics in history I actually like!"

Dior: "Ha ha, ok, Lisa. Go ahead."

Lisa: "Ok, so the very first world war in recorded history, the Liberation Battlefront, was a collaborative effort by the remaining tribes of peoples across the world; marking the end of the age known as the Harvest Period. The purpose of the war was to finally rid the world of reapers and bring about the Age of Sanctuary. The main weapon used against the reapers was a small band of warriors blessed by Ni herself. And they were led by the one and only Liberator."

(After Lisa gleefully finishes the story, Lyone scratches his head, thoroughly contemplating her words.)

Lyone: "Wait, you said the party was 'blessed by Ni?'"

Dior: "That's right. Ni 'handpicked,' sort of speak, the people responsible for bringing down the reapers and making the modern age possible. And guess what those blessed by Ni are called?"

Lyone: "I don't know. What's the answer?"

Lisa: "Champions of Ni!"

Dior: "That's right. So, if we treat Ni with respect, we may be the next to receive her blessing to survive and overcome."

(Lyone comes to a sudden halt, startled at an epiphany, capturing Dior and Lisa's attention.)

Lyone: "Champions of Ni? That's what my parents are."

Lisa: "Hmm? Really?"

Lyone: "You don't remember? Those idiots Champions of Ni captured them called my parents that on the televisual!"

Lisa: "You mean the television?"

Lyone: "Yeah, that thing! Remember? That weird lady with the shiny metal hand and that idiot that was talking too much! They called them Champions of Ni!"

Lisa: "It's a bit fuzzy, but yeah, you're right. They did call your parents Champions of Ni."

(As Lisa struggles to remember, Dior conceals his concern, thinking about her condition.)

Dior: *"Darn it. It's best that I stop erasing her memories for some time to let her mind recover. The last thing I need is to scar the record keeper and compromise informa—"*

Lisa: "WAIT A MINUTE!"

(Lisa's sudden outburst catches Lyone and Dior by surprise, frantically commanding their attention.)

Lisa: "That weird lady on the television! Didn't they call her the Liberator?"

Lyone: "So the same Liberator from the past is turning on the people that she helped? Is that what's going on?"

Dior: "That's enough you two."

(Dior sternly voices his intent, getting the party back on task.)

Dior: "I'm sure we all have pressing questions concerning this situation. But right now, we should focus on making it to our next destination. We still have to travel through a valley before reaching the mountain range. Once were there, we're going to set up a long-term camp and begin training. We could also discuss this situation in detail at that time. Agreed?"

Lisa: "Ok."

Lyone: "Fine."

Dior: "Good. Let's keep moving."

(As Lyone and Lisa follow behind Dior, Olivia prepares to dash ahead of the party, stealthily traveling in and out of cover.

Later in the day, the party travels southwest, noticing the terrain, slowly transitioning from a dry desert climate to a windy climate with big hills, tall blades of grass, and scattered rock formations.)

Lisa: "Finally, no more sand."

Dior: "At this point, it should be smooth sailing. We'll be past these hills in less than a day and reach our destination."

Lyone: "I'm just glad we're done fighting desert monsters. They were all so . . . hungry."

Dior: "If I didn't know any better, I'd say you were one of them, Lyone! Ha ha!"

Lyone: "Ha ha! Hey, that's not all the time!"

(Lyone's stomach unexpectedly growls, catching the party's attention, causing everyone to laugh. Suddenly, Dior hears a loud thump, causing the ground to tremble. He instinctively grabs Lyone and Lisa, disappearing in a burst of speed, avoiding a giant monster rampaging past them. The monster crashes into one of the surrounding rock formations, reducing it to dust upon impact. Dior safely reappears, placing the two onto the ground.)

Lisa: "The heck was that?"

(To their surprise, they face a giant four-legged monster, covered in long dark-brown hairs, and a long multi-pointed horn on its snout.)

Dior: "A duiyu? These monsters are usually peaceful. Unless . . ."

(The giant duiyu drags one of its hoofs across the ground, gathering energy into its horn, emitting a powerful glowing aura. Dior quickly slams his hand on the ground in front of the kids, creating a protective dome of glowing black energy, shielding them from combat.)

Dior: "Stay here, you two."

(While they both watch from a distance, Dior steps forward, taking a heroic stand against the duiyu. The duiyu charges forward at full speed, attempting to gore Dior. But, Dior vanishes at a blinding speed, easily avoiding its assault. Unable to stop itself, the duiyu crashes into another rock formation. Dior dexterously reappears, watching the monster closely.)

Dior: "I'm fairly sure that whatever scared you deserves death more than you do, big guy."

(Dior prepares himself, carefully watching the duiyu turns toward him once again.)

Dior: "Ok then, I'll just tire you out and call it a day."

(The duiyu attempts to gore Dior at full speed. However, Dior firmly catches hold of the duiyu's horn. The fierce monster drags Dior a couple dozen feet, stopping with Dior's back inches away from a rock formation.)

Dior: "You're a lot stronger than normal, aren't you big guy?"

(As the duiyu struggles to ram Dior, it blows air out of its snout, causing him to laugh.)

Dior: "No need to fight dirty!"

(While Lisa watches Dior wrestle with the duiyu, Lyone notices something strange crawling in the surrounding tall grass. The strange monster slithers onto the rock formation behind the two opponents, causing Lyone to urgently tap Lisa's shoulder.)

Lyone: "Hey, you see that?"

Lisa: "Huh? See what?"

(Suddenly, they notice a giant yellow serpent with spotted scales slithers onto the top of the rock formation above Dior.)

Lisa: "DAD!"

Lyone: "MR. KENDRIC!"

(Dior quickly looks up, noticing the serpent monster moments away from striking. As the serpent opens its mouth, revealing its large fangs, it pounces towards Dior. Taking control of the struggle with the duiyu, Dior impales the serpent monster through the head, using the duiyu's horn as his weapon. Then, he quickly rolls away to the side, landing onto his feet. The duiyu backs away, shaking the corpse of the serpent off its horn. Suddenly, Dior notices the surrounding tall grass, trembling with more of the serpent monsters slithering around in a coordinated circle. Lyone and Lisa cautiously looks around them, identifying the distinctive spots on the scales of the serpents that resemble leering eyes.)

Lyone: "We're surrounded!"

Lisa: "How many are there?"

(The duiyu frantically throws itself around, expressing its distress with its horn and face stained in blood.)

Dior: "I see. Guess this explains why you're so aggressive. You stumbled into a nest full of lecros."

(In the distance, Olivia watches the battle through the scope of her rifle, perching herself on top a rock formation.)

Olivia: "Alright old man, let's see what you got."

(While the duiyu draws energy into its horn, Dior confidently cracks his neck, preparing for battle. Suddenly, the besieging members of the lecros' nest unleashes a synchronized assault, firing balls of energy out of their scales, slithering through the surrounding tall grass, maintaining their circular formation. Dior easily deflects the energy attacks with a protective barrier. However, the duiyu is pummeled by the energy attacks, enraging the behemoth, causing it to swing its head and unleash a narrow slash of energy from its horn. Dior steps aside, avoiding the retaliatory attack from the duiyu. The attack soars into the tall grass, causing a big explosion, breaking the lecros' formation. As the smoke from the explosion clears, numerous lecros jump out of the grass, attempting to swarm both Dior and the duiyu.

The serpents also pounces upon the protective barrier surrounding Lisa and Lyone.)

Lyone: "So many of them."

(As a wave of lecros' lunges towards him, Dior raises his pointer and middle fingers at his side. In the blink of an eye, he slices through the lecros, easily defeating them with swipes of his fingers. As more of the lecros' lunge at Dior from behind, they are stricken by a sudden gore from the duiyu. The behemoth rampages across the battlefield, wildly attacking everything in its path.

Olivia comfortably holds her position, finger rested on the trigger of her rifle, witnessing Dior slice through hordes of lecros at high speed.)

Olivia: *"Cocky old bird."*

(At the moment, she notices a great monster rising from the tall grass: a giant lecros covered in long standing hairs that changes coloring to blend into the surrounding environment. The border of the monster's mouth is distinctive in its presentation, positioned as a perpetual sinister red smile. It opens its single eye, revealing hypnotizing circles of yellows and pinks, leading to its black vertical pupil.)

Olivia: "*This should be interesting.*"

(The giant lecros' eye glows with energy, commanding the other lecros to reorganize around it, drawing Dior's attention.)

Dior: "Ah, queen of the nest."

(As the queen lecros postures itself to unleash an attack, Dior prepares himself, strengthening the aura around his two fingers.)

Dior: "About time I ended this."

(As Dior prepares to jump toward the group of lecros, the duiyu rampages towards him at full speed, forcing Dior to evade instead, jumping backwards to avoid. In that moment, the queen lecros unleashes a debilitating screech, causing Dior to cover his ears and the duiyu to freeze in pain.)

Dior: "*Not good!*"

(The coordinated group of lecros moves swiftly, constricting the duiyu, covering its body in a ball of death. Another group of lecros executes the same maneuver upon Dior, wrapping his entire body in a giant ball. As Lisa and Lyone helplessly watches, the lecros nest coordinates, squeezing and biting within their balls of death.)

Lisa: "DAD, NO!"

Lyone: "We have to do something!"

(They decide to run out of the protective barrier, amply preparing to fight, naively alerting Olivia.)

Olivia: "Of course. Definitely didn't see this coming."

(Lyone bravely picks up a rock, throwing it at full strength, hitting the queen lecros on the side of its face, anticlimactically causing no damage.)

Lyone: "Crap! We're gonna have to get close!"

Lisa: "Out of the way, Lyone!"

Lyone: "Huh?"

(As Lisa holds a stance, Lyone turns to her, quickly moving aside at the astonishing sight of a chilly blue light glimmering from her hands.)

Lisa: "Let him go, you idiots!"

(Lisa unleashes a magnificent beam of blue energy from her hands, striking the queen lecros in the face, exploding into an icy mist. Suddenly, a dark-orange beam of energy pierce through the cold mist, slamming into the ground in front of Lyone and Lisa, causing an explosion, throwing the two off their feet. The mist of energy disperses, revealing the queen lecros glaring at the two with a glowing eye, commanding the rest of the lecros nest to attack them. Before either of them can climb to their feet, a group of lecros' slithers quickly toward them, preparing to strike.

Suddenly, the sound of distant gunfire rings out across the field, exploding the heads of three of the pursuing lecros. The shock from the gunfire instantly halts their pursuit. While Lyone and Lisa watches with surprise, the lecros are riddled by a siege of bullets, ripping through the nest. Meanwhile, the death ball of lecros encasing Dior's body begins to struggle, expanding from within, losing their grip. Then, the constricting lecros are untangled and thrown aside, revealing an unscathed Dior protected by a black barrier surrounding his body.

As the barrier converts into his Energy Stream, he quickly notices Lyone and Lisa outside of their protective barrier, provoking the queen lecros to unleash another attack.)

Olivia: "Pierce."

(The barrel of Olivia's rifle transforms on command. Suddenly, the party hears gunfire once again, witnessing the queen lecros's head explodes, stopping its attack and ending its life. After the death of the queen lecros, the rest of the lecros nest fall to confusion, attacking each other uncontrollably. Noticing the turning tide of battle, Olivia readies herself to fire another round.)

Olivia: "Incinerate."

(Upon command, Olivia's rifle transforms once again. Next, she launches rounds into the tall grass among the battleground, setting the parties' surroundings ablaze. The rabid lecros nest are alarmed by the sudden inferno, finally scattering about in different directions in their retreat. With a small flame lingering at the end of the barrel, Olivia comfortably removes her finger from the trigger of her rifle.)

Dior: "You two ok?"

Lyone: "Yeah, we're fine."

(Lisa walks up to Dior, passionately punching him in the stomach repeatedly. Surprised by Lisa, he stands in place, unharmed by her strikes.)

Lisa: "THE HECK IS WRONG WITH YOU? YOU COULD HAVE DIED, YOU IDIOT!"

Dior: "Lisa! It's ok! I'm ok!"

(Dior hugs Lisa, stopping her from attacking him further. She sobs in his arms, wrapping her arms around him in response. Lyone sighs with relief at the restored calm. Suddenly, he chokes on his breath, grimly taking notice to the duiyu. The behemoth painfully cries out, laying on the ground in a puddle of blood, covered by fang bites, barely breathing. While they tensely watch, Dior walks over, kneeling next to its head.)

Dior: "You were at the wrong place at the wrong time."

(Dior examines the duiyu's still-bleeding wounds, noticing it visibly becoming weaker by each breath.)

Dior: "Too much blood loss. Time to return to Ni, big guy."

(He firmly grips the duiyu by the horn, briefly reciting a prayer, finally breaking its neck. Afterwards, he stands to his feet, proceeding back to Lyone and Lisa.)

Dior: "Alright, let's get out of here."

Lyone: "Wait, shouldn't we take some meat? They're still fresh."

Dior: "I suppose you're right."

Lyone: "Good. I bet that big one that fired energy at us tastes great."

Dior: "Maybe. But, if you eat that queen lecros, it's gonna be your last meal."

Lyone: "Oh! Is it venomous?"

Dior: "Something like that."

Lisa: "Hey guys, shouldn't we make this quick? It's already nighttime."

(Lyone looks up at the sky, discovering clouds covering the moons. Dior draws a hunting knife, carving meat from the fallen foes.)

Lyone: "All the fighting was pretty distracting."

(Olivia remains at her sniping point with her rifle strapped across her torso, watching the party with her binoculars. After gathering their equipment, they quickly move along past the burning tall grass. Then, Lisa briefly stops, cautiously looking around.)

Lyone: "Something wrong, Lisa?"

Lisa: "Yeah. Remember those loud gunshot noises during the fight?"

Lyone: "Oh yeah, you're right. Where was that coming from?"

Lisa: "I think we're being followed."

Dior: "Hmmm, I'll search for Energy Streams in the area. You two keep a lookout."

Lisa: "Ok."

(With Lyone and Lisa searching their surroundings, Dior closes his eyes for a few seconds, opening them with a concerned expression.)

Lyone: "Did you find anything?"

Dior: "Unfortunately, I didn't. Whoever it was, they're gone now."

Lisa: "Figures. Now what do we do?"

Dior: "We thank Ni we're not dead, keep moving, and find a good camping spot before it gets too late. Agreed?"

Lyone and Lisa: "Ok."

(While Lyone and Lisa leads the party, Dior briefly hangs back, turning in Olivia's direction, giving her a thumbs up. As he runs ahead to catch up with the rest of the party, Olivia gives Dior a middle finger in response.

Later that night, the party sits around a bonfire, eating the food they gathered, partly sheltered within a rock formation. Clouds cover the skies of the rocky hills, voiding it of light from the planet's moons. Lyone swallows some of his food with a big smile on his face, savoring the quality of meat.)

Lyone: "Wow! Who would have thought that fat horned monster tasted so good?"

Lisa: "Yeah, seriously! Even those lecros taste pretty good."

Lyone: "I mean, gum meat is my favorite, but I think we should kill some more of those duiyu!"

(While the two continue their casual conversation, Dior becomes visibly irritated, listening to their manner of speech.)

Lisa: "I don't know, I say the lecros taste better. Plus, the texture isn't as rough."

Lyone: "That's because you roasted your meat too long. Who taught you how to cook again?

Lisa: "Shut up, Li'l L!"

(Lisa playfully pushes Lyone and he returns the gesture, both laughing at each other.)

Lyone: "I'll shut up when you stop calling me that!"

(As they gleefully push each other, they remain unaware of Dior's growing contempt; until he loudly assert his voice.)

Dior: "ENOUGH!"

(Lyone and Lisa freezes, scared silent by Dior's commanding yell. Dior finishes his food, disdainfully staring into the bonfire.)

Dior: "An adult duiyu could grow to be a one thousand, two hundred-pound behemoth, capable of charging at a top speed of fifty miles per hour without the use of its Energy Stream. Somewhere over a hundred with it's Energy Stream, depending on how well the monster's Energy Stream is developed. But, the most interesting fact is just how peaceful they are to other organisms relative to its own evolutionary family."

(Lyone and Lisa remain silent, watching Dior pick up a stick. He throws it into the bonfire, displaying the same enthralled gaze.)

Dior: "The queen lecros is capable of controlling hundreds of lecros through the exchange of body fluids and pheromones during mating, creating a lecros' nest; an entire organic army of serpents coordinating as one, securing prey and protecting themselves from other predators. Tell me, which one of you wanna take a guess at how many times I've seen something, or someone killed because of monsters like these?"

(Their fear renders them tongue-tied, frightfully listening to Dior, noticing his stern voice lowering to emphasize his point.)

Dior: "The number isn't important, but the reasons why they were killed are. These monsters have lived long lives, far beyond the average. And, by the grace of Ni, they have become powerful by surviving through the trials that Ni has placed before them. If you treat them like weaklings, carelessly allowing them the benefit from your obliviousness, they will kill you. Monsters like these are not mere wildlife in their environments. These are battle-hardened warriors. Therefore, you will treat them as such, with respect, with honor, and without mercy. Even in death. Do you two understand me?"

(Loss for words, their eyes hastily shift about, intimidated by Dior's strict demeanor.)

Dior: "SPEAK!"

(They both flinch at Dior's sudden outburst, frightfully bowing with respect.)

Lisa: "I-I understand dad!"

Lyone: "Yes, Mr. Kendric!"

Dior: "Good. Now, finish your meals and call it a night. We've a long day ahead of us."

(While Dior shift his attention back to the bonfire, Lyone and Lisa silently continue their meals. Feeling the urge to say something, Lyone decides to speak.)

Lyone: "They don't care about respect and honor, you know."

(Upon hearing Lyone's voice, Dior slowly turn towards him, silencing him with a penetrating leer. Lyone stares back at him, clenching his plate of food, trying to control his nervousness. Lisa keeps her head slightly slanted to the ground, shockingly observing Lyone out of the corner of her eyes.)

Lyone: "It's the truth. If there is anything my parents taught me about survival on Ni, it's about survival of the fittest. Monsters aren't going to show us honor, or respect, or pray for us when we're dead. And neither will Ni."

Lisa: "But, Ni blesses us, remem—"

(Dior raises his clutched fist, instantly silencing Lisa. Suddenly, a powerful black aura surrounds Dior's body, causing Lyone to drop his food on the ground, falling to his hands and knees. Lisa remains silent and seated, watching Lyone struggle.)

Lyone: <in Huadi> "What the . . .?"

(Dior rises to his feet, folding his arms behind his back, patiently walking over to Lyone. With each of Dior's steps, Lyone feels more pressure onto his body, struggling harder to remain on his hands and knees.)

Dior: "Remember imperial force, Lyone? This is what it feels like when you're under the influence."

(He steps directly in front of Lyone, grabbing him by the shirt, lifting him up to eye level.)

Dior: "The reason you should treat other organisms with respect and honor is because, unlike certain opponents of any kind or creed that knows nothing of these qualities, when we have the power to bring them to their knees, we solidify the principles which sets us apart from them; by the grace of Ni, the righteous discretion that guides our swords. If they live or die, either occurs by the hands of the righteous."

(Dior withdraws his Energy Stream, indifferently dropping Lyone onto the ground. Crawling onto his hands and knees, Lyone remains silent, catching his breath. Afterwards, Dior turns to Lisa, watching her fearfully stare at the struggling Lyone.)

Dior: "We should all get some rest, Lisa."

(Lisa flinches upon hearing her name, quickly turning her attention to Dior, nervously nodding in agreement.)

Lisa: "O-Ok."

Dior: "Good. Finish your meal. I'll gather all the waste."

(She follows his command, finishing her food in silence. While Lyone tiredly lies on the ground, Dior walks by, gathering Lyone's fallen dinner in a bag of waste. Later that night, Dior holds a conversation on the phone with Jel outside his tent, slowly pacing back and forth.)

Dior: "The move is going well?"

Jel: "Yes, I've already had help from some of my aides from work. There is still a lot of preparation that needs to be done. But don't worry. It's all easy enough."

Dior: "Good. That's good to hear."

(As Dior continues his conversation, Lisa crawls to the front of her tent, secretly listening to Dior's voice.)

Dior: "No, everything's going well. Lisa is just having a bit trouble putting life on Ni into perspective."

Jel: "I see. What exactly is it that she is having trouble with?"

Dior: "How powerless and naive she truly is. Not too long ago, we got into a situation with monsters far stronger than average."

Jel: "Did something happen to her?"

Dior: "Luckily, we made it out alive and without a scratch."

Jel: "Hmm, there's more to this, right?"

Dior: "Right. I believe she is taking the privilege of not having to engage these threats for granted. She also has a problem with showing honor and respect to her opponents; Ni especially."

(After hearing Dior's words, Lisa lowers her head in shame, angerly balling her fist. Consequently, she crawls back into her sleeping bag, forcing herself to sleep.)

Dior: "I'm not too alarmed though. I have faith she'll realize that there is power in being benevolent within your intent; even if that means taking a life."

(At the Kendric family home, Jel stands in her study on the phone. Suddenly, a hand set on Jel's left shoulder. She calmly looks over her shoulder, responding with a nod, continuing the conversation with Dior.)

Jel: "So, how's Lyone?"

(Upon hearing Lyone's name, Dior abruptly halts, momentarily pausing with suspicion.)

Dior: "Lyone?"

Jel: "Yes, dear. Our visitor. He is still traveling with you now, right?"

Dior: "Of course not. He is back with his tribe. I thought I told you about this?"

Jel: "Ah, I see. Don't mind me. I've been a bit more forgetful than usual, ha ha."

Dior: "I see. Don't push yourself harder than you need to, dear."

Jel: "No, don't worry about me. I'll be fine. So, you mentioned a tribe?"

Dior: "Yes. The kid was a part of a nomadic Paration tribe I knew from a long time ago. They were traveling through the southern part of the Yellow Shadow Forest last I checked. Don't know where they are now, but they seemed safe enough."

Jel: "Ah, yes. Now I remember. Thank you, dear."

Dior: "No problem. Well, I better go and get some rest. You get some rest as well, ok?"

Jel: "Of course, dear. Thank you."

Dior: "Goodnight then. I love you."

Jel: "I love you, too."

(Dior hangs up his phone, worriedly folding his arms in silence. At the Kendric family home, Jel hangs up her phone, drinking water from a cup, cautiously observing officers in uniform step out of the room.

The next morning before dawn at the camp, Lisa and Dior prepare themselves for morning training. Once Lisa finishes her stretching routines, Dior rises from his meditation, cracking his neck and wrist.)

Dior: "About ready?"

Lisa: "Yeah."

(As Dior holds his palms open in a defensive stance, Lisa raises her fist to eye level, readying her strike. She charges forward, attacking with a quick right-left jab combo. Dior easily blocks both strikes, countering with a left hook. She ducks under his attack, countering by kicking to Dior's left. He blocks, pushing away Lisa's leg. But, she utilizes the momentum, spinning into a sweep kick from Dior's right. He jumps over Lisa's attack, attempting to counter with a quick palm strike. However, she rolls away, intuitively evading his attack, hopping back onto her feet, fluidly resuming her stance. Thinking about her approach, Dior notices her anxiousness, becoming concerned.)

Dior: "Hmm, you seem a bit—"

(Lisa's Energy Stream erupts into a cool light-blue aura, furiously enveloping her body. She launches herself toward Dior, throwing a strong right punch. Easily blocking her strike with his open palm, he feels the strength of the hit throughout his body, becoming impressed. Suddenly, Lisa floats in the air at eye level with Dior, repeatedly punching his palms in quick left-right successions with energy flaring upon every impact.)

Dior: *"Hmm, what's gotten into her?"*

(Lisa kicks towards Dior's head. He blocks the attack, noticing a following left knee strike. He skillfully blocks her knee strike with his palms, pushing her away. Lisa lands onto her feet, immediately assuming a stance. Next, she begin to gather a large amount of energy, visibly drawing from the surrounding environment, vehemently directing the energy into the space between the palms of her hands.)

Dior: "LISA!"

(Dior breaks Lisa's focus, slowly shaking his head from side to side in disapproval, displaying a piercing glare. Lisa reluctantly eases her tension, carefully releasing the energy back into the surrounding environment. As Yunyi rises across the horizon, Lisa withdraws her Energy Stream, respectfully bowing to Dior, hiding her anger. Dior quietly walks over to her, worriedly kneeling to eye level, speaking to her with care.)

Dior: "Hey, what's gotten into you? Don't tell me you're still mad at me from before."

Lisa: "I didn't know you were still mad at me."

Dior: "What? Why would I be mad at you?"

(Lisa irately fold her arms, resentfully turning away. Dior smiles, placing his hands on her shoulders, attempting to comfort her.)

Dior: "Lisa, come on, don't be like that."

Lisa: "I heard you talking about me last night."

Dior: "Huh? What do you mean?"

(Lisa rolls her eyes at Dior's cluelessness, irritably turning her attention to him.)

Lisa: "I heard you talking on your smartphone."

Dior: "You must have been dreaming or something, ha ha! I didn't talk on a portable communicator last night."

Lisa: "Dad, why you always lying like that? I saw you last night! And stop calling it a 'portable communicator.' I know a smartphone when I see one."

(As she sharply stares at him, Dior laughs nervously, rubbing the back of his head.)

Dior: "*Darn, got a bit careless last night.* Alright, Alright. I'll explain. But promise to keep this between us, ok?"

Lisa: "I'm listening."

(After he cautiously glances over to Lyone's tent, he continues the conversation with Lisa, lowering his voice.)

Dior: <whispering> "Last night on the phone, I was talking to your mother."

Lisa: "So, that was Mom, huh?"

Dior: <whispering> "Shhhh! Whisper, Lisa."

Lisa: <whispering> "But why are we whispering?"

Dior: <whispering> "I'm getting to it. So, right now, your mom is being investigated by Arbitrators."

Lisa: <whispering> "What? But why? What did she do?"

Dior: <whispering> "They suspect that we were helping unauthorized personnel."

Lisa: <whispering> "'Unauthorized personnel?' You mean Lyone? But, Lyone didn't do anything wrong!"

Dior <whispering> "Doesn't matter. If we mention that Lyone is traveling with us when talking to your mom, there's a chance she could get indicted. So, instead of using Lyone's name when we're talking about him—"

Lisa: <whispering> "—you use my name instead."

Dior: <whispering> "Exactly. We weren't talking about you. We were talking about Lyone."

Lisa: <whispering> "Yeah, I guess that makes sense."

Dior: <whispering> "Glad we're on the same page. But remember, keep this between us. Lyone doesn't need to know this."

Lisa: <whispering> "Ok, but, will Mom be ok?"

Dior: <whispering> "Don't worry so much. Your mother knows better than anyone about handling herself in situations like this."

Lisa: <whispering> "Ok, then. Why are you still worried, then?"

(Dior momentarily pauses, firmly standing tall on his feet, sternly posturing himself.)

Dior: "What are you talking about? I'm not nervous. I know your mom is going to be fine."

Lisa: "I know you, Dad. You get all sly and schemey when you're nervous."

Dior: "What? I'm not THAT secretive when I'm nervous. That's just me being professional, ha ha!"

(Lisa remains unconvinced, sassily staring through his facade.)

Dior: "Ha ha, that obvious, eh?"

Lisa: "Well, whatever it is, as long as Mom is safe, we can handle things here."

Dior: "You think so?"

Lisa: "Of course! You have me and Lyone to watch your back!"

Lyone: "Hey!"

(As they're alerted to Lyone's presence, Lyone walks out of his tent, yawning and stretching.)

Lyone: "I heard my name. Is it breakfast time?"

Lisa: "Of course food is the first thing on your brain, Li'l L."

(Lisa looks towards Dior, noticing his stern gaze directed toward Lyone. She cheerfully smiles, deciding to break his focus with a question.)

Lisa: "One more thing, Dad."

Dior: "Hm?"

Lisa: "Ni is also with us, right? With these odds, we can't lose. Ni'Ador!"

Dior: "Ha ha! Ni'Ador, sweetheart!"

(He smiles with relief, lovingly watching Lisa wave at him while she walks toward Lyone.)

Dior: *"Ni is with us more than you know, Lisa. Let's hope you're right."*

(Once she walks over to Lyone, she playfully covers her nose, joking with a mocking tone.)

Lisa: "Eww! Li'l L, ya breath so hot, you need to gargle a fire extinguisher."

Lyone: "I just woke up, so shut up! That joke was lame anyway!"

Lisa: "Your breath is so funky, your tongue emits disco lights."

Lyone: "Laaame!"

Lisa: "Your breath is soooo musty, you could mold a loaf of bread by saying 'hello.'"

Lyone: "Laaaaaaame!"

(Dior cheerfully chuckles to himself, watching the two make fun of each other.

Later that morning, Olivia spies on the party through her binoculars, crouching in the distance, watching them prepare to traverse the valley. Her earpiece buzzes and she quickly answers the call.)

Idol: "Major."

Olivia: "General, sir!"

Idol: "Your report."

Olivia: "Sir! If they were any doubt before, it seems I've been recruited to Dior's party. I ended up covering them against a lecros' nest yesterday."

Idol: "That sounds fun. Did you see him in action?"

Olivia: "Sir, he survived a lecros' nest's death ball without a scratch. I could even tell he was holding back."

Idol: "Holding back, eh? Sounds like civilian life made him soft. Then again, monsters like those aren't that much of a challenge at his level of combat. Anyway, what's your current situation, major?"

Olivia: "Sir, Dior's party is currently finishing preparations to traverse the newly discovered plain A02-S."

Idol: "No need to refer to the newly discovered areas by their registry IDs anymore. Their names have been ratified."

Olivia: "Interesting. Do all the names ratified originate from Dior and his daughter Lisa?"

Dior: "Yes. The Yellow Shadow Forest, the Kipi Family Desert, Valley of Hondra's Breath, and the Hoviros Mountain Range."

Olivia: "'Valley of Hondra's Breath,' huh? That one must have been named by Dior as a tribute to the ancient Cerarian gods."

Idol: "I'd say so, considering it's been tens of thousands of years since those names have even been uttered by common folk. Even most elites don't know the entirety of the ancient Cerarian gods. But, I did hear that once they researched the name and found out what it meant, a significant portion of the World Discovery Committee took offense. They even voted against it. But the Wyvern's Den overruled their objections seven to one, citing the Adventurer's Guild Pact. Needless to say, many of the religious types in our ranks aren't too flattered by the decision."

Olivia: "Sir, seven to one? Which judge was the one?"

Idol: "Isn't it obvious? Judge Iredowan. He is the most religious of them all, of course."

Olivia: "Bet you could cut the tension with a knife."

Idol: "Yeah, well, let's hope it's just tension that's getting cut."

(As Olivia continues her conversation, she notices the party moving forward on their path.)

Olivia: "Sir, the target is on the move."

Idol: "One last thing before you take off, major. At the present, the Federal Union is conducting scouting missions in that area along with escorts from the Adventurer's Guild. They'll be there for an extended period of time gathering intel about the area."

Olivia: "Sir, I'll make sure to stay with the target at all times and avoid detection unless necessary."

Idol: "Good. Up to you now, major."

Olivia: "Sir!"

(She cuts off communications, placing her set of binoculars away into her bag. Then, she takes a firm grip on her rifle case, dashing forward in a burst of speed.

As midday arrives, Dior scans the area with his eyes, following closely behind Lisa and Lyone. Lisa is astonished by the bustling ecosystem, looking around at the many different species of wildlife freely grazing around them.)

Lisa: "Wow, this place is even livelier in the winter!"

Dior: "Seems many of the predators in this area went missing. Maybe they're in hibernation?"

Lisa: "Or maybe they moved to a warmer climate for the winter?"

Dior: "That's a good observation, Lisa. Too bad we don't have enough time to search for clues to support that hypothesis."

Lisa: "I don't know about you, Dad, but I think it'd be fun to solve a mystery like that!"

Dior: "Ha ha! Well, if that isn't a sign of a great adventurer, then I don't know what is!"

(Dior and Lisa shares a laugh, continuing their conversation. Although, Lyone remains quiet, reflecting upon the argument with Dior during dinner last night. The clouds in the sky move away from Yunyi, revealing metals within the surrounding rock formations that reflects the daylight. The party observes in awe, gazing upon the reflections of light.)

Lisa: "Whoa, what is that sparkling in the rocks?"

Dior: "Don't know. If I had to guess, I'd say some pretty rare metals, maybe?"

Lisa: "Hey, Lyone! You see those?"

Lyone: "Yeah. It's pretty cool."

Lisa: "Let's go look at one of them up close!"

Lyone: "What? No! Do you not see all these monsters around us?"

Dior: "Actually Lyone, most of the monster species that live in this valley are pretty peaceful."

(Dior and Lisa stops next to one of the rock formations, examining the shining materials. Meanwhile, Lyone keeps a keen eye on the passing monsters. Suddenly, Lyone gawks at the sight of a giant monster with a long neck and long legs, casually striding over the party.)

Lyone: "How are you so sure we're safe?"

Dior: "Because, conditions are not as harsh as they were before we found you."

Lyone: "This place was different before?"

Dior: "Yup. When we were here before, this place was pretty dangerous. So much so that I had to run through this area carrying Lisa, and another time carrying you and Lisa, ha ha!"

Lyone: "And it's not as dangerous now?"

Lisa: "Not even close! You should have seen it! There were these crazy dark clouds covering the whole sky, lightning was striking everywhere, and I thought I saw something flying above us as we were running away!"

Dior: "Oh you definitely saw something, Lisa."

Lyone: "What was it?"

Dior: "It was a pterior. Kin to the Iai species of monster, their bodies are big and spherical, typically covered in hair with many antennas all over their bodies. One of the amazing things about this species is its ability to use its Energy Stream to convert energy into element from birth. The pterior have evolved to use that ability to float. Otherwise, they'd just be immobile blobs of flesh."

(As Lisa and Lyone consider the frightening thought of a pterior, Dior casually touches the shining metals in the rocks.)

Lisa: "Umm, THAT was chasing us?"

Lyone: "How did you not even remember how THAT looked? It sounds like a living nightmare!"

Dior: "Well, she couldn't see it."

Lyone: "What do you mean?"

Dior: "I was assessing its abilities as we retreated. That particular pterior that sieged us was far stronger than most. It also seemed to have the ability to use its Energy Stream to blend into the surrounding environment."

Lyone: "So, a giant, fat, invisible fur ball with antennas all over it, that floats."

Dior: "And shoots lightning."

(While Dior stand to his feet, Lisa and Lyone look at each other, awkwardly standing silent in their fear.)

Lisa: "Lyone, I'm starting to see your point about kids being out here."

Dior: "Ha ha! Don't worry so much, you two! It's not like I'm going anywhere. If we stick together, we'll be fine."

Lisa: "Agreed."

Lyone: "Yeah."

Dior: "Alright then, let's keep going."

(Dior cheerfully paces along their path, leading in front of the hyperaware Lyone and Lisa. Thirty minutes later, the party hikes past trees and bushes, heading to the top of a steep hill.)

Lisa: "Hey, once we get to the top, can we have lunch?"

Dior: "Sure. I can cut up some of the fruit I found."

Lisa: <Imitating Dior> "'Remember to wash your fruit and check for worms and parasites, Lisa.'"

Dior: "Who was THAT supposed to be?"

Lisa: "The only person I know who has an adventurer's tip for almost everything, ha ha!"

Dior: "Sounds like a wise person! You should listen to him more often and . . ."

(Dior dramatically turns to Lisa, sporting a mocking smirk.)

Dior: <imitating Lisa> "Stop being a hater."

Lisa: "Shut up, Dad! I don't sound like that! Ha ha!"

Dior: <imitating Lisa> "Stay mad, girl! Stay mad!"

Lisa: "Oh my god, shut up! Ha ha!"

(While Dior and Lisa hysterically laugh, Lyone abruptly stops, analytically staring at the ground. He kneels next to a set of footprints, vigilantly discerning distinctive attributes from them.)

Lyone: *"These are no monster footprints. And they're fresh."*

Voice: "HALT!"

(Lisa and Dior are stopped by a group of four soldiers. Lyone reacts almost instantly, hiding behind a group of bushes, undetected. Peeking from cover, he notices the soldiers wearing lightly armored camouflage gear, armed with high tech semi-automatic rifles and earpiece communicators.)

Federal Union Scout #1: "Stop right there, you two."

Dior: "Ahh, I didn't know the Federal Union Scouts made it this far!"

(The soldiers walk closer, pausing with surprise, recognizing Dior and Lisa.)

Federal Union Scout #2: "Mr. Kendric? Is that you?"

Federal Union Scout #3: "Holy crap, it is him!"

Federal Union Scout #4: "The rest of the squad isn't going to believe this, ha ha!"

Federal Union Scout #1: "Alright, men, fall in line."

Federal Union Scout #2, 3, and 4: "Sir!"

(Federal Union Scout #1 takes a few steps closer to Dior and Lisa. Dior takes a good look at the equipment of the soldier, hiding his concern.)

Dior: *"Hard to discern the height of their technology. Something's not right."*

Federal Union Scout #1: "We weren't informed that you two would be traveling through this area."

Dior: "That's weird. I officially filled out paperwork with the Adventurer's Guild a while ago for this expedition. I'm taking Lisa on a training quest. If she's going to take over when I'm gone, it's time that she starts leading the way."

Federal Union Scout #1: "Training, huh? That makes sense."

(Federal Union Scout #1 turns to his squad, giving Dior an opportunity to communicate with Lyone through telepathy.)

Dior: *"Lyone."*

(Lyone is startled by Dior's voice in his mind.)

Lyone: *"Mr. Kendric? Is that you?"*

Dior: *"We don't have much time to talk like this before these soldiers notice the change in my Energy Stream, so listen carefully. You see that large rock formation to the west?"*

(Lyone peers over to the west, noticing the mentioned rock formation, twinkling with the shining metals found in the region.)

Lyone: "*Yeah.*"

Dior: "*Hide there and wait for us. This may take a while but trust me. We'll be there.*"

Lyone: "*Ok then.*"

(Lyone cautiously takes a quick look at his surroundings, clearing his path. Afterwards, he moves towards the west in stealth. Olivia watches the situation from afar through her binoculars, quickly moving to keep an eye on Lyone. While the group of soldiers speak amongst themselves, Dior places his hand on Lisa's shoulder, capturing her attention. He secretly mouthed the words "He's ok", causing Lisa to carefully respond with a relieved nod.)

Federal Union Scout #1: "And make sure the monsters from earlier are in the report as well!"

Federal Union Scout #3: "Sir!"

Federal Union Scout #2: "Sir, by the way, it's already approaching early evening hours."

Federal Union Scout #1: "Already? Darn, time flies around here."

Federal Union Scout #4: "Maybe it's because we're busy trying not to get killed, eh? Ha ha!"

Dior: "Take it from me, that definitely helps, ha ha!"

Federal Union Scout #1: "Guess we better get back to the encampment."

(Federal Union Scout #1 touches his earpiece, opening communications with HQ.)

Federal Union Scout #1: "HQ, this is Squad 4. We're on our way back to camp . . . understood. Also, we've run into some company during patrol. It's Dior Kendric and his daughter, Lisa Kendric . . . they say they're camping and training . . . yup. More or less free roaming, believe it or not . . . ok, then. Understood."

(Federal Union Scout #1 cuts communication on his earpiece, sternly turning towards Dior and Lisa.)

Federal Union Scout #1: "Mr. Kendric, command would like a word with you, if you have a moment."

Dior: "Not like we can say no, eh? Ha ha!"

Federal Union Scout #1: "Well, you can. But, you know how that goes."

Dior: "Indeed I do. Alright then, do you mind if I talk to my daughter for a second and prepare her for command's audience?"

Federal Union Scout #1: "Sure. That's pretty smart, actually. Wouldn't want the kid to speak out of turn."

(Federal Union Scout #1 turns back to his party, allowing Dior and Lisa to walk a short distance away to talk.)

Lisa: <whispering> "He's ok?"

Dior: <whispering> "Yeah. You see that rock formation to the west?"

(Lisa casually looks to the west, noticing the target area.)

Dior: <whispering> "We'll meet him there later. Ok?"

(After Lisa confidently nods, they walk back to the group of soldiers.)

Dior: "Alright, we're ready to roll."

Federal Union Scout #1: "Good. Let's get moving."

(The squad of soldiers lead the way forward, with Dior and Lisa following closely behind them.)

Federal Union Scout #4: "Hey, Mr. Kendric, is it true that you defeated a giant flying fish monster?"

Dior: "You mean that time we were exploring Lake Celodad? You know, Lisa was the one that hooked that sui while we were fishing."

Federal Union Scout #3: "You're kidding!"

Lisa: "Ha ha, I actually thought it was just gonna be another boring fish to catch."

Federal Union Scout #4: "Incredible! A little girl surviving a battle with a monster of THAT caliber!"

Lisa: "Well, Dad did most of the butt kicking, but I made sure to stay out of the way and cause distractions, at least. Ha ha!"

Dior: "If anything, we ate well that night. I could go for some golden glazed sui right now, ha ha!"

Lisa: "Now I'm hungry to, ha ha!"

Federal Union Scout #2: "These two are unreal."

Federal Union Scout #1: "Hey, let's focus on getting back alive, guys. You'll have plenty of time to kiss their butts at HQ."

Federal Union Scout #2, 3 and 4: "Sir!"

(Lisa's and Dior's eyes are glued to the large western rock formation, following the soldiers to the Federal Union Encampment.)

Lisa: *"Be careful, Lyone."*

(Meanwhile, Lyone arrives at the western rock formation, staying within cover, hyperaware of his surroundings. Olivia positions herself on a nearby hill shaded by trees. With the aid of her cylinder cloaking devices, she remains undetected, stalking Lyone without the aid of her binoculars.)

Olivia: *"There's a lot of scouts in the area. Can't risk getting caught due to the glare from my binoculars. I'll just have to stay reasonably close."*

Lyone: *"Alright, just gotta stay here and stay out of sight. Hope they're not in trouble. Didn't seem like it."*

(Minutes later, Dior and Lisa are led by the four scouting soldiers into a large campground filled with warriors. From the crowd, Federal Union Soldiers can be identified by their uniforms and the abundance of Huma Men in their ranks. The other warriors of another group all wear different types of armor, bearing the same crest, with a mixture of both Beast and Huma among their ranks. Many gather around numerous tents offering weapons, armor, and other assortments. Dior becomes increasingly concerned, noticing the Federal Union soldiers specifically sporting high-tech equipment and weapons; which are unavailable at the weapons and armor tents.)

Dior: *"Where are they getting this level of technology?"*

(Lisa looks closely at the tents, crests on the warrior's armor, and the flying banners, noticing the same insignia of a nearly opened door decorated with vegetation and small wildlife.)

Lisa: "The Federal Union Adventurer's Guild?"

(As the two travel through the encampment, Dior briefly locks eyes with numerous soldiers and guild members, staring back at him with looks of admiration. Then, he turns away, focusing on the path through the crowd.)

Dior: "Interesting. I didn't know there was an operation underway here."

Voice: "Information has been withheld at the request of our employers."

(Lisa and Dior turn to the voice, noticing a short stout man, with long light-brown hair, and a thick beard. He carries a sword as large as himself, strapped around his shoulders in its even-larger sheath.)

Lisa: "Alex! I-I mean, Guild Master Bale! Been a long time!"

Alex: "Dior! Lisa! Nice to see you two are as active as ever, ha ha!"

Dior: "You're here as well, Alex?"

Alex: "This is a top priority assignment that I put my best men on. Would be a waste to stay out of this one and lead from a desk."

Dior: "I see. You said you were hired?"

Alex: "Yes. We're hired as reinforcements for the Southern Federal Union Expansion Forces."

Federal Union Scout #1: "Mr. Kendric, Lieutenant General Iesom would like to have a word with you in the Federal Union command tent."

Dior: "Caime is here as well? This must be one heck of an operation then, eh?"

Alex: "You'll learn all you need to know from him. Come, I'll accompany you both."

Lisa: "Nice!"

(Lisa runs towards Alex, giving him a high-five. Then, the three walk together toward their destination, following the squad of soldiers. Upon reaching the Federal Union command tent, the four scouting soldiers salutes and bid their farewell.)

Federal Union Scout #1: "Mr. Kendric, Guild Master Bale, this is as far as we go."

(While Dior and Alex return salutes, Lisa stands by with her arms folded, hiding her disgruntled attitude.)

Lisa: *"I'm right here too you know."*

Dior: "We appreciate the escort, gentlemen. Before we depart, may I ask your names?"

Voice: "That can wait 'til another time, Dior."

(Their attention is captured by a tall slim man, wearing a red-and-black Federal Union uniform, decorated with medals. The commanding soldier steps from the Federal Union command tent, along with escorting soldiers.)

Dior: "Lieutenant General Iesom."

(Caime steps forward with his two guards at his side, saluting the four scouts.)

Caime: "You're dismissed, men."

Federal Union Scout #1, 2, 3, and 4: "Sir!"

(As the four scouts take their leave, Dior and Alex greet Caime with salutes. Lisa continues to stand with her arms folded, pretending to be patient.)

Dior: "Lieutenant General Iesom, been a long time, sir."

Caime: "At ease, the both of you. We have matters to discuss. Follow me."

(Dior and Alex relaxes, following Caime into the command tent along with his guards. Lisa casually walk behind them, aloofly yawning. Caime comes to a sudden stop at the entrance, looking back over his shoulder at Lisa.)

Caime: "Authorized personnel only, Dior."

Lisa: "Huh? Who? Me?"

(Dior pauses, turning his attention to Lisa.)

Dior: "Lisa, stay here for now. I'll return shortly. Ok?"

(Lisa folds her arms, sighing with frustration.)

Lisa: "Fine."

Dior: "Also, seriously, don't wander off."

Lisa: "Ok, ok. I got it."

Dior: "Alright then."

(The group enters the command tent leaving Lisa behind. As Caime's guards remain standing outside the tent's entrance, she rolls her eyes in response. Inside the tent is a strategy table surrounded by five individuals; two of which are arguing with one another.)

Strategist #1: "We can continue the search at the edge of that perimeter. But, that's as far as the men are going without backup and adequate supplies."

Strategist #2: "Which is more than likely going to be too late by the time we have that capability. Are we trying to save our scout or leave him for dead?"

Strategist #1: "Either way, we're here under orders. We can't just break rank as we see fit, Usifkov."

Usifkov: "I know that, Gregory! But time is not on our—"

Caime: "That's enough, you two. If there's any blood to be spilled, it'll be that of the beast responsible."

(Usifkov, Gregory, and the three other people around the strategy table shifts their attention to Caime and his guest. The five quickly settle their sights on Alex and Dior.)

Caime: "I've brought someone that may be able to help us in our predicament."

(Dior steps forward to the strategy table and offers a salute.)

Dior: "My name is Dior Kendric. I'm a freelance adventurer of the Federal Union's Adventurer's Guild."

Gregory: "At ease, Dior. I'm sure we all know who you are."

(Dior relaxes his stance, folding his arms behind his back, waiting for the group to continue.)

Gregory: "I'm Colonel Gregory Dayton of the Federal Union Southern Forces."

Usifkov: "Colonel Usifkov Akive, Southern Forces."

Medical Personnel: "Francesco Amaida, lieutenant of the medicinal unit of the Southern Forces."

Researcher: "Lieutenant Xia Yu of geological research, southern forces."

Tactician: "My name is Peter Howl, lieutenant of the southern division: strategy and tactics."

Dior: "A pleasure to meet you all. Now, someone mind filling me in?"

Caime: "Certainly."

(Caime steps forward, placing his hand on the sphere-shaped object at the front of the strategy table. Next, he focuses his Energy Stream, directing energy into the sphere. The table shines with energy, surprising Dior and Alex with its sophistication. The energy injected into the sphere spreads across the tent, transforming the affected area into a large projection space.)

Caime: "At o-nine hundred hours yesterday, a member of Federal Union Scouting Squad Six went missing in action. We need your help getting him back."

(A holographic soldier appears next to Dior and salutes.)

Caime: "This is the target, according to my last memory of him, Private Ericsson Bradshaw. He was last seen on scouting duty in the eastern part of the Valley of Hondra's Breath."

(As Caime continues the briefing, a large map of the area appears in the middle of the group. Dior's eyes are directed to a glowing blip on the map, marking the area the missing soldier was sent to.)

Dior: "Hmm, if I was a betting man, I'd wager the target is in that nearby swamp to the east."

Usifkov: "That's exactly what I was saying! We should have a team at least scout the swamp."

Gregory: "Not only will they be heading into an unexplored area, but our supply route to this location still hasn't been fully established."

Peter: "I have to agree with Gregory. According to reports I'm receiving from the main army, they're establishing the supply route very quickly thanks to our new technology. But it's still going to take a few more days to pave a sustainable route through the Kipi Family Desert."

Dior: "A few days through that desert? That's actually very fast assuming this camp was established fairly recently."

Usifkov: "That may be so, but the target has already been captured for over twenty-four hours. We can't risk waiting much longer!"

Dior: "Captured, you say?"

(Dior momentarily pauses, suspiciously eyeing everyone in the room.)

Dior: "There's something you guys aren't telling me."

Caime: "It's true that we believe the target has been captured. If this is true, he is more than likely being held captive by the survivors of the beast and monster forces that held the meadow region south of the Federal Union."

Dior: "The survivors that fled the invasion, eh?"

Caime: "This brings us to the second objective. We need you to locate the enemy's stronghold in this region and report back with the coordinates. The sooner the better."

Dior: "And what will be the compensation for this task?"

Caime: "Family prestige will be awarded upon saving the target or confirming his death. Family prestige will also be awarded for scouting the area and identifying the enemy camp."

Dior: "Hmm. I'll do this under two conditions: first, I'm going to need a contract written up including mission details, conditions, compensation details, and collateral compensation to my family if I die. Second, I'm going to need supplies and all the information you can give me about that area as of today."

(Caime pauses, staring at Dior, observing him return an unwavering glare of his own.)

Caime: "I can make sure that a contract is drawn up Dior. However, this is a secret operation. We'll be withholding certain details in the written version."

Dior: "Details like?"

Caime: "Your deeds in aiding our forces and the compensation details, including collateral, will be written. That's all I can guarantee."

(As Alex watches Dior out of the corner of his eyes, Dior breaks the tension with a confident smile.)

Dior: "Ok then. Supplies and information is all I need now."

Caime: "Done. Peter, get him outfitted with the supplies and information necessary."

Peter: "Sir!"

(Peter makes his way towards the entrance of the command tent, stopping beside Dior and Alex.)

Peter: "This way, please."

(While Peter lead their way, Dior and Alex briefly speaks to each other through telepathy.)

Alex: *"Still the savvy negotiator I see."*

Dior: *"Gotta keep those skills sharp somehow."*

Alex: *"Even though you know they're purposely scrubbing this mission from the record, you still ask for a written contract. You're something else Dior."*

Dior: *"Never start from a position of weakness Alex. You know the drill."*

Alex: *"That I do."*

(Dior, Alex, and Peter exit the tent, meeting a bored Lisa. She practices her combat stances until she notices the group.)

Lisa: "About time!"

Dior: "Follow us, Lisa."

Lisa: "Where to?"

Dior: "Good question."

Peter: "Just follow me. I'll lead the way."

(Meanwhile, Olivia remains in cover at the top of a hill, watching over Lyone from a distance. Lyone hides within the large rock formation, awaiting the arrival of the rest of his party.)

Lyone: "*I hope I don't have to stay here overnight. As peaceful as it is now, that could change in a heartbeat.*"

(As Lyone sits silently, he hears the sudden chatter of a group of soldiers, moving towards his location. He urgently jumps to his feet, placing his back to the side of rocks.)

Federal Union Scout #5: "Report."

Federal Union Scout #6: "All clear on the east side."

Federal Union Scout #7: "Same for the west. The monsters in this area are pretty tame in the daytime."

Federal Union Scout #5: "Good. I'll call it in and we'll head back."

Federal Union Scout #7: "Ya' know, I wonder why Dior named this place Hondra's Breath."

Federal Union Scout #6: "Maybe it was his daughter's idea?"

Federal Union Scout #7: "Nah! Why would she know about an ancient Cerarian god? We had to dig through a lot of books to even know who the heck that is."

Federal Union Scout #6: "Who knows? Maybe his daughter is an alien clone from the past or some crap?"

(Federal Union Scout #7 pauses, giving Federal Union Scout #6 a sharp stare, prompting Federal Union Scout #6 to respond with a shrug.)

Federal Union Scout #7: "Have you been smokin' my stash man?"

Federal Union Scout #6: "I swear I haven't touched it since last night."

Federal Union Scout #7: "Bruh, on my momma, my stash better be there when we get back!"

(Lyone grows anxious the longer the soldiers linger. Suddenly, He slips on gravel below his feet, causing a sound loud enough to alert the two conversing soldiers.)

Federal Union Scout #6: "Did you hear that?"

Federal Union Scout #7: "Yeah."

(As the soldiers point their weapons in Lyone's direction, he remains hidden behind the cover of rocks, nervously covering his mouth.)

Lyone: *"Crap, I think they heard that."*

(Olivia quickly devises a plan to aid Lyone, readying her high-tech sniper rifle, tensely aiming towards the approaching soldiers.)

Olivia: <whispering> "Silent Mode: Distraction."

(Olivia's rifle transforms on command. Next, she fires a silenced round, hitting the ground a few yards away from the group of soldiers. Suddenly, the round emits a hi-pitched chirping noise, drawing the attention of all the soldiers.)

Federal Union Scout #5: "Hold up, command, something just came up."

(Federal Union Scout #5 turns off his earpiece, immediately drawing his weapon.)

Federal Union Scout #5: "Hey, what's going on?"

Federal Union Scout #6: "We don't know! That sound just started!"

(Suddenly, the entire rock formation begins to tremble, throwing the squad of soldiers off balance.)

Lyone: <in Huadi> *"What the heck?"*

(While Lyone struggles to keep his balance, Olivia places her rifle away, preparing to rescue him. But, a sudden sandstorm violently whips into the air around the rock formation, forcing her to take cover. The rock formation begins to rise, causing a massive tremor and sandstorm throughout the area, revealing a giant tortoise like monster hidden beneath the valley's ground. At the Federal Union camp, everyone's attention is captured by the giant tortoise-like monster, bearing the huge rock formation on the back of its shell.)

Alex: "The heck?"

Peter: "What is that thing?!"

Lisa: "No! Dad!"

Dior: "Yeah, I know!"

(Dior hastily throws off his equipment, capturing everyone's attention.)

Dior: "I'll be back!"

(Without looking back, Dior fearlessly takes off in a burst of speed toward the monster. Meanwhile, as the giant monster continues its rise from the ground, Lyone desperately attempts to hold on, losing his balance. While the group of soldiers are tossed to the front of the monster, Lyone is tossed to its side. Once the giant monster stands upon its massive limbs, the sandstorm halts. Finally, the squad of soldiers stand to their feet, finding themselves in front of the towering mammoth.)

Federal Union Scout #5: "Crap."

Federal Union Scout #7: "W-What do we do?"

(Dior appears a few yards away from the group of soldiers, quickly looking among them, finding no sign of Lyone. To everyone's surprise, the giant monster slowly turns its body away from them, causing great tremors with every step. As they cautiously gawk, the monster ignores them, gradually walking away from the group.)

Federal Union Scout #5: "Well, that could have ended badly, I supp—"

(Suddenly, a horde of tall, yellow, eight-legged, spider-like monsters emerges from the giant hole in the ground, stampeding toward Dior and the group of soldiers.)

Federal Union Scout #5: "What the . . .!"

(The group of soldiers open fire upon the horde of spiders, mowing down a few. Although, the large horde remain wholly unaffected, continuing their unrelenting march.)

Dior: "It's too many! Get out of there!"

Federal Union Scout #5: "Retreat!"

(One of the soldiers throw a grenade to cover their retreat, frantically running away during the explosion. Federal Union Scout #5 looks back, coming to an sudden halt, astonished at the sight of a strange event. Soon after, the other two soldiers also come to a halt, looking back in amazement. Dior's black Energy Stream resonates ferociously, sapping what little daylight remaining within the surrounding area. He firmly stands with his right arm crossed over his left, focusing a massive amount of energy into his right arm.)

Dior: "Nightfall."

(Dior swings his right arm horizontally, unleashing a massive slash of black colored energy, passing through the horde of spiders in the blink of an eye. The energy attack leaves behind a dark trail along its trajectory, flinging severed body parts of the horde of spiders into the air. Dior stands victorious before the corpses of the horde; his right arm dripping blood from the recoil of the attack. As the three soldiers remain frozen and speechless, Federal Union Scout #5's earpiece continuously buzzes. Federal Union Scout #5 answers the call, standing about with his mouth hanging open.)

Command: "Hey! What's going on out there? Are you guys ok?"

Federal Union Scout #5: "He killed them all."

Command: "What? Who killed what?"

(After Olivia sighs in relief, she suddenly remembers Lyone, calmly scanning the area for any signs of him.)

Olivia: "Where are you, kid?"

(Olivia's gaze land on the huge hole in the ground; previously filled by the giant tortoise-monster.)

Olivia: "Don't tell me—crap."

(Lyone lies at the bottom of the hole, half buried under sand and gravel. He slowly regains consciousness, lifting himself above the dirt, opening his eyes to find himself surrounded by the glowing blades of spears. The spears are held by the tongues of bipedal frog-like beast. Their bodies glow the same bright-orange light as the blades of their spears, oozing from a coat of slime. Nervous at the encounter, Lyone doesn't move a muscle, hearing the familiar voices in his head.)

Faint Voice: *"Lyone, don't move."*

(One of the frog-like beasts, body glowing a dark red, steps forward commandingly, communicating with the rest of its kin. Next, the commanding beast places its hand in front of Lyone's face, emitting a yellow aura, causing Lyone to become increasingly drowsy until he is completely sedated. Once subdued, the beast carries Lyone by the shirt, and the group walks into the depths of a cavern.)

(Minutes later, Dior arrives at the Federal Union Encampment along with numerous soldiers and guild personnel, returning from patrol due to the emergency event.)

Lisa: "DAD!"

(Dior is greeted by Lisa and Peter, urgently running toward him. Alex stands near the three, addressing two high-ranking Adventurer Guild officers.)

Lisa: "Dad, are you ok?"

Dior: "Yeah, I'm fine."

Alex: "Good. Let's be prepared for anything."

(Alex and the two officers share a salute, crossing their chest with their right arms, dismissing them with their orders. Then, he turns to Dior, gratefully confirming his safety.)

Alex: "Dior, glad to see you're safe, but we have a situation on our hands."

Dior: "What's the situation?"

Peter: "We've received reports of large, eight-legged monsters rising out of the ground from numerous places throughout the valley."

Alex: "I'm guessing it's because of that giant tortoise monster causing tremors with every step."

Dior: "It disturbed the monsters that lived underground. If I had to guess, I'd say they were probably hibernating for the winter."

Peter: "Whatever the case, they're above ground now, attacking any and everything they come across."

Dior: "Then it's probably best to gather your forces and retreat."

Caime: "Unnecessary."

(Caime gains the attention of the group, walking towards them with his two guardsmen. Dior, Alex, and Peter salutes, standing at ease once Caime waves his hand.)

Caime: "We have all the equipment and supplies we need to hold this position successfully for quite some time."

Alex: "Sir, with all due respect, my guild isn't equipped to fight such long, drawn-out battles in the middle of the wilderness."

Caime: "My forces will see to it that this location is secured."

Alex: "Sir, but how? Your forces consist of mostly scouts and scientists. We're going to be up against a horde of monsters overrunning this location!"

(Keeping his eyes on a skeptical Alex, Caime speaks to Dior.)

Caime: "Dior, your task hasn't changed. Please track down the refuge of the beast and save our man if you can."

Dior: "Alright. Considering the circumstances, I'll make this quick."

(Dior turns to Lisa, kneeling to eye level, noticing the visible concern on her face. He remains calm, confidently smiling to ease her fears. Next, she gives him a hug for comfort.)

Dior: <whispering> "He's missing. But I'll get him back."

Lisa: <whispering> "Ok, be safe. Ni'Ador."

Dior: <whispering> "We will. Ni'Ador."

(After their hug, Dior stands on his feet, turning his attention to Alex with unease.)

Alex: "Don't worry. I'll make sure Lisa's safe."

(Alex notices that his words are ineffective at addressing Dior's concern.)

Alex: "My men will be ok as well, Dior. You have my word."

Dior: "Very well. Ni'Ador."

Alex: "Ni'Ador."

(Dior turns away from the group, moving toward the front gate with zeal, capturing everyone's attention.)

Peter: "Hey! What about your supplies?"

Dior: "No need! I plan to make this quick!"

(Lisa teems with inspiration, watching Dior courageously stride out of the Federal Union Encampment.

Meanwhile, Olivia holds a conversation with Idol on her earpiece, watching the activity around the Federal Union Encampment.)

Idol: "If the target is dead, we have to confirm it. It's too risky to leave the area without confirmation."

Olivia: "Sir, I'd knew you'd say that. Alright then, I'll jump into that whole."

Joshua: "Major, you might want to be hyper vigilant in there. Monsters in cave areas usually have adapted to dark, damp, close-quarter environments. I'm afraid your rifle won't be much help."

Olivia: "Thank you, Joshua. I'm prepared to handle this the old-fashioned way."

(Olivia abruptly finishes her statement, noticing Dior positioned outside of the Federal Union Encampment's entrance staring in her direction.)

Idol: "Major, something wrong?"

(Dior takes off in a burst of speed, reappearing next to Olivia, sitting on the ground with his legs folded and his head hanging low.)

Dior: "I'm gonna need your help."

(Briefly surprised, Olivia turns to her side, finding Dior sitting next to her.)

Olivia: "Of course you do."

Idol: "What was that, major?"

Dior: "Any clues of his whereabouts?"

Olivia: "Not from the view of my scope. However, I was just about to conduct an extensive search now that the soldiers are in the encampment."

Dior: "I see."

Idol: "Olivia, is someone there with you?"

(Without shifting her eyes away from Dior, Olivia replies to Idol.)

Olivia: "Sir, its Dior. He's here with me."

Idol: "Ah, I should have known."

Olivia: "Sir, he's requesting my assistance to recover the target."

Idol: "Confirmed. Utilize Dior and recover the target. But remember, no contact with any Federal Union soldiers."

Olivia: "Understood, sir."

(Olivia turns off her earpiece, turning her attention to the giant hole left by the great tortoise-like monster.)

Olivia: "I last remember seeing Lyone fall off the back of that giant monster carrying the rock formation on its shell. But, I couldn't get to him due to the sandstorm around it. I searched the area surrounding the hole of any signs of the target, but that yielded nothing. My only guess at this point is that the target fell under the monster and into that hole."

Dior: "Then let's move in. Be prepared for CQC."

Olivia: "Understood."

(Olivia puts her binoculars away, drawing a combat knife from its holster at her lower back. Dior stands to his feet, cracking his neck. Once prepared, the two take off in a burst of speed. At the bottom of the hole, they find a dark cavern filled with the pink webbings of spider like monsters. Sand and gravel litters the cave floor, falling through the hole from the surface.)

Olivia: "This cavern must be filled with those monsters."

Dior: "Looks like they're arachnid species of monster. The pink webbing is very distinctive."

(Dior and Olivia carefully survey their surroundings, ready to defend themselves.)

Olivia: "We're clear."

Dior: "Alright then, let's look for clues to Lyone's whereabouts. But stay on guard."

(As the two begin to search for Lyone, they periodically pause, readying themselves for combat at the sound of monsters echoing from the depths of the cavern, only to find themselves alone in the dark. Yunyi fully sets below the horizon, causing the cavern to become pitch black. Olivia gathers energy from the environment, focusing the energy at the fingertips of her right hand, creating five small orbs of light. She releases the orbs and they slowly float around the area, providing a modicum of vision, revealing long pathways leading to other areas of the cavern.)

Olivia: "These pathways are incredibly long. There's no doubt these reach far across the valley."

Dior: "Hm."

(Dior kneels over a section of the cavern floor, examining something of interest, capturing Olivia's attention.)

Olivia: "Find something?"

Dior: "Yeah."

(She walks over to him, detecting the trail of multiple large slimy footprints in the sand and gravel.)

Dior: "I'd expect footprints in a far-reaching cavern infested with arachnid monsters, but these are definitely not the footprints of the monsters that call this place home."

Olivia: "You think these are the footprints of kidnappers?"

Dior: "I wouldn't be surprised, considering there are already reports of a missing soldier. This cavern could be how they come and go through the valley quickly and undetected."

Olivia: "Looks like we have a lead, then."

Dior: "Agreed. But, before we follow them, it's best to know what awaits us on the path they took through this cavern."

Olivia: "And how are we supposed to do that?"

(While Olivia observes with skepticism, Dior follows the footprints to the beginning of the tunnel taken by the kidnappers. Next, he closes his eyes, positioning his right ear toward the pathway, focusing energy into his Energy Stream. Dior snaps his fingers, echoing the sound down the pathway until it reaches the end. He snaps a few more times in slow intervals, finishing his technique, calming his Energy Stream.)

Dior: "Hmm, there are no detected lifeforms that seem like a threat to us. But there may be traps. Be on guard during transit."

Olivia: "Understood. But before we take off, you mentioned a missing soldier. Mind elaborating?"

Dior: "I was given an assignment by Lieutenant General Caime. He wants me to locate a scout that went missing some time ago during a mission on the east side of the valley."

Olivia: "And the soldier's name?"

Dior: "Private Ericsson Bradshaw."

(Olivia reacts to the name with a quick sigh and look of disappointment.)

Dior: "An acquaintance of yours?"

Olivia: "He's a new recruit to Scouting Squad Six, under my training."

Dior: "That's unfortunate. However, this is the life of a soldier. Nothing more to it. Right?"

(Olivia composes herself, stepping forward, feeling Dior's eyes monitoring her.)

Olivia: "We have a task to accomplish. Do we not?"

Dior: "That we do."

(Dior and Olivia prepare themselves, taking off down the pathway in a burst of speed. She follows behind Dior, carefully analyzing his movements.)

Olivia: *"What technique was that? Was he using sound waves to extend his vision like a kind of sonar?"*

(Olivia takes notice of Dior's Energy Stream, studying him from up-close, pressing forward through the narrow cavern pathway.)

Olivia: *"He is moving slowly enough for me to keep up. It's annoying."*

(Dior keeps his attention fixed on the path forward, keeping a determined expression.)

Dior: *"Hang in there Lyone."*

And so, the little lion was captured, thrusting him and his party onto the warfront of an expanding empire. Although this little lion was taught to be as adaptive as possible within his environment, he will soon learn that environments are similar to any living organism. They have limits that can be broken.

www.ingramcontent.com/pod-product-compliance
Lightning Source LLC
Chambersburg PA
CBHW021143310726
48971CB00002B/454